FOXGLOVE

ROBERT E.L. TROWBRIDGE

USA • Canada • UK • Ireland

Note for Librarians: A cataloguing record for this book is available from Library
and Archives Canada at www.collectionscanada.ca/amicus/index-e.html
ISBN 1-4120-8019-3

Photograph Page 129, Kevin Trowbridge, photographicilluminations.com

*Printed in Victoria, BC, Canada. Printed on paper with minimum 30% recycled
fibre. Trafford's print shop runs on "green energy" from solar, wind and other
environmentally-friendly power sources.*

Offices in Canada, USA, Ireland and UK

Book sales for North America and international:
Trafford Publishing, 6E–2333 Government St.,
Victoria, BC V8T 4P4 CANADA
phone 250 383 6864 (toll-free 1 888 232 4444)
fax 250 383 6804; email to orders@trafford.com
Book sales in Europe:
Trafford Publishing (UK) Limited, 9 Park End Street, 2nd Floor
Oxford, UK OX1 1HH UNITED KINGDOM
phone 44 (0)1865 722 113 (local rate 0845 230 9601)
facsimile 44 (0)1865 722 868; info.uk@trafford.com
Order online at:
trafford.com/05-3017

10 9 8 7

FOR ERIC

CONTENTS

"Ah but a man's reach must exceed his grasp,
Or what's a heaven for?"—Robert Browning

CHAPTER 1

"I Still Haven't Found what I'm Looking For"—U2

THE PINK SLIP

"Foxglove Farm in the sevens!!" screamed the pink slip.

My receptionist, long a candidate for a pink slip of her own, had scrawled this message from Judy. It occupied my worn, leather swivel-chair and greeted me upon my return from lunch. As a rule I get voicemails or emails; seldom written directives to call my wife; even less often in my chair. Clearly this was important; a communiqué not to be overlooked, nor to be sat upon.

Memory failing, I fired up Yahoo and searched *foxglove farm,* finding spreads with that name in Virginia, Kentucky and Ohio on the first page alone. America was *rotten* with Foxglove Farms.

One finger typing "foxglove farm canada," I searched again. Bingo.

Saltspring Island Realty offered a Foxglove Farm on their site; one-hundred and forty-nine "arable" acres with an elderly farmhouse. The spread was pictured on my laptop, and with tractor and livestock in the foreground, seemed to smack of working as opposed to hobby. That would certainly not do. I don't do working.

Saltspring is a gorgeous and artsy isle about a two hour, mind-numbing ferry ride from Vancouver. A few years back Judy and I checked out a number of Saltspring properties, taking that ferry on our first trip. The *Queen of Nanaimo* was full of touring Japanese schoolgirls and the smell of bad soup from the galley. On our second excursion we opted for a half hour floatplane to Ganges Harbor where a hopeful Saltspring realtor named Angelo waited at the dock. He Volvoed us for thirty minutes to a waterfront hideaway for our inspection. He was at least seventy-five and creaky arthritic and it was all he could do to show us around the rocky terrain of the subject property. It was a weary fifties bungalow, fixed to a concrete slab, perched on an overgrown acre that tumbled to the sea. For Judy, the fact that the house and gardens needed work seemed to add to their appeal. It could become one of her projects. I can relate, having been one myself for thirty-three years now. But I'd been turned off by the first Volvoing; then the return trip to Ganges cooled her ardor.

Three hours later, Angelo left us back at the floatplane. We left *him* with a nasty lowball offer that all three of us knew would amount to a waste of his time. Bobbing wharf-side on the pontoons and buckling up, we felt an eerie sense of just having dodged a bullet. Saltspring wasn't for us; I guess we're just not islander material. It's always all about the getting there, and then it's all about the getting back.

But this Foxglove Farm on Yahoo was far from in the sevens, as per the pink slip. At one million four hundred and ninety-nine thousand it sought over ten grand per bucolic acre, "arable" or otherwise, and it wasn't even on the sea. If you're going to be on Saltspring or Hornby or Galliano, or for that matter on any Gulf island, you've *got* to be waterfront, and that bloated price, even with our anemic late-nineties

Canuck loonie, was well beyond our comfort zone for a second home.

Maybe I should have called Judy first thing. Four hours later she had set me straight as we drove out to Langley Township in the Fraser Valley. The subject of the pink slip was a mere fifty kilometers east of our Vancouver townhouse on Kitsilano Beach, and now her forest green Range Rover idled outside an imposing iron gate which straddled a pair of stout stone pillars.

A worn metal plate on one pillar gave fair, albeit faded warning to *Beware of Dog*. The country mailbox said FOX-GLOVE FARM.

CHAPTER 2

"She's got to be somebody's baby"—Jackson Browne

THE GAP

MY WIFE IS BETTER LOOKING THAN ME. WE'VE ALWAYS HAD this gap.

This was marginally true in 1972 when we met at Brock University in St. Catharines, Ontario. Through a sweet, smoky haze and the din of Cat Stevens, Neil Young, Led Zeppelin and Humble Pie, the gap was apparent to me. But in early '72, when I was twenty-one and Judy was eighteen, no one assumed I was her father; a shocking conclusion to which one or two people have jumped in recent years, as the gap widened.

She was a grade "A" knockout.

Five-five, one hundred and six pounds and a waist-length cloud of hair, the shade of a one-cent piece, fresh from the Ottawa mint, with natural blond highlights that danced in the sun. The face of a cheerleader which, with just a touch of blush and eyeliner, could easily be the cover of *Vogue*.

Eyeing her from a safe distance, I liked the way she would toss her copper cloud over a shoulder with total nonchalance. Sometimes, when she carried her Brock cafeteria lunch tray, Judy would do a double-toss; first one shoulder, then the other. If soup were on her tray this maneuver, I supposed, would prevent her perfect un-split copper ends from dipping in the cream of mushroom.

The twelve guys in my residence dorm would sit around and often the topic of conversation was the girl with the copper cloud of hair. We'd play Hearts or Risk until dawn with pizzas and beers and share leering visions of what we would do with her if we only had the chance. This went on from September to nearly February; but each of my residence mates also had a gap when it came to Judy Radford; gaps greater than mine.

One guy's gap, in particular, yawned wider than The Grand Canyon.

Kurt "Bags" Bagnall had long, stringy dishwater hair, often more than a few days removed from a washing. His preferred beverage was a "boilermaker," Molson's Export Ale with a two-ounce rye chaser. Bags always slept in past noon, never seemed to go to any classes and made a habit of helping himself to beer and food in the communal fridge, never checking or caring much about to whom it might belong. Toiletries and cigarettes were fair game too. If three or four of us chipped in for a Dino's pizza, Bags would show up just after the delivery boy to scavenge. Bags "borrowed" a burnt orange corduroy shirt jacket of mine in September and made it his own for the next two terms. As a matter of fact, I think he still has it.

Bags was given to being roughly outspoken, spewing even more profanity than the rest of us. One evening, Bags was the central figure in a spiteful shouting match over a disputed call in our table hockey league. Then he pocketed our only puck and stormed out, heading for the campus pub. That night I semi-affectionately christened Bags as "The Lowest Form of Human Life," and his new name stuck.

But Bags was just like the rest of us when it came to

obsessing about the copper-haired girl who was oblivious to our existence; or so we all thought.

One day, with six of us lolling around the residence, a pleasant coed, Joanne Picinin, who played on the Brock women's volleyball team, knocked on our door with a petition to sign.

For what, I don't remember; students had causes in 1972.

The last name on the list was Judy Radford; her ink barely dry. I heard myself saying, "I don't mind signing for *anything* next to her," and taking Joanne's pen, scribbled my name. "It's funny you say that," came Joanne's reply, "because *she likes you*."

A thunderbolt; one of life's pivotal moments.

There was a dance that night in the residence cafeteria and I was looking from the mezzanine down to the dance floor to get a bird's eye view of my co-petitioner, still cautiously conscious of the gap.

Perhaps Joanne was mistaken, or maybe my residence mates persuaded her to set me up with a cruel hoax. An act that vile, I knew, was not beneath them. Well, certainly it wasn't beneath Bags.

Then there was a tap on my shoulder.

I turned and saw the cover girl smile through the copper cloud.. Downstairs near the he dance floor we sat and talked. We never did dance. It turned out she knew Joanne from volleyball. I would have figured the copper haired girl was far too aloof for digging, setting and spiking. After all, she could break a nail.

After ten minutes we went to her residence and we smoked a little hash. Unlike President Clinton, I think we might have inhaled; or at least I think *I* might have. She had a guitar that I strummed, drawling my best Bob Dylan, *A Hard Rain's Gonna Fall* and *Don't Think Twice*. I offered the guitar and she was reluctant and I asked her again. Then she took it and played Joni Mitchell's *Michael (from Mountains)* and *Circle Game*. We harmonized on *Circle Game* as if we'd teamed on the chorus a hundred times before, trading the lead and harmony back and forth. We moved to the stairwell for better acoustics. Her angelic voice made my rough vocal almost sound okay.

I gave her an innocent back rub and we must have had the munchies.

I can recall her making me a folded-over white bread bologna sandwich on a plate on the floor of the common area of her residence; kneeling, and on perfect haunches in bone colored corduroys.

Double-tossing her long hair back over each shoulder, she wiped the excess mustard off the knife onto the outside of the bread. Later she would make the same mark on the peanut butter sandwiches of our four children. I would come to call this a "badge."

Fifteen years later I was a speaker at an insurance conference at The Intercontinental Hotel in Paris. Our room wasn't large but oozed elegance. The nightly tariff on its door was posted at close to three thousand francs, approaching nine hundred dollars in 1987.

There was a speaker's dinner in a fabulous private room, bedecked with chandeliers. Judy and I were seated with a dozen others. The impeccable service was white glove; no expense was spared.

There was a Pouilly something white wine that was so savory each sip was like biting into meat. Foie gras, shrimp and lobster starters, then sorbet for sullied palates, and Chateaubriand that dissolved on the tongue. There were gallons of red wine of a quality I'd never tasted before or since. Marvelous pungent cheeses with Burmeister Port followed iced soufflés and petit fours all washed down by a special Remy Martin you'd never find at the liquor store; and you wonder where your premium dollars go.

I guess that this was among the top dining experiences of my life; but remains a distant second to that bologna sandwich of January 28th, 1972, with its golden mustard badge.

A few of my residence mates hated me for a while but they got over it. Some even came to our wedding, six months and a day after I signed that petition. Bags didn't show.

Standing at the altar I awaited my bride.

My hair was trimmed for the wedding from the middle of my back to just below the shoulders. The groom wore navy blue velvet, an Edwardian bell-bottom suit that I'd found in a little store on Yonge St. for sixty-nine dollars. The store wasn't exactly Holt Renfrew. Besides a few suits, they also sold tie-dyed tee shirts, water pipes, pet rocks and Iron Butterfly posters.

"Now it's not too late, you know we can just keep on driving over that hill dear," said Judy's Dad, as their car approached the church.

Back in 1970, before my time, Judy was Reine du Carnival in her Ottawa Valley birthplace. It was a small town but this was no small achievement. Someone had talked her into entering her sunny good looks against a slate of Gallic beauties.

Hawkesbury was ninety percent francophone and her competition had names like Chantelle Parizeau, Yvette Tremblay and Monique Villeneuve. Pretty girls; pretty French-

Canadian girls. Soon after marrying Judy I saw an old Polaroid of her riding on the back of a white Lincoln Continental convertible waving to the throngs that lined Main Street, her new crown perched atop the copper cloud. She was seventeen. Judy Radford had kicked ass; pretty French girl ass; or derriere I suppose.

So yes, there's always been this gap. And the gap widened with each passing year. Four pregnancies throughout the seventies saw each of us put on weight throughout the gestations. Post-partum she'd work hers off in no time. Sit-ups and weighted leg lifts at bedtime, fastidious housework and keeping up with four rug rats occupied her days.

My regimen was Scotch and beer, pizzas and submarine sandwiches following sedentary days at the office. I *kept* the weight that I had gained in sympathy with each pregnancy. As my waistline widened, so did the gap.

While on the subject of gaps, I have always found Judy's space between her front teeth rather fetching, sort of Lauren Hutton-esque. She doesn't share my appreciation for *this* gap, however, and has recently taken steps to have it closed with retainers, dental "appliances"…those kinds of things. She was worried that one of the teeth was weaker and the space was getting more prominent. Her gap was growing. When I testified to my love of the space, she would have none of it.

"I feel like I'm one baguette away from being a sea-hag!" she said one day.

CHAPTER 3

"She's got legs; She knows how to use them"— ZZ Top

GETAWAY STICKS

I'M A LEG MAN AND OUR FRIEND ANGIE READ ADMIRED JUDY'S at a charity function we attended along with Angie's husband Calvin, one of my golfing buddies. The evening called for cocktail dresses…. for the ladies of course.

"Judy's got great getaway sticks," bubbled Angie after a few Chardonnays, who, for the record, owns a decent pair herself.

"I hope you take *very* good care of them, Bob."

I wondered how I could do that…. it wasn't quite like taking my Lexus in for a service. By this time I was fifty-two and Judy was approaching the big "Five-O," and had already taken steps toward gam maintenance. She had recently put one getaway stick in the care of Roxanne. Roxanne made veins go away by injection.

Judy, upon meeting Roxanne at her Vancouver clinic, cited mixed feelings. Birthing four babies and riding horses since trail-guiding in her teens kind of made a visible leg vein a medal of honor. In a way it was a blue badge of courage.

While Roxanne's handiwork restored Judy's leg to a Reine du Carnival state of perfection, their easy banter turned to horses. Roxanne had a couple of them on her farm. Judy had Mickey, an aging but noble Irish warmblood that she boarded down on the "flats" in Southlands, an equestrian Mecca in the heart of Vancouver.

The horse-speak continued on Judy's next appointment.

"Did you ever think about buying a farm?" Roxanne had asked.

"Oh yeah," Judy mused, "but we only like old properties; you know, something with a bit of history, and there aren't many of those in B.C."

"Well my friend's farm is a hundred years old," perked Roxanne, syringe in hand. "It's right across the road from our farm *and it's for sale.*"

Judy raised a skeptical copper eyebrow. "I thought I knew of all the heritage farms…. There's so few of them…...but there's just one property I really love…I forget exactly where it is…. but my husband and I drove out to see it a few years ago…. I'd seen it in a magazine…it's gorgeous, but it's been turned into some kind of dried flower business."

Roxanne shrieked at the coincidence. "*That's* my friend's place!!! That's Foxglove Farm!!! It's an exclusive listing, but she's putting it on M.L.S. tomorrow!"

It was in the sevens.

CHAPTER 4

"I'm goin' to the country"—Canned Heat

THE DRY RUN

It was approaching seven p.m....and inky black on that February night.

And it was all the darker on that no-exit country road where Foxglove Farm awaited at the dead end. I shut off the Rover and killed the lights. As our eyes adjusted to the darkness, déjà vu crept up. Judy and I crept out and approached the gate.

We *had* been here before. Three, maybe four years back; summertime then. Foxglove Farm had been featured in one of Judy's magazines; *Country Living* I think, or *Victoria,* the type of glossy publication that profiles an urban couple renovating a dilapidated gem; a rustic find upon which they stumbled on a fall Sunday afternoon, scouring rural antique shops for that perfect armoire.

"Denise, 42, is a partner in a major accounting firm and Bruce, 39, switched from architecture to Early Childhood Education. He now runs a school for gifted children when he's not restoring rare grandfather clocks." That kind of thing.

Slim chance *we'd* stumble on a gem. Certainly not on a Sunday. While sharing Judy's appreciation of country real estate, I was even more passionate about The National Football League and it's smorgasbord of Sunday afternoon televised offerings. While my stack of fantasy football rags was still dwarfed by Judy's thirty year pile of decorating monthlies, that was a gap that wasn't so much growing as holding its own. The NFL's appeal was just enough to keep me out of the antique stores and fall fairs; and on Sabbath mornings my foursome tees up religiously at 7:28.

But when Judy eyeballed the Foxglove Farm pictorial that summer a special pilgrimage was in order. British Columbia's dearth of such properties sparked curiosity. Foxglove looked so old; British Columbia, while beautiful, is just so damn young.

Lori Bogen hadn't minced words.

It was 1990. Lori and her banker husband, Michael, had been posted for a year or so in Vancouver and the Royal Bank saw fit to move them back to Toronto. Our two daughters had become fast friends with the Bogen girls and were sorry to see them go.

Lori and Michael hailed from New York City and Lori was African-American. Black would have been okay in 1990 and knowing Lori I expect it still would. She wrote interesting music on her synthesizer and had a voice like Roberta Flack.

Judy had asked whether uprooting from the ocean and mountains of idyllic Vancouver to "the big smoke" concerned her.

"Naw," smiled Lori "Vancouver's like Arnold Schwarzenegger, gorgeous, but so what?!!

Gimmee Danny Devito any day!!!"

It was tough finding Foxglove for the first time on that summer day back in 1998 or 99. As navigators go, my soul mate and I are hardly Lewis and Clark; probably more like

Lewis and Martin.

Finally there, we had never made it past the same pillars and iron gate that now loomed in the night. Just inside the gate there was a brown shingle gatehouse that served as an office for the flower business. On our previous visit the office was CLOSED and so it was now.

Four years back we had peered through the wrought iron bars up a long narrow ribbon of a driveway that ran a gauntlet of freakishly tall, skinny trees, their lacy tops swaying in the slightest breeze. The leaves were long gone on this nocturnal visit but the treetops still danced fifty yards overhead. While each stout trunk stood a respectful twelve feet from his neighbor, their anorexic tops scratched at each other with the insistence of a tomcat at a screen door, wanting out.

When it comes to her passions, Judy wastes no time. She goes straight from point A to point B. As the owner of the shoulder that got tapped at Brock in 1972, Judy's sense of urgency offered me no surprise.

Now lusting for Foxglove, she had snapped into action. A few minutes from Roxanne's clinic she was working the phone. Ferreting out the realtor with the exclusive listing, she'd lobbied hard for a viewing *this* evening. His name was Gary Hooge, but he pronounced it *Hoagie* like the poor boy sandwich.

But Gary was a pro. Foxglove drew its share of "Looky Loos" and curiosity seekers in the daytime when you could see the damn place. Rebecca, the owner, was in Vancouver tonight…and Rebecca *hated* short notice. And besides, the Canucks were on the tube against the Avalanche and the archrivals were in a tooth-and-nail scrap for top spot in the

NHL's Western Conference.

Unused to defeat, Judy slammed into overdrive. Leveraging her case with Hooge's chance for a "double-ender," she applied the fulcrum of his expiring exclusive listing. She had the Hooge carriage turning into a pumpkin at midnight. She said we'd settle for an outside tour tonight and come back to check out the house tomorrow.

But *no*, Hooge anchored his heels. "Tomorrow at 1 pm. See you then. Park just outside the gate."

But Hooge's lack of eagerness wasn't about to deter us from night riding down that dead end road right up to that very gate. And we could listen to the Canucks on the radio. Anyway, Foxglove *was* hard to find…and it had been at least four years. This could be a dry run for tomorrow; we could grab a bite in Fort Langley.

My stomach growled in the darkness and I was the first to turn from Foxglove's gate. It was well past happy hour too and we were in serious arrears. We had some catching up to do.

Judy tore her hands from the bars of the gate and turned to join me as I fired up the Rover. Suddenly the black night lit up like Hiroshima.

Six hundred meters from our dead end, high beams blazed toward us. The jig was up. We were caught like escaped Allies in the path of a Panzer tank. I was anonymous behind the wheel, and assessing an urgent three point turn on the narrow ditch-lined road. Maybe I could at least save myself. It was too late for Judy.

Seeing Judy bathed in the lights like Renee Zellweger in her signature piece in *Chicago*, I half expected my spouse to start high-kicking and belting out *Roxie*. Cornering us, the silver SUV rolled to a stop. The passenger side window floated down as we awaited our fate. One of Langley's finest?? Perhaps an irate Hooge?? Or, God forbid, Rebecca the Empress of Foxglove???

A pretty blond head leaned over from the driver's seat. A generous open-mouthed grin revealed a snapping wad of beige chewing gum. "Hey Judy! Come on in for a glass of wine!"

"Sounds good Roxanne!" was Judy's laughing reply.

CHAPTER 5

"Roxanne!!"—Sting

ROXANNE

Foxglove's wrought iron gate was a poor cousin to Roxanne's. Straight across the narrow road from ours *(ours??),* it was a spiffy two door that opened inwards, saloon-like, after Roxanne punched in a four-digit code from the seat of her SUV. Her pillars were bigger and newer than ours too; just about a century newer. Atop each pillar squatted a dignified concrete dog. Each dog's mouth held a basket of flowers; "winter pansies," Judy told me later.

We followed Roxanne's taillights up a long, meandering crushed stone drive that wove through an orchard and past a three-story barn. We finally parked beside her in front of a faux sandstone dwelling that was more manor than house. An oversized clock face presided over the courtyard, high on the front of the triple car garage. The hands were at 7:25. Roxanne had put in a long day shrinking veins.

The whole scene evoked a sense of Avignon *au sud de la France*, where the Popes had hung out for a few centuries, and did full justice to the long driveway and the twenty acres. A house that was built new to look old.

Inside the manor there was pandemonium. A riot of golden

retrievers greeted Roxanne with unbridled glee. It seemed to me like four at the time but in retrospect there must have only been two; Ben and Brooke, the two I have since come to know. They welcomed their mistress with all the joy of a large Asian family reuniting at Vancouver International Airport.

Judy got in there and stirred the doggy pot. Right on her knees, nuzzling their ears and rubbing their flanks; baby talking her approval. "*Well aren't you a beautiful girl…yes you are!*" Ratcheting up their frenzy.

My wife loves big dogs.

Roxanne, blonde and trim in a crisp, navy dress, worked the cork out of a Pinot Gris and poured. Her husband, Peter, was playing tennis that evening at his club in Vancouver. He was a vascular surgeon. Our prospective neighbors were both in the vein business. And arteries too in Peter's case.

"I had a great-uncle who was a tree surgeon," I lied in exchange for a chuckle.

Roxanne asked about Foxglove and Judy rolled her eyes and filled her in about having to wait a day. Roxanne topped up our glasses and there was that grin; the one with the wad of gum. "I can take you guys through tonight; Rebecca's my best friend and she makes me dinner when I work late. She's a sweetheart. I have to go over and get it anyway. Bring your wine."

Retrievers in tow, the three of us ambled through the winter chill up Roxanne's driveway and eventually came to her gate, crossed the narrow road, then released the rubber bungee cord that held the Foxglove gate shut.

Judy poured what was left of her pinot gris into my empty glass.

A pale, hesitant moon winked through the shuffling cloudbank.

CHAPTER 6

"Working on the Night Moves"—Bob Segar

"WE ARE SO BUYING THIS PLACE"

MY WIFE IS A NEGOTIATOR PAR EXCELLENCE. AND WITH EACH passing year her bargaining muscles seem to grow stronger. Judy's will is cut and buff when it comes to getting what she wants.

Final Sale stickers in retail outlets amuse her and she takes *no cash refund* caveats as a personal challenge. Upgrading an airline ticket is child's play to my wife.

Indian rug dealers hide in the back room when they see her "truck" pull up in front of their gaudy emporiums. I swear that in thirty-two years we have never or seldom bought an Indian or Persian carpet. Our homes have enjoyed a tremendous variety of the best of them, mind you, every size, pattern and color. Judy has two magic words that melt these rug floggers…*On Approval.*

God help the schoolteacher that might consider flunking one of my children. After parent-teacher night that kid would be in line for a Rhodes scholarship.

And when it comes to real estate, let's just say that Judy and I buy low and sell high. Well, most of the time. Feeding off each other's boldness.

It wasn't always that way.

In our early twenties we had paid the builder's full price for a 1,040 square foot bungalow in Edmonton. Borrowed the ten percent down payment from my parents. It was the lowest priced new house in town at $44,500; the most basic model from Key Royale Homes. We had to drive by the stockyards and rendering plants of northeast Edmonton to get to our subdivision of Hermitage, a daily source of nausea to Judy who was expecting Dylan at the time. But we made that trip whenever we could; just to see the hole in the ground and then the foundation and then the frame. "This'll be *our* bedroom, honey!" I bawled out, flat on my back under the stars on the frosty plywood floor of our future boudoir, while Judy sized up the roughed–in kitchen. Mark, not yet two, was always with us, and I'd hoist him into the seat of the yellow excavator, left idle in the evening or on the weekend, on the site of our dream home. He called it a "bo-zozer" while he tried to slam it into gear.

This was a bare bones starter home with one rather than one and a half bathrooms, no lawn and no fence. Most of our neighbors grew potatoes in their front yards. We weren't certain, but figured it was a Ukrainian strategy that enriched the gumbo soil prior to sewing grass seed a year or two later. Any edible spuds were value added.

Judy's dad was handy to the point of building houses himself. Built them, lived in them, and then rented them out after building another. Determined that I could be the same kind of man, she encouraged me to build a fence, and then a recreation room in the basement. The latter assignment cured her once and for all, when she came to the conclusion that my studding, insulating and paneling efforts were actually devaluing our property. Before that debacle, she had given me the green light to create a feature wall in our dining area with mirrored tiles, having deemed the illusion of more space to be a *good thing* for our shoebox of a bungalow. Having no experience in this kind of work, I took the same approach that I would to a jigsaw puzzle, having slapped a few of those together as a youth. I'd do all the outside tiles first, and then methodically fill in the middle. On my frequent breaks to quaff well-earned O'Keefe Ales, I'd get Judy to come and admire the progress of my work, a gleaming outline of a square, first one and then two rows deep. The third row brought trouble, as any true handyman might expect. A perfectly square and mitered dining room would have been fine, but perfection wasn't a hallmark of Key Royale Homes. As I tried to jam each new square-foot of tile flush to its brethren, the mirrored corners would bust off and hurtle toward my un-goggled eyes.

The day was saved by our neighbor, Kevin Hanna, who with his wife Edith and their baby boy, occupied their own Key Royale shoebox, right across Homestead Crescent from ours. Kevin was a glasscutter by trade and a damn good one, skillful enough to spend his weekend salvaging our wall, in exchange for a few O'Keefe Ale. Grateful, and wanting our relationship with our new neighbors to be a two-way street, I helped Kevin and Edith over at their house the very next day, and for all I know that *Family Protector* life policy is still in force.

When my insurance career returned us to Ontario in 1977 we paid too much for a back-split with a pool in Barrie; seventy-six thousand, just nine-hundred less than asking. Our daughters Harmony and Taylor were born at the Royal Victoria Hospital, sisters for Mark and Dylan, and we brought them home to that back-split. My efforts to stain our deck in Barrie didn't go that well, provoking an impromptu visit from a posse of Varden Crescent neighbors who pointed at my streaky handiwork and laughed. That would be at us, not with us.

Four years later we were in the Toronto suburb of Scarborough with a nineteen percent mortgage on a new two story with a few fancy features. Full price this time. Still a couple of babes in the woods; but babes with a bidet now.

But lucky timing in a move to Vancouver in '82 caught a wave. We moved and renovated a lot just for the fun of it. Bought in the suburbs at $155,000 sold after three and a half years at $222,000. Took a Sunday drive in '87 and on a whim bought prime in the city at $360,000, sold in one year at $705,000. Then we bought an old money Shaughnessy estate at $850,000 and sold after another twelve months at $1,388,000. Having only *new money* and not much of that, we paid off our $618,000 mortgage and bought a smallish waterfront log home in West Vancouver; finally for cash.

The kids constantly had to learn their new phone number and make new friends. They could only shake their heads at their nomadic Mom and Dad's priorities and screwed up value systems. But the six of us had each other and today, as adults, our children embrace change with zeal. Plus they have lasting friendships from all over B.C.'s Lower Mainland.

Our won-loss record was like the U.S. Army's; twelve and one.

The one loss was brutal and came in 1989-1990. If you care to read about how a family of six can live in a one-bedroom log cabin for one full year with a retriever, a black and tan Kansas Bloodhound, and a couple of cats…and *still* lose $210,000…please be patient.

Calamity like that deserves its own chapter.

But my point is that Judy knew better than to show her cards. She knew *so* much better.

Our collective experience in residential real estate deals, our hard lessons from the seventies, the string of victories, the odd setback, could have been bound into a text book; required reading at the community college…*Getting A Helluva Deal 101.* Judy just couldn't help herself when it came to Foxglove Farm.

Maybe it was the dark stroll down Foxglove's tree lined drive and the way we flowed into the interlocking brick courtyard. Parking for twenty cars and memorable parties.

Or the ancient fountain in the courtyard's center? Imported? Italian? French? Or the formal pond just beyond the courtyard wall, dappled with moon gleam.

Maybe it was the fact that this was not so much a *farmhouse* as it was a European country manor. Bony vines covered every inch of its splendid proportions and were halfway through annexing the roof. "Virginia Creeper," Judy mentioned on the ride home. She was familiar with that particular creeper from her gardening magazines; a big-time bloomer in the spring, then leafy through December.

Winter allowed the shutters to emerge. They were there that night; faded French blue.

Perhaps it was our failure to buy the Trotman Farm. Or rather it was *my* failure.

We'd just moved into Vancouver after that Sunday drive

in 1987. A few weeks later the Trotman farm came on the market. This was a heritage home with tasteful, countrified décor that would become Judy's preference for the next decade. Ten acres dotted with hay bales, neatly wrapped in white plastic.

She already stabled Boozer at the Trotman barn, close to the ocean, by the dyke at Boundary Bay. Boozer was our nickname for Newcastle Brown, a dark chocolate colt that Judy had bred and helped birth in 1986. Birthed him at Trotman's and could ride him right on the beach beyond the dyke.

Enjoying the move to the city after four years in a bedroom community, my feelings were mixed, and our offer reflected my tepid enthusiasm. Trotman's farm would be basically the same commute I'd been tackling since we moved to B.C. in 1982.

We came in second best to a foot doctor from Maryland or Minnesota who was setting up a new practice in Vancouver. A fifty-thousand dollar *gap* if memory serves.

Steeped in Judy's simmering disappointment, I contacted Dr. Russell directly. Turned out *he* was having mixed feelings a week after trumping our offer. Thought he might prefer the city. I proposed $35,000 cash for his interim agreement and said we'd trade our house on Angus drive if he wanted to check it out. I drew up the details myself and took the papers and our cheque straight to the hospital where, for all I knew, he was shaving bone off somebody's arch.

But the podiatrist's wife was cool to our plan. Mrs. Russell was already scouting for a pony for the kids. That was seventeen years ago. I think they're still there. I thought we had put the farm thoughts out of our mind and moved on; but maybe it was unfinished business.

Roxanne and her retrievers led us away from the grand

front of the home to a French door on the East side. We stepped in onto the Tuscan tiles of an unlit mudroom that led past a pantry into a white kitchen with a marble center island.

"Normally I'd take my shoes off, but what the hell," shrugged Roxanne, leaving hers on. We followed suit.

"Some things are going to have to change after *we* move in, Roxanne!" declared a beaming Judy.

There was an outlook to a generous dining room, lined in French windows on three sides. Roxanne slid the dimmer switch upwards to locate her take-out dinner, revealing a ceiling that was all dome and clad with copper on the outside. Judy saw what she saw and turned to me, possessed.

"We are *so buying* this place!" she exclaimed, in full earshot of the vendor's best friend.

CHAPTER 7

"These are the days"—Van Morrison

THE VIEWING

12:50 PM THE NEXT DAY.

We had sworn a pact to never reveal the events of last night. Roxanne's clandestine tour was safe with us.

Like most realtors with a last kick at both ends of a thirty-thousand dollar commission, Hooge was punctual. Tall, forty-sixish and craggy Dutch, he waited at Foxglove's gate as we arrived in my white Lexus 430 SC. I shut off the CD player before rolling to a stop.

Even though it was February I'd convinced Judy to let me put the roof down and crank up the heated seats to the max. We were wind-tossed but toasty as we rocketed down Highway 1 with Van Morrison bellowing "These are the Days," over the blow of the climate control set at 32 Celsius. Taking the two-seater for a winter *al fresca* was an easy sale. After 30 wedded years I knew when to pick my spots; and Judy was going to see Foxglove Farm today.

Of course that was *before* Brutus. After Brutus we'd always take her Range Rover, an outrageously unreliable export of the United Kingdom that she refers to as her "truck."

In the daylight at the dead end we could see the charming

old cottage next to the gate. The French paned glass in its windows was at odds with the rustic touch of an old rack of antlers above the side door. A large glass greenhouse with a brick floor was to the right of the cottage.

It was loaded with dried flower displays, garden gnomes, and various antique implements. A rusted hand scythe was propped against a concrete bullfrog. This was Rebecca's store; the shingle gatehouse was her office.

Ivy or creeper or *whatever* was everywhere and had married the woodsy brown gatehouse to the greenhouse. Invading through gaps in the glass-paneled ceiling of the latter, it had then journeyed earthward, dangling in mid-air, halfway down to its old, red brick floor. Wisteria, Judy confirmed the next day.

Hooge said we should leave my car next to his, outside the gate. He didn't have a prayer. I glared "why?" and before he could answer Judy said "Gary, if we're going to buy this place we want to see what it feels like to drive right up that driveway." Silence was consent and I slowly tooled up the long, narrow drive.

You could hear the crunch of what was left of a thin layer of tiny crushed stone on each hardened tire track. Between each track a strip of grass tickled the undercarriage of my low-slung roadster. Behind us trudged Hooge, his car still outside the gate.

The trip down the drive was supervised by thirty-two of those tall, bare, freaky trees. There were sixteen per side; Acacia trees, alias Black Locusts, Judy had learned. Most likely one hundred and one years old. Foxglove's house had been built in 1901.

We crossed a bridge over a creek and entered the courtyard guarded by two brick sentry houses, both sporting leaded windows and coach lights. Their faded French blue doors mirrored the shutters on the main dwelling. Each steep, shingled roof had long since surrendered to moss.

Any sentries on duty that afternoon were evidently A.W.O.L.

We parked by the fountain, got out and stared at the whole scene, waiting for Hooge in stunned silence, as Judy's hand crept into mine. This must be a dream. Only in a dream could a country road in the Fraser Valley lead us to an eighteenth century estate in Provence or Sussex.

"I'll bet she's got a butler," I whispered to Judy, half-expecting a tuxedoed Anthony Hopkins to swing the front door open.

Daylight revealed the courtyard's generous expanse bordered in boxwood hedge, the principal house, and a long, ancient barn-garage combination that was delicious in its charm but needed work. This somewhat sagging structure defined the entire west end of the brick courtyard, at right angles to the house on the South side, and the three foot curving brick and mortar wall that outlined the pond to the North. Quite a few shingles on the old barn were missing in action.

You could drive right between the garage and barn underneath their mutual second story that housed its own clock. This one was old, unlike Roxanne's, and accurate just twice a day, with hands stuck at twenty past four.

If you *did* drive through you'd run into the *new* barn about a hundred feet further. There were hot showers and a birthing stall. Three other stalls each boasted ample space for a seventeen-hand beast to find room between its steaming manure piles to recline among the shavings. Kick back and chill after a long day grazing and munching, amid all the amenities that the modern horse demands.

Hooge caught up and turned the tarnished brass knob of a heavy pine door; no key…folks don't lock up in the country. The front door housed a red and green stained glass oval and a brass slot, whose flap invited *LETTERS*. I imagined all the bills, due and past due, that must flow through that slot. Then I remembered the country mailbox on the dead end road. A five-minute hike for those bent on troublesome tidings.

We stepped inside onto the heaving curve of the red *fir* floor.

"Can you believe they didn't use hardwood, Jude?" was my first comment.

Gary advised that in the *country* the grandest of homes had main floors of fir. Harder wood was a city thing. I fought the urge to a roll a nickel on the swell of the entrance hall. "Just more character," was Judy's take.

Off the kitchen and dining room, which we had visited with Roxanne the prior night, was a long sunroom, totally glassed. The floor was new, a heated stretch of golden biscuit tiles with a weathered look. "Like a narrow street in Tuscany," I conceded to Judy.

Behind it, with a lookout to the kitchen, was a square interior room that French windowed on to the Tuscan street.

A tearoom perhaps, or an arena for my chessboard? Bridge anyone?

Across the fir hallway was a family room, or perhaps a library, with more French windows and doors that opened to all the patio you'd ever need. And sweeping from the patio was a lawn right down to the narrow river. Foxglove boasted seventeen acres and Hooge reckoned that four of those were on the river's other side. The family room was lined with built-in bookcases that framed an etched, concrete fireplace with emerald, marble trim. Green carpeting here sank into a swale near the double French doors, suggesting trouble beneath.

Carpeting usually lasts about forty-eight hours when Judy snaps into action on moving day. I wish I had a loonie for every staple I've pried from the oak floors of our city homes over the years and another buck for every time I've gouged a knuckle in the process.

"That fir floor needs work Jude! It's probably going to have to be totally replaced," I said to no one in particular. Judy and Hooge were ahead of me, mired in discussion.

The family room led to yet another that was behind a closed door. "The ballroom," announced Hooge as he opened the door to an icy blast. "The ballroom has its own furnace, outside of the house, the vendor doesn't use this room too much these days, so maybe she sees no point in heating it."

"The heating bill must be astronomical," was my input, "hey Jude check this out, you can see my breath!"

The ballroom had a Roman pillared entrance area, a hardwood floor, and nearly as many square feet as our entire Edmonton bungalow.

"We've never been to a ball, much less thrown one!" I whispered to Judy.

No less than five-dozen leaded panes of high arched French-door glass provided a checkered, downhill view toward the river. Counting these, detached from the patter between Judy and Hooge, I returned to the library and counted panes there. Once again, there were sixty.

A carpeted ramp from the library eased the six-inch drop to the ballroom and its oak parquet. The ramp was kind of a tacky touch but the ballroom must have been in use for some purpose. There was no furniture, just dried flowers everywhere. "Hydrangeas," Judy said.

"They shoot a lot of movies at Foxglove" remarked Hooge.

"Rebecca had *The Linda McCartney Story* and parts of *Legends of the Fall* and quite a few others. The ramp is for their equipment."

"*Legends of the Fall* had some good parts," I offered, "but I can't recall seeing this place in it; it seems to me they were on a spread in Montana," a stream of skepticism which Hooge ignored.

A door led from the ballroom down a long narrow hallway with four stained glass windows. Sharing the ballroom's idle furnace, the hallway and its granite floor held a chill. The hallway led to the chapel. Yes…the chapel; tiny and frigid, with more stained glass and granite floor. Looking up, we could see the invasion of tendrils of Virginia Creeper, poking through the upper window over the altar. Judy and I exchanged a quirky look.

I had been a server in the Anglican Church at age fifteen. A reluctant conscript to the calling, fresh from my own confirmation, I had lacked the sense of self to just say "no."

When the late Reverend David Milne suggested I cut my hair it was 1966. The Beatles were chart toppers that year with *Magical Mystery Tour* and The Stones had answered with *Their Satanic Majesties Request*. Hendrix and The Doors were just emerging. "Clapton is God" graffiti would soon appear on the brick wall of my high school.

I got a new Sears Silvertone electric guitar for Christmas and started a band with four of my friends. After much deliberation we called ourselves *The Phyve*. Our business cards proclaimed that *The Phyve* specialized in "The English Sound." We were lousy, but after a gig at The Purple Pad in Essex, Ontario, a group of about five girls asked us for autographs as we packed up our equipment. A couple of them had me sign on the underside of their forearms. One said she liked our rendition of *This Could Be the Last Time*. Another said she liked my hair.

Reverend Milne's personal hairstyle was fringe plus naked spit shine scalp. A friend of mine refers to this genetic misfortune as a "horseshoe cut." I let Reverend Milne know that my serving days were over. I turned in my red cassock, watched the Detroit Lions and Tigers on early Sunday afternoons and avoided barbershops.

A server was the Anglican version of the Roman Catholic altar boy, but without so much of the buggery. But the sad revelations of our RC counterparts, along with a study of the Inquisition, drove a further wedge between organized religion and me. Burning folks is really bad.

Judy and I attended Church for baptisms, weddings, funerals, Christmas and Easter. We were like a tour pro that just played in the majors.

We even stopped doing that when in the eighties the Minister started asking the congregation to shake hands and say "God bless you, neighbor," to the strangers in the pews ahead and behind. Screw that. I had no interest in pressing flesh with a clammy hardware store manager and his trench-mouthed wife. We were Anglicans for God's sake not Baptists. Canada's branch of The Church of England must have hired consultants in the seventies who told them to remove the stick from their collective ass and loosen up. They probably formed a "focus group," that recommended the paraphrasing of the starchy, cryptic prose in The Morning Prayer

Book into understandable pap. My ewe and I strayed from the flock before they replaced the shot of Holy Communion wine with Welch's Concord grape juice. I'm sure that would have been next.

The potentates of the Anglican Church changed things to make their services more accessible. These days corporate lingo would call it "re-branding." If they'd bothered to ask me I would have said…"Now hold on here, I kind of like you inaccessible and I'd probably like you even more if you weren't here at all!"

Even before my short and agonizing career as a server, I'd honed a technique that enabled me to survive the tedium of Reverend Milne's Sunday sermon.

Moving to Windsor in 1961 I fast became a rabid supporter of the Detroit Tigers. They won a hundred and one games that year, usually a pennant winning record that earned a berth in The World Series. But the Yankees had Maris and Mantle chasing Babe Ruth's homer record and I think they won about a hundred and nine times, leaving my heroes a distant second.

It was during those sermons that I would strategize how the Tigers could improve and vanquish the Bronx Bombers in '62.

I'd picture the team in their snowy uniforms with the olde English *D* on the emerald turf of Tiger Stadium. My squirming in the pew would subside, as I could almost smell the fried onions, hot dogs and cigar smoke; the presiding aromas of the old downtown ball yard.

As the sermon plodded I'd check my lineup.

Dick Brown behind the plate, Frank Lary on the mound, "Stormin'" Norman Cash at first and the speedster, Jake Wood, at second. Chico Fernandez and rookie Dick McAuliffe shared shortstop as Chico was a bit of a weak link. Another rookie, Steve Boros occupied the hot corner. The great Hall of Famer Al Kaline patrolled right field; swift Billy Bruton was in center, occasionally spelled by Bubba Morton if the opposition was starting a southpaw.

My personal favorite, number seven, Rocco Domenico Colavito was the Tiger left fielder. He was the real deal, a slugger, crushing forty-five homers and a hundred and forty RBI's in 1961 and was more than adequate in the field. Opposing base runners rarely tested Colavito's arm. Rocky had a cannon.

Colavito's trademark was a pose he struck in the on deck circle and sometimes at the plate between pitches. With both hands he would hold his bat at each end and place the barrel behind his neck and stretch and flex his lanky 6-foot-3-inch magnificence. Six-three was pretty tall in 1961.

The Reverend Mr. Milne was in his pulpit going on about something…"In Peter's letter to Paul he wrote etc. etc. etc." and "Paul wrote back to Peter blah, blah, blah." Or Milne was litanizing the afflictions that beset old Job. I daresay even Job's patience would have worn pretty thin during one of Mr. Milne's Sunday blowhards.

I'd run out of big league Tigers so I turned my thoughts to their farm team, The Toledo Mud Hens. Which Mud Hen should make the jump to the big team? Purnell Goldy, Jimmy Northrup, Willy Horton?

After the '62 season there was trade talk. The Tigers were actually thinking of dealing Rocky Colavito.

It was probably a contractual issue, but hey, I was twelve. What did I care about payroll concerns? That Sunday I spent Milne's entire sermon in deep prayer. I prayed my guts out. "Please God, don't let them trade Rocky. Don't let them deal number seven!"

Prior to the 1963 season the Detroit Tigers traded Rocco Domenico Colavito to the Kansas City Athletics for second baseman Jerry Lumpe (pronounced *Lumpy* like Fred Rutherford's son in Leave it to Beaver), and journeyman pitcher, Dave Wickersham. The Tigers, mediocre in '63, slid into three years of stinking. The Yanks went to the Series five years in a row ending in 1965. This was an early nail in the coffin of my regard for organized religion. Clearly, God was a Yankee fan.

In 1980 Judy and I brought our youngest daughter Taylor to the Anglican Church in Barrie to be christened. We were familiar with the drill, having baptized our first three children.

When second son Dylan was christened in Edmonton, the Minister expressed his regret that Judy and I had declined to attend the pre-baptism course that his parish offered. He tried to change our mind.

But my bride and I weren't course takers; neither pre-marital nor pre-parenting. Other young couples seemed to have long engagements, big weddings and planned conceptions. Once they "pulled the goalie," and announced "we're pregnant," they'd take a course together on how to breathe during labor. Meanwhile Judy was whelping pink joy without so much as a whimper.

Take a course on baptism? Hell, I don't even read the manual when I assemble a gas barbeque. Well one time I tried. Followed step one through five to the letter. Wearying, and, in retrospect, probably suffering from attention deficit disorder, I jumped forward to the last five; steps one hundred and sixty-seven to one hundred and seventy one. Then I fired that sucker up and damn near vaporized the family.

We managed to avoid the baptism course for the boys and for Harmony, but at Taylor's christening the reverend dug in his heels. On the phone he had seemed a little testy that, save for this baptism, we hadn't set foot in his church.

Judy's family had made the seven-hour trek from Hawkesbury for the ceremony and my parents had flown in from Vancouver. The regular Sunday congregation had filed out and our family was gathered in the first pew with the swaddled main attraction. This timing in itself was a red flag. The baptisms for the other three kids had been part of the regular service in the presence of the entire flock. When Harmony was christened in Hawkesbury, Father Lawlor had crafted his upbeat sermon around her name. "God bless Harmony!" the congregation called back in one full voice.

But Taylor's ceremony seemed to be set up as an afterthought, and then the man of the cloth told us how it would be. "I'm sorry you didn't attend our pre-baptism course but, provided you and Judy do so after the fact, I'll still perform the ceremony." It'll be five weeks, one evening per week."

I envisioned our parents returning to their distant homes, their little pink granddaughter still a heathen; but I didn't wilt. Loins girded by the outrage of the Inquisition and sodomized altar boys, Milne's sermons and the gutted, pasteurized prayer book, I glared back at this puffed up cleric with my own brand of hellfire.

"Sir, are you blackmailing us?"

He paused, scalded and skewered.

He grabbed baby Taylor from Judy's arms and jerked her towards the font. He sprinkled holy water on her brow with an indignant backhanded gesture and scowled a blessing.

She started to cry a little.

Maybe we'd convert the chapel into a wine cellar. Lord knows it was cold enough.

The chapel's acoustics were like Carnegie Hall. I delighted in how my words seemed like they were coming from James Earl Jones. I stepped up on the small raised wooden platform where a pulpit could have been and drawled some fire and brimstone like a Mississippi pastor. "Brother, Sister, the Day of Reckonin' is approachin'…. It's time that y'all repent!"

Then I baritoned the first verse of *Amazing Grace* and wasn't surprised when Judy failed to step up and lay on her soprano harmony. We usually have to go through a mating ritual of persuasion before she'll sing, and besides, she was occupied, telling Hooge that Foxglove was overpriced; a beautiful property for certain, but one that just needed "*so* much work."

A leaded, paned door led from the chapel outside to the back of the ballroom. As the three of us strolled by, the heavy-duty external furnace shuddered to life. Seconds later its hot breath was cozying both the ballroom and the icy chapel.

"Well that's *just* what a husband needs to see!" I quipped to Hooge, "his wife walks by and the furnace kicks in!"

Feigning a swat to my cheek, Judy chuckled too.

CHAPTER 8

"I've got the man I love beside me,
We love the open road"—Joni Mitchell

NIGHT RIDE HOME

FOXGLOVE FARM *DID* NEED A LOT OF WORK. I WAS RECITING its deficiencies to Judy on the ride back to Kit's Beach. The hardtop of the Lexus was up and Van the Man sang *I'm Tired Joey Boy*.

The upstairs was tacky; every bathroom needed doing. The roof was suspect under all that creeper and what about the plumbing and wiring? The ballroom ceiling was water damaged by rain that had collected on its flat turreted roof. Then there were those heaving fir floors! The horse set-up was hardly state-of-the-art, with an overgrown riding ring that sprouted dozens of saplings.

"Half a million," I said, "for starters."

"Offer half a million??" Judy asked.

"No, it's going to take five-hundred grand to fix that place up."

"No way would it be that much," Judy countered, "we'd move slowly, take our time; I'd be happy to move in and live with it just as it is."

"Yeah, right" was my reply. That's what she had said in

1988 about Pine Crescent, the Shaughnessy estate with the $618,000 mortgage. It needed tons of work but we'd take our time. The basement was tenanted and that would help with the payments.

The day after we moved in she'd called the painters and a handyman; the day before she booted the tenant, paying him off for the short notice.

"If we do this, you might have to choose you know," I said as we soared westward over The Port Mann Bridge.

"Choose??" Judy pondered.

"Well, especially if the business doesn't sell." I was referring to our insurance brokerage that we started five years back. Lately there'd been some serious acquisition interest from a large U.S. firm.

"Maybe we can manage the townhouse and the farm," I explained, "but worse case scenario it's going to be one or the other. Do you really want to live in Langley?"

We fell silent and after a few minutes I cranked the volume on Van.

CHAPTER 9

"Big Time!!"—Peter Gabriel

SIZE MATTERS

I GUESS I SHOULD HAVE KNOWN THAT SOONER OR LATER WE'D get a farm and not just a paltry acre or two.

Judy has a thing for big things. Even in my case she has often declared "I likes me a man with a little meat on his bones," drawling like Foghorn Leghorn, the cartoon rooster.

Our townhouse on the ocean on Point Grey Road is tiny; three floors, five hundred square feet per floor. Judy has defiantly filled it with big things like an immense oak fireplace surround, a Grand Piano and a full-sized AGA stove in British Racing Green. Then there was a Saint Bernard named Bernice. Her theory is that the minimalist *less is more* approach actually makes a small space seem even smaller. I agree with her. I've drunk that kool-aid and so do most of our visitors who admire her bold stroke style.

Although, I guess I *did* have some reservations about Bernice.

Bernice joined our family when we were on the rebound from Agatha, the bloodhound from our hellacious year at the log cabin. We had made an impetuous decision to buy Agatha two years prior, when we were still grieving the loss of Steisha. Steisha was a golden retriever, quiet and gentle, a genuine lady, struck down by a cluster of abdominal tumors when we lived in Tiddley Cove.

A few weeks after Steisha's demise, Judy and I were strolling down Marine Drive in Dundarave when we saw a doggy chart in the window of a veterinarian office. There were hundreds of canines illustrated, every breed that has ever slobbered or scratched a flea.

Suffering a brain glitch, it was *I* who zeroed in on the bloodhound. Minutes later we were breaking speed limits and running amber lights to get to Richmond. A cellular call to The House of Puppies had verified that they indeed had a bloodhound on the premises, a black and tan Kansas bitch. She was only a few weeks old and The House of Puppies closed at five o'clock.

We made it to the H of P just under the wire and were led to a bin that was teeming with pups. There were four-legged toddlers from more than half a dozen breeds. Boxers, Terriers, two shades of Labs, German Shepherds, Afghans and Bulldogs were all well represented within this wriggling mob of juniors. From the rabble, with a leap, emerged the bloodhound, escaping the bin, *in fact* choosing us.

"That Boxer's cute too, Jude," I said, too little, too late.

There was a book, in effect an owner's manual, for each of the breeds offered by "The House of Puppies." Well, for each of the breeds except the bloodhound.

"We're out of the bloodhound book but we'll order it for you if you like," proposed the young lady behind the counter. "It'll take about two weeks."

We said that'd be fine and she wrote up the deal. Meanwhile young Agatha was running free about The House of Puppies with a geranium plant in her mouth, dropping clumps of soil here and there. While we were ordering her manual she had seen fit to uproot that two-foot plant, with its bright red bloom, from a clay pot near the Chihuahua section.

If the bloodhound book had been in stock we would have never opted for the bloodhound.

Two weeks later I already knew more about the blood-hound than I could ever want to know. Then the book arrived in the mailbox of the log cabin. The first sentence began, "Congratulations on choosing your bloodhound!" and continued, "your life is about to change forever!"

Agatha was hyper and obsessed with escape. It didn't matter where we were living, West Vancouver, Shaughnessy or Dunbar, Agatha bolted through the skinniest crack in the door. Pursuit was futile; they're called hounds for a reason.

Judy urged me to give chase on foot while she combed the streets in her red Jeep Grand Cherokee. We soon learned where to find Agatha and it became my job to journey to the East Vancouver Pound off Venables St. to bail her out. On no less than six occasions, in one year, it fell to me to spring Agatha from the clink. Each time there was paperwork of some length and one of the screws at the pound would roll my visa card for ninety-one dollars.

The pound's employees came to know me pretty well and would call me directly at my office when they received word that Agatha was en route to the hoosegow in the paddy wagon. On my final visit I showed up twenty-five minutes before she did and I'll be damned if I didn't have to insist that they start the paperwork in anticipation of her arrival.

The desk clerk's nametag proclaimed that he was Floyd. His left eye had a small tic that jumped to life every fifteen seconds.

"We have no way of knowing that it's your dog sir. You have to identify her."

I grimaced, my resolve rising with my blood pressure.

"You did say it was a bloodhound," I established.

"Oh it's a bloodhound sir, a black and tan bitch."

"Oh, then it's a female. Now Floyd, you're sure of that??"

"Yup sir, the dogcatcher mentioned that he'd picked up a lady when he called in, and it's pretty hard to mistake the gender, her being a short haired breed and all." Mutts of every description were whining, yelping and stinking from the cell-block behind him. Floyd's eye tic was beginning to percolate.

"Now tell me Floyd, do you ever get any other black and tan bloodhound bitches here?" (Salesmanship 101; only ask a question where you already know the answer.)

"Nope, just that one of yours," came his cautious reply.

Through lethal eye slits and gritted teeth I quietly said "No, of course you don't, why would you? No one else would have a bloodhound would they?" The eye tic was doing jumping jacks, leaping around like O.J.Simpson's polygraph needle.

I pushed my visa card on the counter, right under his nose.

"Fill out that freaking paperwork…*now*."

Fifteen minutes after everything was signed the paddy wagon turned off Venables into the pound parking lot. The driver jumped out and swung the back doors open. He'd brought in two suspects and they were side by side in a couple of cages. They were sitting, each with a length of pink tongue dangling, looking out the back. On the left was a full grown Black Labrador whose great grandmother may have had a dalliance with a German Shepherd. On the right was a black and tan Kansas Bloodhound bitch; my bitch; my paid for bitch.

I nodded to the dogcatcher and winked at Floyd who'd carried the paperwork out to the parking lot to get a jumpy eyeful of the proceedings. "That's my dog," I said, pointing left to the Lab-Shepherd cross. "That's Agatha."

Judy found Agatha an ideal home on a farm in Abbotsford, a bit of a bible-thumping town that lies halfway between Langley and Chilliwack, further east up the Fraser Valley.

"If Agatha bolts from there, that farmer's going to have one helluva drive to the East Vancouver Pound," was my reminder to Judy of my former responsibility.

The last we heard, our bloodhound had her own bedroom and a steady diet of lean ground beef and rice. It was still tough to say goodbye for Judy who never gives up on a kid or a dog. Husbands? The jury's still out.

When we billeted Agatha out to Abbotsford in 1993 we had just moved on to Alma Street into a charming Tudor home that was smaller than what we were used to, with the exception of the log cabin in Tiddley Cove. The back yard was all pool and spa and pool house and glazed aggregate concrete. Inside it was bleached hardwood and open concept, bay windows with cushioned window seats; a home suited to adults who liked to entertain, and maybe okay for children back for a while from university. It was clearly unsuitable for bloodhounds with their tendency to gnaw on things; particularly upscale items. At the log cabin one afternoon, I was mortified to find my burgundy calfskin Ralph Lauren wallet had been more than half consumed and my Platinum American Express Card was punctured beyond legibility of the expiry date. Suspicion of this misdemeanor was only one transgression on Agatha's lengthy rap sheet.

This, even more than the costly visits to the pound, hastened Agatha's dispatch. An easy decision for me; it was a tough call for Judy, whose keen devotion to Agatha went so far as holding her long, silky ears high and dry above the bitch's head when the latter wet her whistle in our toilet.

But Judy still hankered for canine companionship, even though she had vowed that Agatha would have no successor.

No more than six weeks later we were at the Oakridge Mall and she beckoned me to venture into a pet store. She walked me straight over to a glass cubicle where an earnest little white dog seemed to recognize her. A Shih Tzu I think it was; a small breed. I recall its price being about three or four hundred dollars. Swiftly I drew my credit card from my wallet to close the deal; I could only guess that size no longer mattered.

But no, she was just softening me up. "Let's think it over," she suggested.

It was a classic sales technique through which I should have seen. Get agreement on a minor point. Whether or not we would get another dog was no longer in question; now it was just a matter of size…and size mattered.

A couple of weeks later I came home after work and found no Judy. As per usual, I poured a double Chivas. Then the phone rang and it was a call from her Jeep. Harmony and Taylor were about fifteen and thirteen then and I could hear them giggling in the background.

"Where's my dinner!!??" I demanded to know, in a way that she'd never take seriously.

"I'll make you a nice dinner, but I've been *bad* honey," Judy confessed. "Don't be mad."

"Did you buy a dog?" I asked, thinking of the low maintenance Shih Tzu.

"No, I bought a *big* dog...a *really big* dog."

"Well that's just great," I muttered, hung up, and freshened my Scotch.

Moments later they arrived, the girls reveling in my discomfort. "Can we keep her; can we Dad?" they chanted a parody of something they'd probably seen in that Beethoven video with Charles Grodin.

Judy had seen her in another pet shop. At six months she had signs of hip displasia. "Her cage was so small and cramped and at her age nobody's going to buy her. She was half-price...they'd reduced her twice...two hundred and fifty bucks...for a purebred St. Bernard!!...It was *so* pathetic! We're not going to keep her; I just wanted to get her out of there. Don't worry, I'll find her a good home."

Right; a temporary measure; just like when they introduced income tax around the time of The First Great War.

The girls were rolling on the bleached oak floor with this huge ball of orange and white fluff. Shafts of sunset filtered through the California shutters and I could see tens of thousands of little doggy hairs floating in the family room.

I sulked for an hour or so and the fact that they had actually named her really grated on me. The girls called her "Nana," like the English sheepdog in Peter Pan.

"We're not keeping her," I finally announced "but if we were keeping her, her name wouldn't be Nana, it would be Bernice."

"Bernice!!!" shrieked Harmony. "I love you Bernice," purred Taylor.

CHAPTER 10

"Give to me your leather; Take from me my lace"
—*Stevie Nicks*

THE OFFER

"WHAT SHOULD WE WRITE?" ASKED JUDY AS I CRACKED OPEN a Semillon Blanc in the kitchen at Point Grey Road.

After that "we are so buying this place" comment, we may as well write full price," came my reply as I poured, "or maybe fifty grand over asking!"

The asking price for Foxglove Farm was $789,000 and Judy phoned Hooge to let him know our offer was $239,000 less. He sounded like he was sucking on a lemon when he said, "My vendor won't even respond to $550,000. You saw the property; you know how unique it is."

"But it still needs a ton of work, Gary," countered Judy, "I don't even know where to begin; haven't got a clue." Without calling her a liar, I do remember thinking she probably had some idea of where to begin.

Hooge made a few points about the prices of comparable properties, but added that Foxglove Farm was truly incomparable. That asking price was "less than land value," for seventeen dry acres, especially with a good spring well and water rights on its very own river. Plus there were views of the snow-capped mountains on the north side of the Fraser; the old house, with all its history and charm, in essence, was free.

We were adamant and faxed Hooge the lowball. Sure enough, no response. We came up a hundred grand and she came back at $775,000.

I ran to the liquor store for a Mumm's Cordon Rouge while Judy faxed another counter offer to the ReMax office. Back at Point Grey Road I shoved the bottle up to its neck in the cubes of the icemaker. Twenty minutes later our big, outdated Brother Fax machine beeped to life, paused for an aching moment, and then coughed up a blotchy page. Next to Judy's $758,000 and her J.T. were the initials R.B. and just like that we were farmers.

Then there was a semi-chilled champagne toast, a hug and a high-five.

"That Becky drives a hard bargain," I said.

CHAPTER 11

"When we walked in fields of gold"—Sting

WE'RE BAAAACK!!!!

YUP, WE WERE FARMERS; OR AT LEAST WE WOULD BE IN FOUR months.

Daunted by the financial acrobatics I'd have to perform to own a second property without selling the first, I'd convinced Judy that possession of Foxglove Farm should be deferred as long as the vendor would endure. It turned out this suited Rebecca just fine, because after twenty years at the farm and running her flower business there, moving out was a task of monumental proportion.

The deal was struck in mid February; the possession date was June 23rd.

The day after our offer was accepted, Judy told Hooge we wanted to go through again, measure for furniture and drapes and take a few pictures.

Rebecca stayed outside the house while we were inside, and, when we were strolling the gardens and walking the fields, we could see she had gone inside; probably annoyed by our first lowball offer. We never did meet Rebecca that day.

Hooge waited patiently for at least a couple of hours but hey, that only works out to about seven minutes per acre. Judy had a couple of disposable cameras and used up all the shots. Out in one of the pastures, far from the house, she held the camera at arm's length, grabbed me and pressed her right cheek against my left.

"Smile honey!" she said as she snapped.

She keeps that photo at bedside these days. It accentuates our gap. I'm smiling but distorted, rubber faced and bewildered, photographed right up the nose. She's photogenic, as always, and beaming the purest brand of joy.

"I've never seen so many blackberry bushes," I enthused. "We're set for life!!" I love blackberries; there were masses of their brambles near the house, around the barn and the mother lode was in the back acreage, where our fence intersected the river. Judy nipped this in the bud. "If you want blackberries, go to the IGA. Blackberries take over everything. Absolutely invasive; we're taking a chain-saw to most of these."

"You know we could put in a couple of golf holes over there," I pointed to the most remote corner of our fiefdom, "just par threes. I could work on my short game like Peter."

Our friend Peter Wardle has a six-hole par three course on his waterfront property on Hornby Island. Peter's short game's pretty sharp. He usually takes a few bucks off us at Shaughnessy.

"Horses and golf balls don't mix," was Judy's solemn response, "it just takes one for a broken leg."

We turned to stroll hand in hand past the overgrown riding ring and headed back to the courtyard. We saw a sprinting pheasant barely manage to get airborne in time to avoid a lunch date with a coyote. Just another day at the farm. Our farm.

We said goodbye to Hooge in the front hallway of the house and I lingered for a moment in the den that opened off it through a couple of French doors. It had an old marble floor, wainscoting and deep paned windows overlooking the courtyard fountain and the rhododendrons. I wondered what color their blossoms would be on June 23rd.

"I can write my book right there Jude."

"That'll be cool," she nodded with a smile.

Parting from Foxglove was sweet sorrow.

Hooge must have sensed something and let us know that we couldn't keep doing this. This would be the final tour until June 23. When the reality of the long wait until midsummer sank in, Judy and I called Hooge to see if we could move up the possession date. I limbered up for some of those financial acrobatics I'd been trying to avoid.

But June 23rd was just fine with Rebecca. It gave her time to have a "going out of business" sale. Besides, she was getting remarried in June to an architect from West Vancouver. They were tying the knot in our chapel.

CHAPTER 12

"The Waiting is the Hardest Part"— Tom Petty

GREAT SCOTT!!

As THE DAYS AND WEEKS CRAWLED BY JUDY AND I WERE LIKE a couple of five year olds eager for Christmas morning. "Only a hundred and thirteen more sleeps!" I told her on the first of March.

I kept thinking of that brawny den and the book that I might finally write, or *at least* finally start, a dusty and faded notion, tucked away in a corner shelf of my head for almost thirty years.

In fall of 1972 Judy and I left our summer jobs in Toronto and returned to Brock for our second year; only this time we were Mr. and Mrs. Trowbridge. We had rented a one-bedroom basement apartment in Thorold, a small town not too far from campus. It was one hundred and ten dollars a month.

Our landlord was Mr. Bosco, Tony Bosco, a short and keg-like bald Italian who worked in the factory in Thorold. At least I think he did. I was never sure what the factory produced, but the whole town of Thorold smelled like vanilla.

Mr. Bosco had a permanent, squinted-up grin, through

which, on those rare occasions he spoke, his fractured English would emerge. His wife, Lillianna, talked enough for both of them. She made a rectangular pizza every day, soaked it in olive oil and used it as legal tender.

"Juduh"…she would say. Helpa Beana with her matha and I'll bakea you a pizza." I dunno whya Beana is so badda inna math. I makea her pizza. She eatsa good."

Beana was their twelve-year old daughter who had trouble with figures.

"When it comes to mathematics, I got static in the attic," confess the lyrics from "Raised on Robbery." At least Beana Bosco had a kindred spirit in Joni Mitchell.

Tony was proud of his dog, a beagle that was rarely out of a small cage in the back yard. His name was Snoopy…they thought real hard on that. No model prisoner, Snoopy was a barker and a whiner.

"Snoopa, heasa huntinga dogga," beamed Tony through the squinty grin.

The Bosco's were okay I guess, but when we were back from class or from Toronto for the weekend we'd invariably be greeted by a sometimes flat and occasionally frothy bowlful of yellow urine. Somebody was using their key in our door and having a whiz in our toilet…anda no flusha.

My money was on Tony.

Judy and I signed up for six courses each and five of them were the same; mainly English Literature and Dramatic Media courses.

We couldn't get enough of each other. A week has 168 hours and we were spending 165 of them together.

Bags, alias "The Lowest Form of Human Life," had led

our floor's intramural squad to the Brock Flag Football championship the prior year. But Bags was a dropout after just one year of cutting classes and I suddenly had big shoes to fill when I inherited his job as quarterback.

But Judy pitched in to build my confidence. Not only did she cheer us on from the sidelines, she actually practised me up between games. We'd scrimmage with just the two of us.

"Go deep Jude!!! Long bomb!!" I exhorted, pounding the pigskin into my left palm on the front lawn of the Brock tower. I could see the copper cloud bouncing off her shoulders as she ran a fly pattern fifty yards downfield. I stepped up and launched a perfect spiral against a crisp blue autumn sky. I guess I should have yelled "turn around!!" but I was transfixed by that precious moment.

The bouncing hair, framed by the scarlets and ambers of that October day. My best girl going deep. Twenty bucks to our name. Not a care in the world.

Her head felt okay after a few minutes. It was a tight, sixty yard spiral and the pointy end had nailed her right where her downy "soft spot" would have been, nineteen years prior; but fortunately those Radford girls grew up to be hardheaded women.

For the rest of our scrimmage we confined her pass routes to the shorter patterns. When we huddled, I only called for the screens, flares and buttonhooks. My arms over her shoulders, though we were quite alone, I whispered each play through the fragrance of her hair.

Then it was time to go to Romantic Literature 205. Turn our thoughts to Wordsworth, Keats, Shelley and Byron. We headed towards the tower. I jogged beside my teenaged wife, tossing up the football every few steps, running under it to haul it in myself.

"Next time I still want to go deep again honey," chirped the plucky wide receiver.

The head of Brock's Faculty of English was Professor Michael Hornyansky, a tallish, slim be-speckled man who drove a Renault or a Peugeot.

C'est le même chose, n'est-ce pas??

He had a ginger goatee with a bit of silver dusting.

I only know what he drove because we had an Austin Mini-Cooper conversion circa 1967. On one of the many times it wouldn't start I hitch-hiked from Thorold to class. Hornyansky pulled over. He knew Judy and me from his small creative writing class.

"Why not a French car?" he queried when I bemoaned ever driving a British Leyland product. Grateful for the ride and hopeful for an "A" in creative writing, I quelled my candor and shrugged.

He dropped me by the tower at the centre of the campus.

It would take almost as much of an idiot to drive that French crap too, was my thinking at the time.

Hornyansky's writing class was on Monday evenings at seven. It ended just in time for Monday Night Football, at the time a new phenomenon. I looked forward to Mondays in those days. About a dozen students gathered around a table with the Prof. By each Thursday we had to submit whatever Hornyansky had assigned at the end of the Monday session. It had to be typed. Professor Hornyansky's secretary would remove the names and mimeograph copies of everyone's work for the whole class. This, at least at Brock, predated the advent of the photocopier. Then everyone, with the author's humiliation or occasional pride shrouded under the cover of anonymity, would pick each submission apart.

Hornyansky himself was often one of the more savage critics, but a tall, pink-faced kid with a dusty blonde Afro could be real nasty too, if he didn't take a shine to your short story or poem. I think his name was Mr. Crane. Hornyansky addressed us all by our last names.

One Monday, our assignment sounded easy enough but some of the class found it tough. "Write a serious limerick," was the edict that came forth through the ginger goatee. Just one verse was adequate.

Back at Casa Bosco I flushed the toilet then got started straight away. With one eye on the football game I scratched away on a notepad and had a couple of false starts. The cadence of the limerick cries out for the word "Nantucket," and that wasn't going anywhere serious.

Then I thought of groupies.

"The Pleistocene Lady of Dances
To dignify decibel trances
Reshapes overnight stands
And encounters with bands
Into artfully molded romances."
(I couldn't stop at one verse.)
"With cellophane smile she enhances
Her hopes of successful advances
With the patched denim prizes
Who buy the disguises
Of the Pleistocene Lady of Dances."

The following Monday night the class was assembled around the table and Hornyansky handed out four fresh and fragrant mimeographed pages with a dozen limericks. One was a two verser.

Even Mr. Crane liked mine. Judy dutifully pitched in with her endorsement, as did a few of the more outspoken of our fellow poets and novelists in training. Hornyansky's brief approbation was precious nectar to my ears. He referred to the author establishing "pathos" and grasped any subtleties I intended, and maybe some I hadn't.

Judy had slapped her limerick together on Thursday, just beating the deadline. It recalled a poignant Hawkesbury scene.

"By the train track down by the river
The wino sits rotting his liver
And as he huddles against
The broken snow fence
The cold winter wind makes him shiver."

There was utter silence for about thirty seconds as each of us read our copy. Certainly she'd done well in the pathos department, I thought, holding my breath. I snuck a peek at Hornyansky. He commanded the head of the table; impassive behind gold rim glasses, tamping tobacco in his pipe. Mr. Crane broke the long silence. Starting with a repressed series of snorts, Mr. Crane sounded as if he was doing his best to hold in a toke. Then his pink face cracked out of control, as tears streamed down his cheeks, which flushed even pinker than usual.

"I'm sorry," he grinned, "I really am," shaking the dirty blonde Afro.

"But I just can't get over the image of this wino sitting by the river, holding his liver in a tin cup."

All the students laughed with the exception of Mr. and Mrs. Trowbridge. Well, I chuckled just a little, so as not to blow our cover. Hornyansky smiled behind his pipe and moved on to the next limerick.

But every worm has its day and the dog has a way of turning.

Another one of our classes was Dramatic Media 295.

This course was actually an excuse to watch movies. Just about every movie ever made. It was three weeks before we even got into the talkies.

"The Battleship Potemkin" led to a passel of other silent flicks and then some Rudolph Valentino, just to see what all the fuss was about. We were soon into the "oaters," all the John Wayne pictures, several weeks of Hitchcock and cheesier horror from William Castle.

When our assignment was to analyze a recent movie, Judy and I began a lifelong custom of sitting in the center of the theatre's first row. Right up front, we were totally absorbed in the sights and sounds of the film, undistracted by any Afro sporting popcorn muncher who might otherwise dilute the experience. Hell, we were married, we didn't have to neck in the back of the theatre. We could go home to the Bosco's, flush the toilet and jump into bed.

Later, through the eighties and nineties, we'd double date with our great friends Don and Shirley; dinner and a movie.

Don and Shirley preferred to sit in the back and loved movies as much as us, but as our savvy lawyer, Don was no stranger to compromise and easygoing Shirley's always been an angel. Judy and I weren't hard to get along with either, so we'd all sit in the second or third row from the screen. Sometimes you've just got to give a little.

(We still see Don and Shirley, but not nearly so much these days. Over the years Liberty, Yum Yum, our Golden retriever Steisha, Agatha, Bernice, a fat cat named Zsu Zsu, Dornoch, Mickey and Matt have played havoc with Don's asthma and allergic afflictions. Don would be in tears five minutes after coming over, and not just because he was glad to see us. Matt, by the way, arrived at Foxglove about a year after we did. Another seventeen hand chestnut gelding, Matt was the spitting image of Mickey, an absolute clone, with the exception of one snowy knee-length sock that set Matt apart. Judy had recruited Matt from Southlands despite her opinion that he was a bit of a dullard. "Matt's stupid," was her assessment as she wrote his name in chalk on the stall next to the one with the glossy brass nameplate that said *Mickey*, "but horses are herd animals; Mickey needs company…. Matt'll be your horse," she added as we strolled back to the house.)

At the lectern for the Brock film course was our English 101 professor from first year, one Professor Maurice Yacowar. While Hornyansky drove a French car, Professor Yacowar straddled a Harley Davidson to get to and from the lecture hall.

From neck to foot, Yacowar was every inch a Hell's Angel.

A black leather jacket with silver chains, worn black chinos and black motorcycle boots were his daily lecture garb. From the neck up he could have been a Palestinian terrorist. A thick black Smith Brothers beard, (for those who remember their licorice cough drops), matched a thatch of the blackest hair, always pony tailed on campus. Glasses with thick, black frames, a la Woody Allen, completed the look. While only five nine, tops, Yacowar cut quite a picture.

Some students said he had studied at Oxford and was a Rhodes Scholar.

In English 101 first year students were awestruck by his incisive, almost surgical dissection of a best seller known as The Holy Bible. He offered no moralizing, no theology; just criticism of the literary work.

Yacowar had a unique speaking voice that was juxtaposed to his appearance. I could imitate it flawlessly then and still can.

He spoke formally, enunciating each word separately yet with a bored croaking timber, as if it were great trouble to have to speak at all. Most of us hung on every croaky, nasal word, aware of his master stature as a critical analyst, and his fondness for flaunting his craft, sometimes frame by frame.

Occasionally Professor Yacowar would pull the collective leg of the sophomores that took his course.

During a classroom viewing of Godard's "Breathless" with Jean Paul Belmondo, Yacowar made a big point of getting the projectionist to freeze a frame where Jean Seberg was strutting down a Parisian street in a simple white shift that wasn't even that short by 1972 standards.

"Roll that back!" he croaked, "Stop it there!"

Jean Seberg sashayed backwards down Rue St. Germaine and froze.

Many in the room poised their notebooks and pencils at the ready, awaiting a Yacowarian pearl of insight.

"Nice legs, don't you think class?" came the croaking assessment.

Our major paper in the second term was an essay, critically analyzing any movie we wanted. Judy chose King Kong, not the remake with Jessica Lange, the original black and white classic starring Fay Wray.

Perhaps subliminally influenced by Yacowar's glasses, I chose "Everything You Always Wanted to Know About Sex But Were Afraid to Ask," at the time, one of Woody Allen's more recent zany comedies. I thought it was chock full of edgy, multi-level angles to grab on to and it would make for a slam dunk A Plus, to go with the one that I got from Hornyansky for my serious limerick. This essay would write itself.

The day the class handed in our papers Yacowar had a little fun with Judy and me. "Here's a husband and wife team," he croaked with each word separate, "he's written on *Everything You Always Wanted To Know About Sex But Were Afraid to Ask*...she...*King Kong*!"

We beamed from the front row of the lecture theatre where we usually sat as the class enjoyed a good laugh.

Three weeks later we had just occupied the same seats and were five minutes early, glad to get out of the cold. About a dozen students were sliding into the seats behind us.

Judy looked extra "hot" that day as the young people say, though our long walk to class was chilly. That Niagara Escarpment wind could be raw and wet.

Normally she'd throw on a pair of jeans for class but that day she'd worn a very tiny plaid kilt. "McKinnon tartan," she told me back at the Bosco's. She topped it with a soft oatmeal sweater and pulled it all together with matching over-the-knee socks. For perspective, if her chunky heeled loafers were in Baton Rouge and her cable knit knees were in Kansas City, the flirty hemline of that kilt was just south of Saginaw, Michigan. A lot of slim, bare getaway stick was glowing pink, fresh from a righteous nipping by the February air. The guys in the class gawked a little and a few days later a couple of the girls came to class in similar outfits. Some days, don't you just feel you could chop a mountain down with the side of your hand?

Yacowar entered stage right and moved towards his chair off to the side behind the lectern. He'd worn his black-on-black motorcycle getup and lugged a stack of papers under his arm. He piled the papers on a table by his chair, sat down and crossed his legs. He adjusted his thick glasses and took on a bored countenance as the balance of the class filed in. The boot that he had set upon his knee revealed a sizeable wad of what was certainly canine excrement, wedged in the arch by the stacked heel.

From my vantage point in the front row I heard myself in full voice, "Professor Yacowar, you have dog shit on your boot!"

Without missing a beat the croaky, bored response volleyed back, every word separate…"Great Scott, I must have stepped on your essay."

～

Yacowar wasn't kidding. He awarded my essay a D minus or maybe a plus.

Recently I typed "maurice yacowar" and looked him up on Yahoo.

He was Dean at University of Calgary now and an author of several publications including The Sopranos on the Couch, a critical analysis of the award winning TV series. He was pictured with a copy of his first novel, a biblical satire titled "Bold Testament." The trademark beard and ponytail had survived these thirty-two years, gathering some frost along the way. Only the thick frames of his glasses remained black.

I found the last copy of The Soprano's analysis at Indigo Books in Yorkville and it was thirty-two ninety-nine well spent. Each paragraph lectures with that same nonchalant croaking timber, every word separate; about a dollar a year to turn back the clock. Yahoo also revealed that Yacowar had authored "Loser Takes All: The Comic Art of Woody Allen." My feeble essay never had a prayer. I'd been rolling my dough in the heart of Yacowar's kitchen.

～

Judy got an "A" for King Kong. That night we celebrated her "A" and I think, inadvertently conceived Mark, our first son.

Maybe it was an "A" plus.

CHAPTER 13

"And Brutus is an honorable man"—William Shakespeare

BRUTUS ET AL

BRUTUS WAS MY IDEA.

Well, not his name, but the whole idea of getting a big dog.

We were considering names like Cromwell, Churchill, or even Chauncey, if a male took our fancy. Chelsea, or perhaps Camilla, if we came home with a bitch. The thing is, when 150 pounds of six-month-old English Mastiff answers to Brutus, then Brutus it is.

We discovered Brutus in Chilliwack a month and a half after buying the farm. The "Wack" can be found where the Fraser River spills out of the mountains into a lush valley that ushers it west to the Pacific. Chilliwack is corn country, the pale, tender "peaches and cream" kind.

His owner had returned Brutus to his breeder after a month or so; just too much of a commitment for the poor fellow, who had lost his job and his wife in the same week. "Probably in that order," was my comment to Judy. "We'll check him out, but I wish it was a female." was her response.

I'd taken kind of a bum rap over the past three decades, as a bit of a dog hater and even a cat hater. Let me go on record that the latter allegation is absolutely unfounded. Well, with the exception of Liberty, and really only for the last ten years of her ridiculously long life. Living things tend to thrive under Judy's care.

I admire cats. I respect their aloof deportment and I have a particularly high regard for the fact that they bury their bowel movements. Dogs, on the other hand can be trained to ride unicycles, lead the blind, and shoo geese from airport runways before jet engines inhale them. Dogs prevent plane crashes. Dogs sniff out explosives and expose smugglers of illicit drugs. A dog is man's best friend.

But dogs crap all over the place. Just ask Professor Yacowar.

I do despise the whole idea of kitty litter and see its very existence as a billboard to the masochism of our species.

If I were to host a dinner party for any guest from history or fiction, yeah, I'd probably invite Jesus Christ. Get his take on Mel Gibson's film, "The Passion," presuming he's checked it out. "No, really Lord, don't rent the DVD; it's one of those flicks you've simply got to see on the big screen."

And okay, probably Adolph Hitler. "So, Fuhrer, tell me. Where do you feel things went wrong? Yah, mitz der Reich, Yah, mitz der master plan. What did you see in that Braun girl? Wasn't she just a little chunky in the calf? Now I could be wrong, but she looked like she was fighting herself under that dirndl skirt. You don't have to answer this but how come *you* had the Luger *and* the capsule in that bunker while your young frau just had the cyanide? Was she cool with your undescended testicle? Do you mind if I call you Dolph??"

Now; what would we serve? Probably Judy's moussaka, always a reliable "go to" dish when we're entertaining, though we seldom have it when there's just the two of us; but only if she can find the extra lean ground lamb at the Fort Langley IGA. She might have to check out Heritage Meats in Langley; she's got Eugene, that nice young butcher there, wrapped around her finger.

"Special cut for Mrs. T? No problem!"

Maybe a Greek salad for starters. Save-On-Foods carries a tasty one in their deli section, but, for this occasion, Judy'd probably want to buy those little roma tomatoes and green peppers and the feta cheese herself and make it in the farm kitchen. She can be real fussy about things like that. Adhering to the Greek theme, dessert could be that sticky pastry thing, the name of which I always get confused with the ski-mask accessory that thugs wear when they rob Seven Elevens. On second thought it's pretty hard to go wrong with Haagen Daaz. Perhaps we'd get each of our guests their own chocolate almond crunch bar on a stick.

Or maybe I'd barbecue. The marinated rack of lamb at Meinhardt's on Granville is marvelously spicy, soaking for hours in an Asian hoisin sauce. It always gets rave reviews provided I don't overcook it, and that can happen once in a while, if I've had a few drinks or get distracted. Maybe we'd better stick with the moussaka, because I would have quite a bit to say to our third guest.

Rounding out our table would be Ed Lowe, an eighty-year old Minnesotan whose claim to fame is the invention of Tidy Cat in 1964, which he later branded as Kitty Litter. Ed would be seated at my left elbow while his wife Lulu sat knitting in their rental car by the fountain in the courtyard. "Old Lulu's going to come in later to help your little lady with the clean up," Ed whispers to me as I greet him at the door. "She's keen to meet the Lord but I think she might still hold a wee grudge against the other fella. Whaddya going to do?" Ed shrugs.

Dinner well underway, everyone nicely relaxed; the moussaka, a hit.

"So let me get this straight," I'd begin as I topped up Ed's Shiraz, then mine. "Our feline friends have evolved enough to actually meow to be let outside to do their business. They insist on going out. They have enough dignity to carefully bury what they've done and enough shame to look furtive and embarrassed while they do it. Now Ed, if it ain't broke…don't be fixin' it!! Don't be bringing all that nasty business inside the house, reversing countless centuries of progress!"

I'd break eye contact for a second, concerned about neglecting my other guests. Though civil, their conversation seems stilted, sort of spinning its wheels.

"There's plenty more of that moussaka, fellas, and it's not going to eat itself! Don't stand on ceremony, go right ahead and dig in!"

I'd drain the Shiraz into their empty glasses and turn back to business.

"Don't be placing that malodorous tray in the kitchen where we eat, or the laundry room where we clean our clothing. Don't even think about putting that foul stink box in the darkest corner of the furnace room so our forced air heating can suck up its vapors and have the whole damn house reeking like a bus stop shelter!

Ed, what in the hell were you thinking??!!"

My respect and tolerance for cats hit a wall in the last decade of Liberty's obscenely long lifespan. Judy found her at the SPCA in Barrie and brought her home to that back split with the pool; one of the homes for which we paid too much.

A charcoal puffball during infancy, Liberty soon turned

into a typical nondescript gray cat. A female cat.

We soon moved to that new house in the Toronto suburbs; the one with the 19% mortgage. Liberty's head spun with the move to the big city. I suppose she fell in with a fast crowd. Maybe with our money worries and the pressure of my new job, we weren't paying her enough attention. I blame myself.

Still no more than a kitten herself, Liberty dropped five babies on the brand new linoleum in our laundry room. I never did meet the father. Reasonably sophisticated in these matters, I was more disappointed for Liberty than with her. I got along fine with the fluffy single mom for another decade. Enduring our sometimes yearly moves within Greater Vancouver, she was steadfast in her devotion to Judy and to her dish. She'd follow us anywhere, her tubes, you might guess, long since snipped and cauterized.

Even the arrival of Yum Yum in 1984, while causing her some concern, was further proof of Liberty's willingness to adapt. Yum Yum, a mocha Siamese, is our current matriarch, although she weighs less than a pound and looks like a stooped Kerrisdale widow trying to cross 41st Avenue, her soft, bent bones wrapped in a tattered mink. Judy had rescued a young Yum Yum from an indifferent owner, just prior to Reagan's second term.

It was after I got our big screen that Liberty went wonky.

It was sixty inches of Electrohome heaven with a blond oak cabinet and folding doors. I'd admired it for a few months in the lower level of Woodward's, back when they were still in business. It was 1991 and we had a house full of teenagers. We had a room built in the Dutch colonial on Angus Drive, specifically for the big screen. Commonplace now, five foot screens, then, were rare and coveted possessions. That TV was my pride and joy and the kids loved it too.

The wide screen with its eleven-speaker stereo satisfied two of my senses. But I hadn't gone for the olfactory option. I wasn't into smelling a daily pile of fresh cat turds in the narrow space behind our family entertainment center.

Liberty had taken a turn. Maybe she was trying to tell us something. This went on for years. Years I tell you.

But there's more.

Not content with fouling our nightly ritual of "Jeopardy," Liberty began to take a keen interest in my closet.

I'd bought a new pair of Churches; fine English shoes, the best black calfskin, worthy of a nightly treeing. But plenty of time for that; I'd only worn them once.

Today they want seven hundred dollars for those same Church shoes; plus tax.

Next morning I showered, shaved against the grain, and tucked a crisply laundered Jack Lipson shirt into the sharply creased trousers of my new Warren K. Cook pinstripe suit. I tortured a crimson and cream striped Oscar de la Renta tie into a Windsor knot, and decided I'd stir Judy from her slumber with coffee and an English muffin. The least I could do was let her see how sharp I looked before heading for work. My outfit was a "power" look and women do love power in their men. In that, Judy was no exception. Stretching my executive socks tight to the kneecaps, I was ready for those gleaming Churches.

The left one went on just fine, the calfskin caressing my foot like a long time lover. Those limey cobblers at Churches really did know their business. The right one was wet. My sock was soaked.

Naïve, I searched my closet for a broken pipe, a drip through the roof, a spilled glass of water; anything to make sense of things.

But then...oh...Oh yes...

I peeled off my saturated Wolsey and brought it to my face and sniffed deeply, seeking but dreading to find.

That cat must have squatted over that shoe like it was a porcelain throne from American Standard. Clearly she was out to get me.

So it came to pass that I hated Liberty; hated her right back.

Judy, though, took great pains to ensure Liberty would live forever. Tolerantly bemused by the nightly stink behind the Electrohome and the indiscretions in my closet, her reaction was sympathy for the perpetrator rather than the victim.

"Poor Libby's senile," she said.

When Liberty was around twenty-one she came to sport a lump on her head about the size of a Titleist ProV 1.

The vet, mindful of the fact that that Liberty was one-hundred and forty-seven in cat years prepared us for the worst. "It's either an abscess which we can remove at a cost of three hundred and fifty dollars, or it's a tumor. If it is a tumor, I'm afraid we should put the old girl down."

"Looks like a tumor to me," was my diagnosis.

Judy wasn't so sure.

I sat in the waiting area reading "Field and Stream" while Judy accompanied Liberty to the O.R. The vet probed and pricked that hard nugget on Liberty's noggin to no avail. Money on the tumor was looking like money in the bank. Then Judy had a go and hit the mother lode...a stream of hot pus shot skyward. She'd done this once before when some critter, probably a West Vancouver raccoon, had bitten Liberty in the head. She sterilized a sewing needle, put the cat in a loving headlock, over some protest, and lanced it herself.

There's no substitute for experience.

Liberty, like Clinton, survived past the end of the Clinton administration. When she finally succumbed we opted for the individual, personalized cremation as opposed to the more popular group incineration. Quite a bit more money but, hey, we know that our jar of soot is the genuine article.

But as a rule I liked cats; my loathing of Liberty was an exception.

Dogs were another story; and I like dogs too. It's just that the smaller our dwellings, the more determined Judy was to commit to the larger breeds. It was when we were crammed into the log cabin and then the townhouse with first Agatha and then Bernice that I was branded as a dog hater. Foxglove Farm, though, was seventeen acres.

With pure heart I pounded Highway 1 to the "Wack," Judy at my side, to check out Brutus, following up on an ad in the Vancouver Sun classifieds. Reaching the Chilliwack exit, we headed south across the valley toward the mountains until we found a split-level house with the address that Judy had circled in the paper. A fat, tawny dog waddled across the front lawn to greet us, flaunting more teats than the Saturday late show at The Follies Bergere. A busy tail showed little evidence of post-partum depression.

"You know, this may not be our boy, honey," I deadpanned. "That just might be a female, whaddya think?"

"Would you grow up?" Judy whispered as a tall, young lady emerged from the front door and told us she'd fetch Brutus from out back.

The English Mastiff is the largest breed, kind of like a Great Dane on steroids. Brutus approached the size of a small pony. He was the yellow version of the species, and was missing half of the licorice skin on a nose that was the size of a child's fist.

The breeder handed Judy a tube of ointment which she began to apply to the raw, red meat of the afflicted area, starting the sweet talk. Brutus was a "beautiful boy."

"How long do they live?" Judy asked, still crouching, dabbing the ointment. "Well, they *are* big dogs," shrugged the breeder with a small, sad smile; "but English Mastiffs can go to eight, even ten sometimes."

Judy, pierced with a needle of pain, kept dabbing, eyes shining.

"This guy doesn't lift his leg yet," laughed the breeder lady with another shrug.

Wary of a second-hand dog with a mangy nose that pees squatting, I still scratched a cheque for $650. I was a farmer now, and farmers have big dogs.

We'd checked out Great Danes earlier that week and they were hyper freaks commanding twelve hundred. Their grossly obese breeder looked inbred herself, lived in squalor, and fed them only raw meat.

When she asked us in the house for coffee we begged off.

Halfway back to Vancouver, the exit for Foxglove Farm was approaching. Brutus was softly snoring on the back seat of the Rover.

"Shall we show him the farm?" I asked, the left turn signal already flashing. "Absolutely!" was Judy's reply.

CHAPTER 14

"I'll be watching you"—Sting

THE STALKING

224ᵀᴴ STREET IS THE DEAD END ROAD THAT TURNS SOUTH off Highway 10 and ends where it meets the Nicomeckl River. One of the Lynch's referred to it as Old Stone Road when chatting with Judy recently. Bob and Bill Lynch comprise the father–son team who cut our fields a couple of times a year with their old Massey Ferguson tractor.

As the Rover slowed near Foxglove's gate, Brutus stirred and stretched himself up with a yawn, his two-tone nose shining with ointment. We could see movement in the gatehouse, probably Rebecca. "Don't stop," said Judy. I fashioned a three point about face and headed back towards the highway.

"Pull over here honey, he might have to pee," she said about three hundred yards from Foxglove's gate. Her instincts were spot on and it was a matter of seconds before Brutus was squatting near the ditch that borders Old Stone Road. This seemed to last for almost two minutes.

"He's got quite a tank on him for just six months, Jude!" I observed.

"Were you a good boy Brutus?" Judy asked, "Brutus is such a good boy," Judy answered.

You'd think he had just won Best in Show.

"He'll be a better boy when he lifts his leg," I murmured.

That little drive by was just the start. We motored out to Old Stone Road the next day, then the next and the next. In those four months between the offer and moving day we would make that trek to Foxglove about six days a week; sometimes seven. We'd always bring Brutus. Sometimes we'd bring a picnic.

We'd park a few hundred yards from the gate and walk Brutus on his leash. Or we'd let him run free in the adjacent field. Brutus would bound joyously through the chest high golden grass, velvet ears all aflap.

Sometimes no one saw us. Most times someone did. Roxanne waved the first few times; then she stopped.

Rebecca never did wave.

Judy and I told each other we just had to stop it. Over the years we had always taken a daily drive past houses we had bought or were having built, but this was a dead end. You couldn't just discreetly cruise by.

Then the next day I'd come home from golf or the office and ask her, "so what do you feel like doing?" "Go check out the farm!" she'd say. I'd say "Okay!" and we'd be on our way.

We were embarrassed but didn't care; at least not enough to stop. And the last time I checked, Old Stone Road was a public byway in a free country.

Cedar Rim Nursery is a massive plant emporium to the west of the farm on Glover Road. We'd been there quite a few times since the offer and had bought a few plants and various garden items. Once we were exploring their vast stock while Brutus slept in the Rover. We reached the eastern extreme of the nursery's public area where trees and other plants were actually for sale, carrying price tags.

We came to a sign that said "Employees Only" that separated items for sale from trees and shrubs that were future inventory.

With hardly a word to each other, we pressed on past the sign. We moved briskly eastward through conifers and cedars, ferns and spruce. Wary for vigilant security guards and snarling Dobermans we must have jogged a thousand feet into the restricted area.

At last emerging from the rows of shrubbery we reached a rise in the terrain, traversed a wet ditch, and pressed ourselves, breathless, against a fence at the nursery's eastern border. There was a long stretch of golden field and, well in the distance, a red roof peek-a-booed through a copse of trees.

"That's our barn, honey," Judy smiled.

One time our strategy was to park right in front of Rebecca's store at the greenhouse and buy something. I stayed in the truck with Brutus and watched Judy engage with the proprietor through the greenhouse glass.

To my dismay, Judy beckoned me in. The conversation was civil with no more frost than a couple of certifiable stalkers might expect.

To her credit she hadn't served us with an injunction or a stay order.

Judy emerged with a brass frog.

Rebecca rang it up in her till.

CHAPTER 15

"A bridge over troubled water"—Simon & Garfunkel

POSSESSED

JUNE 23ʳᵈ ARRIVED AT LAST.

On the phone, Hooge's real estate office said we couldn't pick up the keys until end of business at 4:30. The deal was with the lawyer; closing was some time today and that's just the way it was. Brutus and I waited in the Rover around noon as Judy went in the ReMax office to see about that. Emerging in two minutes, she triumphantly jingled an envelope in her hand. Smiles all around.

When we turned down Old Stone Road our shame and embarrassment from our stalking days seemed like a dream, a distant memory. I stopped at the gate and we both got out. Judy planted a tender kiss on the worn plate on the pillar; the one that said *Beware of Dog*. I unhooked the bungee and opened the gate.

There were about thirty-five options of places to park in the brick courtyard and I chose a jaunty angle by the fountain. It made for an exhilarating contrast to our tight city parking on Point Grey Road. I'd had tickets there right in front of our house.

Nature hadn't been idle in the four months since our last

trip down that narrow drive. Not only were the bony Acacia trees in full leaf, they sported tiny white blossoms, hundreds of feet over our heads. A few days later the flowers would begin to fall. Every year in June, for about ten days, we were showered with a fragrant blizzard of Acacia blossoms. The petals would settle thick on the crushed stone drive, clinging to our shoes as we strolled to the mailbox to get the paper.

The bare woody vines that were grasping the house in February were hiding now under their own layer of leaf. The new barn, cold and quiet in winter, was percolating with swallows; dozens of nests, each with five or six tiny, black-faced occupants. White swallow crap was everywhere.

"We're going to need a power washer," Judy observed, eyeing the swallows with some concern.

Their parents swooped from the rafters and along the concrete floor, furious at our intrusion.

Back in the courtyard, near the pond, a large wire mesh cage melded into a rustic wooden structure. "That's a dovecote," said Judy, "years ago they used to keep doves here. Eventually *we're* going to have doves in there."

I'd only seen one dove in my life. It was a white one, released at a peace rally at the University of Windsor in 1969. "Where would we get doves?" I queried, envisioning some specialty order from a Middle Eastern dove broker. "You can order them at Petsmart," came her reply, "they're about twenty-five bucks each." Judy had been doing her homework.

A throng of ducks and geese made a splashing, honking exit from the pond. I hadn't noticed them gliding through the jungle of reeds and rushes. Their party had been crashed by four blue heron, rasping their vocals and dangling pre-historic limbs. "We've got to get in there and clean that out." Judy's disapproving eye was assessing the overgrown state of the pond. "We'll need some hip waders." Judy's blue eyes were focused on my hips. "Remember our deal honey," was my response.

Before offering on the farm, I had said, "If we buy that place it's on the condition that you understand *I* am not lifting a finger."

"Remember our deal?? I want it in writing!" jabbed a smirking Judy, a comment on my deplorable track record as a handyman.

"There's a radical new approach these days," was my counter punch. "Maybe we should check it out; it's derived from the barter system. Everybody does just what they're good at in exchange for something they call legal tender; apparently they say it's good for the economy."

"Don't worry," came her assurance, "we'll hire some guy with waders and a chainsaw."

We walked back through the barn and through a couple of pastures toward the corner of the seventeen acres where the river narrowed. Through chest-high grass we crashed our own trail, Brutus in the lead. A trio of slippery logs had been fashioned into a makeshift bridge across the river and I was first to try to cross. Nearly slipping twice I managed to avoid a drenching in the Nicomekl and once across, beckoned Judy to follow. "C'mon Jude, this is our land too!"

Always a gamer, Judy's crossing was slow but sure. Now we could make our way up the hill to the fence that marked our southern border. Check on the neighbors, assuming we had them.

Brutus, though, was having none of this. Long yellow legs trembling, he took one faltering step onto the mossy log surface, slipped a bit and backed right off. "Come to mommy!!" exhorted my spouse. "C'mon Booty Boy. You can do it!"

Brutus began a pathetic whimpering sound that signified he wasn't coming to mommy at all.

"Let's just keep walking," I advised, "he'll follow; he won't want to be left behind."

Judy, though, has never shared my taste for "tough love" for kids and pets, although she wasn't always averse to dispensing it upon me.

Brutus made a second nail-clacking venture on to the log slipped a bit and made a full retreat.

The whining cranked up to a small crescendo.

"If he slips off that log, he could drown, you'll have to jump in and save him," was Judy's assessment in a nutshell.

The Nicomekl River was thirteen maybe fourteen inches deep at that narrow crossing. Booty Boy was about four and a half feet tall and growing daily.

But the power struggle was over before it began. Brutus was ecstatic as Judy and he were reunited on his north side of the river. I slipped on the mossy log on my return trip but grabbed an overhanging branch to avoid a soaker.

Brutus was happy to see me too; glad that I had come to my senses.

His powerful yellow tail cracked against the leg of my Levis like a bullwhip. A long cord of drool had coiled itself over his nose and around an ear. A jowl flapping headshake flung it skyward and he looked as good as new.

The property tapered to a point where the fence met the river. The blackberries were at their thickest there, no fruit yet, but somehow fragrant just the same. Five or six beaten paths descended the grassy terrain like arteries into the heart of their dense, thorny mass.

"Coyotes," Judy said, with a cloud across her brow. "That must be their den. We're really going to have to watch the cats."

I nodded with all the solemnity I could muster.

"And Brutus too," she went on. "With a big dog, sometimes the pack sends out a female in heat to lure the male in. Then they gang up on him and tear out his hamstring. They "hamstring" him and then its game over. He wouldn't stand a chance in those brambles. Bastards!"

"Maybe Bert would give us one of his rifles," I mused. "You want I should open a can of whup-ass on those critters?"

Judy's dad, Bert Radford, had described his arsenal to me in a quiet man-to-man talk in his parlor, as he called it, thirty years back, on the day he learned of our wedding plans. "A Marlin and a 303 that could bring an elephant down; and if my little girl ends up unhappy; if she *ever darkens my door,* I'm telling you now son, you can run, but you can't hide."

"It's against the law to discharge a firearm in Langley Township," cited Judy, "even on your own property."

"Oh well, I guess the coyotes have to eat too," I said.

I didn't add that after forty-five years of Roadrunner cartoons that once, just once, I would have enjoyed seeing Wile E. Coyote catch, cook and eat that obnoxious speedster, complete with all the fixings.

I looked at Brutus who was still in afterglow from avoiding the bridge. A full foot of tongue dangled and drool was regrouping in his rubbery black gums. He liked his dog food just fine and had put on about thirty-five pounds since adopting us in April. The vet's scale had said one eighty-five.

The coyotes that I had seen over the years skulked around the fairways of Shaughnessy Golf and Country Club. Rail thin and scruffy, I doubted a legion of them could pose a threat to Brutus.

(One Saturday morning my regular foursome was putting out on the ninth green when four of the mangy cowards encircled a small gray squirrel. They co-operated on the hunt, until the unfortunate rodent dashed into the waiting jaws of one of them.

Any teamwork ended there as the lucky coyote dashed off to dine alone. I can still hear the staccato "EE!!EE!!EE!! of the distressed squirrel as its assailant snapped him back and forth by the neck as he loped away.

My partner, Howard, missed his three-footer and blamed the cruelty of nature.)

Foxglove had dozens of fruit trees growing at random throughout the seventeen acres. There were pear, plum, cherry, chestnut and a variety of apple. One ancient apple tree, laden with embryonic Macintosh, caught Judy's eye on the walk back to the house. It was just north of the stump and barbed wire fence that divided our land from Jessell's.

Brian Jessell was a BMW dealer and Rebecca's ex. He had bought the land as a buffer back when they were still married. It was seventeen acres too; flat, but vacant and unserviced. It guaranteed that the burgeoning greenhouse complex at the entrance to Old Stone Road was going to keep its distance from Foxglove Farm. BEVO's greenhouses were multiplying at a rate that would put Foxglove's bunnies to shame.

When Rebecca got Foxglove, Brian kept the buffer land.

Judy had called Jessell within a week of our offer and asked if he'd sell; not right now but somewhere down the line. He claimed to be "easy to deal with" and was "sure we can work something out."

We hadn't done the deal by June and still haven't though it's been two and a half years. But ever since that phone call we kind of felt that his land was ours. In our "stalking" days we'd damn well walked that field like we owned it, and the puppy Brutus had trespassed too.

I mentioned the irony to Judy as she scrutinized the apple tree.

"What irony?" she had absently asked.

"Well, the last thing we want is to have those greenhouses right next to our property, right?"

"Right," she agreed.

"But if we buy Jessell's seventeen acres, isn't that exactly what we'll have?"

I waited in vain for a guffaw. "You always could make me laugh," she had often chuckled over thirty years of witticisms, many lame and some pretty damn funny; but not this time.

The irony was lost on Judy who was zeroing in on Jessell's tree. We could see part of the trunk through the brush and blackberry thorns. She pointed an accusatory finger.

Two feet from the ground the denuding had started and stretched another two feet up. Not a scrap of bark was left on that prolific old Mac.

"Beavers!" Judy snarled. "That's the work of a goddamned beaver. I knew there were beavers when I saw the river's hardly moving. It's killing that tree."

She raised the barbed wire on a broken patch of fence and snaked under it. Brutus and I stepped over a low section.

I quit counting the unripe applets after several hundred and assessed the naked trunk. Somewhere from Grade 10 Science I recalled something about fibro vascular bundles. Little organic canoes that paddle against gravity upwards through the bark; backpacking like Radisson and Grossiers; supplying the essential nutrients from the earth to make leaves and blossoms and apples; delivering the stuff of life.

The trunk was stripped white all the way around.

"I hope to God they know how to portage," I murmured.

Then I recalled I had achieved just 56% in grade ten

Science one term and invariably did much better in history.

Back on our property Judy led a purposeful march through the grass and brush, down to the river, closer to the house. We were the beaver patrol. Brutus cast a wary eye in the event our mission involved another bridge. With the long grass uncut for years, finding the dam was mostly guesswork. Scuttling downward to a marshy footing, we paused to catch breath and get our bearings. Then we heard the waterfall punctuating the quiet that soaked Foxglove's backland. Wanting to "man up" and contribute I forged the trail toward that sound, crashing through the last of the brush and wet soil that bordered the Nickomekl. "Don't fall in honey, its mooshy there," warned my concerned helpmate.

But I wasn't to fall in; not on that fine day.

CHAPTER 16

"Take me back"—Van Morrison

A TALE OF TWO LANGLEYS

THE CHAMPAGNE CORK POPPED AND I LET IT RICOCHET OFF the wall in Foxglove's unfurnished kitchen. Brutus chased it down and handled the sniffing honors then went back to lapping well water from a stainless steel bowl.

We'd forgotten our champagne flutes in the city and I poured our bubbly into plastic glasses more suited to Granny Clampett's bedside dentures.

Our search had turned up two beaver dams and had worked up a thirst. We had beavers all right and we had 'em bad.

"We're talking rodents here!" was Judy's response to my pointing out the status of the beaver as Canada's national symbol.

I'd scared up the champagne at the cold beer and wine store in Langley and it wasn't half bad. The young woman behind the counter was well pierced; her ears, eyebrows, lips and nose recalling an open tackle box. When I paid with Visa she asked to see a second piece of I.D., a bit of a culture shock for a middle-aged gentleman from Kitsilano. The four-man queue behind me smelled like an ashtray.

"Concerned I'm under age?" I riffed, getting no smile through the metal. "You know, I get that all the time. Curse of the gene pool." "Yeah thure," was her tongue-studded comeback.

Of Foxglove's many charms, its location was high on the list.

A few minutes south of Highway 1, the farm was equidistant from Langley and Fort Langley, about a seven-minute drive either way and a civilized fifty minute commute to Hornby and Georgia on weekdays. On weekends I could rocket to my 7:25 a.m. Shaugnessy tee time fresh from planting a kiss on the slumbering Judy at 6:30.

As a young couple Judy and I had often taken Sunday drives northwest of Toronto. From our yellow 1973 Beetle we'd covet the stone century homes and horse farms embroidered into the green fabric of the Caledon Hills. Twenty years later we were contemplating a career move back east and checked out some of those same places, as semi-serious buyers.

One farm had special appeal for Judy; a solid old Georgian commanding a hundred and fifty acres with a skookum horse setup. There was an equestrian club across the road that wanted to run their hunt right across the property with our consent. Such a thumb up would have been forthcoming, as Judy was eager to don black velvet helmet and jacket and join in the chase.

My zeal for the deal was tempered by the prospect of a seventy-five minute commute to Richmond and Bay on a good day; over ninety minutes in an icy winter rush hour. The nearest convenience store was a twenty minute trek to the hamlet of Belfountain at the Forks of the Credit River and that sounded damned inconvenient if you ask me. I envisioned any time that I wasn't commuting, schlepping to the store for razor blades, cat food and toilet paper.

It wasn't as if Judy and I were ever "stock up at Costco" shoppers. First, I'm not a joiner unless it's the right golf club and we wouldn't dream of buying Christmas cards on sale in January. Planning that far ahead, besides being boring, seemed to smack of conceit and an ill-advised temptation of fate. It was kind of like saying, "Who knows what slings and arrows await us in the next twelve months? Who can forecast colorectal nightmares, bloody moles, shadowed lung x-rays, aneurisms and flesh-eating disease, jackknifing semi-trailers in the morning commute and 747's liquefying the World Trade Center? We have no idea whether these or worse blind-sidings lurk around the corner...but we do know that we're all set for greeting cards."

"It's a nuclear age, we could be vaporized on the weekend," have long been my words to live by.

What *did* vaporize was the career move, and with that

I was spared a tedious new beginning in the Hills of Caledon.

By contrast, the convenience stores in the Langleys really were.

In a Patty Duke Show sense, Langley is Patty and Fort Langley is Kathy, her identical cousin, the product of private British schooling. Patty Duke, of course, played both parts, the idea poached from the big screen's *The Parent Trap*, where Hayley Mills likewise did double duty. If you're too young to remember, check it out on the Internet.

Kathy was a demure, cultured teenager with a lame affectation of a high society English accent and a tight-ass hairdo. The sitcom's catchy jingle had a verse that began "Kathy adores a minuet, The Ballet Russes and crepe suzette," or something like that. Patty was her mop-headed American cousin who couldn't give a good goddamn. Patty had a taste for hot dogs, hot rods and rock and roll.

Every week the premise was the same.

For half an hour minus commercials Patty would get herself into some kind of trouble, I think they called it a "jackpot" in 1963, from which Kathy would extract her. I seem to recall The Patty Duke Show won a string of Emmys; but I could be wrong.

Fort Langley is all about gentility and stepping back in time. There's no Wendy's, nor Subway, nor any chain to be found; not even a Starbucks.

If you want a good latte or Americano there's plenty of choices, but most folks line up at Wendel's, a bookstore cum cappuccino hangout where the eggs benny and fresh baked strudel incite something just short of a Fort Langley frenzy on lazy weekend mornings. Brunchers and book browsers all seem to know each other, making Wendel's the lively epicenter of Fort Langley's *je ne c'est quoi*. Judy and I ended up at Wendel's daily during our "stalking" period and Brutus was a fixture there too, curling up under one of their outdoor tables while we sipped a glass of off-dry Bacchus from the nearby vineyards of Domaine de Chaberton. "Anytime you come back from the city and you can't find me, I'll either be here or in the barn," beamed Judy, as we ordered two Italian coffees, one tiramisu and two forks.

While there's a dearth of Big Macs, Whoppers, and Brazier Burgers, Fort Langley's got them all beat at a retro fifties ice cream parlor joint called Planet Java where the Elvis Burger is Judy's favorite. Each booth has its own mini jukebox menu and, while your burger gets fresh cooked, you can lay a harmony on Kathy's Clown by the Everly's or boom out the bass "Duke-Duke-Duke" from Gene Chandler's Duke of Earl.

My appetite usually requires the extra patty, cheese, mushrooms and bacon that define the Jerry Lee Burger. Then there's those obscenely thick milkshakes with the creamy excess chilling in the stainless steel shaker; just to top you up. You know the three flavors. Oh well. There's angle parking at Planet Java, a prerequisite for great small towns, and a cool dish of water for your big yellow dog.

Litigious Fort Langleyans needn't head for the big city. The firm of Cherrington, Easingwood, Kearl, Critchley, & Wenner not only have a very wide sign, but a saber-rattling web-site that proclaims their willingness to "pit" their litigation lawyers against the "best barristers" that Vancouver has to offer.

"Pay at the Pump" hasn't shown up in Fort Langley. The one gas station is an Esso where the petrol pumps bring to mind the animated dancing kind that gassed up the grinning jalopies in early Mickey Mouse cartoons. After all, change isn't always for the better. Pay at the pump is so impersonal. Before Pay at the Pump, you'd have to go inside where you might pay some kindly Texaco veteran name-tagged "Vera," and Vera would show you pictures of her grandchildren and she might counsel you on the kinds of beef jerky and she might call you "hon,"…er…maybe "Pay at the Pump" *is* a good thing. Far be it from me to stand in the way of progress.

Among the shops that sell old stuff in Fort Langley there's one that I actually like. Well, that's not to say I like it in the sense that I ever want to go there. It's just that on those occasions when Judy drags me into The Village Antique Mall, once inside, I never want to leave. It's not really an antique store per se, although there's quite a collection of old furniture. You don't really shop there as much as you rummage through someone's attic. Your attic.

A sprawling warehouse structure, it has more nooks and cul de sacs than a Tunisian medina. Most people like to take their time at The Village Antique Mall, so they've got a little snack bar if you're inclined to make a day of it. Further inside there's a rat's maze of multi level rooms, each with its own nostalgic theme. Toys here, old vinyl albums there, a drink Coca-Cola poster that says "Lifts the Spirits!"

Great old music is a constant, piped through speakers throughout the store.

One rainy April day during our stalking phase Judy and I left Brutus snoring in her Rover while we got a coffee at The Village Antique Mall and started to "poke around" as she likes to say. That day the Platters were singing Smoke Gets in Your Eyes and they just let the whole album keep on playing.

We went our separate ways.

After an hour or so I'd been fondly reacquainted with a Meccano construction set, a Viewmaster, an old miniature steam engine and a selection of slinkies. I vaguely recalled never having my own slinky and wondered why. Then I re-called that we pretty much always lived in bungalows when I was a kid.

There were toys to which I'd given no thought for forty-five years. Plastic rockets where you unscrew the weighted nose and insert a red gun cap like the kind we'd load in our six shooters. Then you'd hurl the rocket as high as you could and it would land on the street with a small explosion. There was a helicopter where you'd pull hard on a string to get the propeller whizzing. Damned if that copter didn't hover in the dining room before crashing into the good china.

There was a board game with a hollow map punched with holes called Gusher where you buy land and drill for oil. Each game you'd shake the board to rearrange the location of the "oil." Strike black crude with the little oilrig and you'd enjoy a big payoff from the banker. My brother John, five years my senior, was always the banker.

John and I learned, first game, that you could sort of tell upon peeking, which holes had oil and which were dry. So we'd only buy land where the holes on it seemed a shade darker from the black wood blocks under the surface of the board.

Gusher soon gathered dust in our closet.

Then I chanced upon a pile of Topps baseball cards dating from the fifties. I searched vainly for the Rocky Colavito card but found an Al Kaline and then Jake Wood's rookie card from 1961. Fast and skinny, he could steal you a base, but Jake was prone to striking out. The stats on the back of his card confirmed my recollection that he fanned 141 times in his rookie year, at the time a dubious new American League record. My dad used to call him "Whiffer Wood."

Jake had played a key role in my baseball education.

In that marvelous pennant run in 1961 the Yankees were in Motown for an August weekend showdown. The great southpaw Whitey Ford was, as usual, at his stingy best, allowing no runs and very few base runners. Somehow Jake managed to land on first. Whether he walked or scratched out an infield single is a little beyond my recollection.

Whenever Jake got aboard the throngs at Tiger Stadium would stand up and slam down their hinged seats in unison, chanting, "GO!! GO!! GO!!" Like I said, Jake could steal you a base. I think he pilfered about thirty sacks in 1961.

Bob Hicks and Larry McConnell, my eleven-year old buddies and I were out of our seats and slamming them down, exhorting Jake to GO!! GO!! GO!! as the masterful Whitey Ford stared over to Moose Skowron at first base where Jake's leadoff was about half its normal distance from the bag. In our youthful exuberance we hadn't noticed that the rest of Tiger Stadium, while not totally silent, was leaving us to chant alone. We were about to learn that Whitey Ford possessed the greatest pickoff move in major league history. The future hall of famer was a lefty whose delivery to home plate was indistinguishable from a cobra-like move to the initial sack. Base thieving speedsters like Jake just couldn't get a decent leadoff.

A three-hundred pound black man turned in his seat to face Bob and Larry and me still yelling "GO"! GO! GO! and slamming our seats. He was munching a Hy Grade Ballpark Frank and held another one in reserve covered with mustard and fried onions. A generous grin split his leathery face as he shook his head.

"Jake ain gun go wif Wy Fo on de mound!"

Jake *didn't* go and a couple of innings later Yogi Berra jerked a Don Mossi slider off the yellow grill of the right field foul pole to nip our heroes 2 to 1. Bloody Yankees!!

Focusing back on the Topps card there was a dazzling smile on Jake's ebony face under his Tiger hat with the old English *D* and it washed me in something bittersweet. "Enjoy it while you can Jake," I whispered. His strikeouts and erratic play at second base had Jake in a utility role by 1963. Detroit sold him cheap to Cincinnati and by '67 he was done. Whiffer Wood probably ended up parking cars. Shoulder checking to be sure I was alone I brought Jake's card to my nose and inhaled. There may have been the faintest hint of that pink sheet bubble gum that Topps used to pack in with their cards.

Another room sprouted book bins. There was one dedicated to a scarlet-coated "Dale of the Mounted" which I despised. My well-meaning Auntie Jean in Calgary sent me the first volume when I was about seven. That was where a young Dale enlisted in the RCMP. I read the first four pages and never opened it again. Neither did I open the two copies a year of Dale's further adventures that arrived every birthday and Christmas until I was about twenty-one. Auntie Jean never got a thank you note and never clued in. Hmm.

"Oh, oh...Yes, I'm The Great Pre-te-en-der," began the next Platters tune. No sign of Judy.

Another bin was full of Classics Illustrated. These were the epic works of Dickens, Tolstoy, Hawthorne and Victor Hugo and other great writers in comic book form. As a boy I read a few; kid friendly versions of The Last of the Mohicans, The House of Seven Gables and The Hunchback of Notre Dame. You could whip through those or something like Crime and Punishment in about fifteen minutes and get the general idea.

From the Hardy Boys bin I cracked open "While the Clock Ticked" and, before I knew it, had read three chapters and skipped forward to the ending. I'd read that book in 1957.

Frank and Joe Hardy were the teenage sons of Detective Fenton Hardy and gumshoeing ran in their blood. They were always bringing justice to miscreants twice or thrice their age and then catching the dickens from their Aunt Gertrude when they got home late for dinner. Their plump, good-natured cliché of a sidekick was Chet Morton who usually got underfoot and slowed the Hardy's down, only to redeem himself in one of the later chapters. Could you have a fatter name than Chet Morton?

The Platters were crooning "My Prayer" and I remembered the final round of The Masters was probably under way. I was wondering where Judy could possibly be and began to consider a search of the rat's maze when I saw the Nancy Drew bin. While admiring Nancy's wholesome girl-next-door looks for about forty-five years I'd never read a word of her sleuthing.

I picked up a dog-eared copy where a fresh-faced, copper-haired Nancy looked particularly appealing on the faded cover, as she unearthed some clue. I turned to a jaundiced page one.

"*What* are you reading??!!" came Judy's voice from behind my elbow. In her hand was a rare and ancient plastic grapefruit juicer. I shuddered and the Drew girl leapt from my hand back into her bin like the business end of a branding iron.

The other way I can make Judy appear out of nowhere is on those rare occasions when I might pass wind. I've talked to other husbands about this phenomenon and more than a few say it's the same thing with their wives. Your woman could be at the opposite end of a six-thousand square foot house and one innocent little fart, discreetly emitted in apparent solitude, will bring her running like you dialed 911. I guess it's just one of life's corollaries.

There was a small lineup at the cashier and I was keen to get back to the city to catch the last few holes of The Masters on TV.

"My family had a juicer like that," I remarked, "just like that."

Judy stopped in her tracks and gave her new found treasure a second once over. She assessed the length of the queue, then headed back into the maze, returning empty handed.

She grabbed my hand in the rain, as we crossed the street to her truck to rejoin the slumbering Brutus.

"One thing you know about that place," she said, "that juicer's going to be there tomorrow."

Fort Langley's nice for walking. In Langley you drive.

What Fort Langley lacks in strip malls, fast food, and chain store shopping, Langley provides tenfold. There's a Highway 10 diversion around Langley known as the Langley Bypass. Along that strip you'll find several golden arches, Dairy Queen, Red Robin, Arby's Roast Beef, and every one of their competitors. There's Safeway, IGA, M&M Meats, and a cheesecake specialty house called "Desserts." Judging from their girth, I daresay that most of their clientele are bucking for a bypass of their own.

There's a Winners store where you can get silk Hilfiger ties for twenty-nine bucks and a Future Shop where upon entry you feel like a maggot that's been tossed into an aquarium of starving tropical fish. One day I ventured into Langley's Future Shop to check out plasma screens for the wall above the fireplace in Foxglove's library. Six salesmen inquired after my health in the first five minutes. Browsing was impossible. When the seventh asked "How are you today?" my reply was "Over served!" as I exited for A&B Sound.

Oh well, at least you could get a nice cold bottle of Champagne if the occasion suited; French no less.

We polished it off in the chapel where Judy might have said a small silent prayer. There were grains of rice on the chapel's marble floor. We supposed they were from Rebecca's wedding.

Judy had brought an old futon that we laid on the heaving fir floor in the library and covered with a downy quilt. I stoked up the fireplace over which our plasma screen would preside one day. Brutus curled up on an old blanket a few feet away.

It was our first night at Foxglove Farm.

CHAPTER 17

"Lay your head down on the ground"—Don Henley

THE END OF THE INNOCENCE

IT WAS INCREDIBLY DIFFICULT BALANCING ON ONE FOOT ON top of the fountain in the center of the courtyard. More so since I was naked, absolutely starkers. It was seven-thirty on the morning of June thirtieth, 2002. My fifty-second birthday.

On Point Grey Road it never occurred to me to pose in front of the house in my birthday suit. The joggers and dog walkers might well object. Most of them do gawk from the sidewalk, through the slats of our California shutters, into our little ivy clad townhouse; but that's when we're inside and fully dressed.

"Judy!!!," "I cried, hoping to roust her from the actual bed that had recently been delivered to our upstairs bedroom. Our futon days were over. "Judy!!!" you've *got* to come see this!!!" The effort of calling had me teetering on my left foot while my right foot was shaking, airborne behind me like a statue of Mercury, afflicted by some terrible palsy.

My arms had been stretched straight out behind me like mercurial wings but were now waving in circles to keep my balance. Judy appeared in the front doorway, *her* nakedness bundled up somewhere in her fluffy housecoat.

"You're nuts!" is what I think she exclaimed.

"Come on birthday boy, let's make some coffee."

There was something expansive about moving to the country. Almost like having chains loosened that have shackled and squeezed your temples for decades. You could pose naked on your own fountain. You could make love in the hot sun on your back lawn as the dammed river made best efforts to flow by.

If you wanted to you could urinate on your own land. The cavemen undoubtedly used to do this on a daily basis just to mark their territory in a time that preceded land titles, surveyors and fences. Plus if they had a leak in the cave they'd catch hell from the old lady.

In business I've heard the phrase "pissing on stumps" for many years to describe a grasping of control of certain areas of responsibility or staking claim on clientele. Come to think of it, it's me that says that. That must be where I heard it.

Judy doesn't fully approve of this practice on my part, and to my knowledge doesn't partake in it personally. Don't get me wrong; if two or three Heineken are busting my bladder in the back five acres, she doesn't expect me to shuffle back to the house. But if I enjoy a gratifying pee two hundred feet from the barn, she carries on as if I was relieving myself in the chapel. She likes to nip this kind of thing in the bud, if you'll excuse the expression.

It's probably just as well that she does return to the house when nature calls. Idolizing Judy as Brutus does, I'm just as glad he never sees her squatting, presuming she indeed squats. One time I tried to be a role model and called Brutus to watch while I lifted my leg, but that's tougher than it sounds and I had to throw my Levis in the wash. Maybe

Brutus is on to something.

But having land was a wonderful thing.

You could shout or scream at the top of your lungs and no one could hear. Not even the neighbors. "We're just going to have to fight louder honey," I quipped, pleased with my joke and with my birthday.

After coffee, bacon and eggs and toast Judy gave me my present. A brilliant gift I hadn't asked for, but something I had wanted since I was ten. It was a pellet gun; a Swiss-made pellet gun that looked like a twenty-two but was still an air rifle. "Anything more powerful would require a gun license," Judy advised, relaying what she'd learned at the Langley gun shop. It was all heavy oiled wood and cold steel barrel. It brought me joy that day but would soon deliver shame and primal pain.

It was a one-shot-at-a time barrel loader. My first targets were the occasional leaves that were floating slowly down our beaver-clogged river, a hundred feet away. You could see the pellet splash in the water and adjust your aim to deal with the wind. Then I graduated to sniping at a Coke can in the crotch of a tree behind the house. First time lucky, I hit the can from thirty yards and upon inspection was thrilled to see that I'd ripped a hole right through the aluminum.

That's when Judy stepped in. "The cats are out there somewhere and if you keep that up, sooner or later you're going to hit Brutus with a ricochet."

"You'll *really* be concerned when I get my crossbow for Christmas," I countered.

Brutus was nowhere to be seen, probably having his afternoon bowzer in our upstairs bedroom.

Judy put Don Henley's "End of the Innocence" CD on the stereo then tapped me on the shoulder. I was her choice for a slow dance on the Tuscan tile floor of our kitchen. That great song has a political message but Bruce Hornsby's trademark piano chording throughout always got us to dancing, and we're not really dancers if you know what I mean.

A week or so later, Judy was gone shopping and I patrolled the farm with pellet gun in hand. The freedom was delicious; I could shoot at anything I wanted. I started with the leaves floating in the river. I saw my aim wasn't far off as I missed by a few inches from a hundred feet. I was just getting started. My jean shirt pocket bulged with about thirty pellets; I guess you could say I was packing.

Moving to the courtyard I rang a couple of pellets off the ivy-covered iron cupola that adorned the house over the aged front door like an onion with glandular issues. I guess the immigrants that built Foxglove in 1901 must have been homesick for St. Petersburg. The little guardhouses each had a metal bracket at the peak of their mossy shingle roofs and I fired a couple of pellets there.

Most living targets were off limits, both from Judy's instructions and my own inherent decency. In truth I wouldn't even aim at a robin, let alone shoot. Okay, just that one time I aimed, but pulling the trigger never came close to entering my mind. We've got a ton of robins at Foxglove Farm.

Judy hated frogs though, ever since her sister Linda had dropped a plump, wet one, with frantic, dangling legs, down the back of her tee shirt when she was eight or nine. From March to July, Foxglove's pond was a cacophony of frog smack. They just never shut up. From afar, their collective racket sounded like wind chimes. From the house they sounded like the bulked up sexual athletes they are. You'd hear a deep bass croak that was surely a male. Then it would be answered by something two octaves lower, right from the

balls. Then you'd realize the earlier call was from a pert debu-
tante, all gussied up for prom night. While Judy never made
it official I think it would have been okay with her if I shot a
frog. But while we heard, them I seldom saw one. Can't shoot
what you can't see.

I hate crows and would have been happy to shoot one of
them or even do a whole murder, if you can forgive the pun.
When the Lynch's cut our fields they would start from the
outside, circling ever tighter, eventually turning their smoky
old tractor on a dime. Dozens of mice and small brown rabbits
would pathetically leap from the newly shorn swath toward
the grassy island in the center, where Bill or Bob Lynch had
yet to cut. The Lynch's were blowing their cover and crows
were noticing.

From nowhere they gathered, lining up in our trees like
Boxing Day bargain hunters. There were hundreds of inky
bastards who knew distress when they saw it and swaggered
in their group dynamic. They bided their time until that old
tractor shut down and then they moved in for a leisurely
brunch. Judy, though, discouraged me from shooting crows.
She claimed they were mystical spirits and I would bring us
bad luck. The crows had a healthy respect for my marksman-
ship nonetheless, giving a wide berth any time I appeared in
the courtyard, brandishing my birthday gift. One day I fired
a warning pellet over the heads of a noisy klatch of them and
they were gone for weeks, preferring the hospitality over at
Peter and Roxanne's.

Judy wasn't back from shopping yet and I moseyed into the
barn. She'd been increasingly concerned about the mess the
swallows made and had mentioned that all their white drop-

pings could present a health hazard. She hadn't trailered
Mickey over from Southlands yet and I wondered whether
the swallows were part of the reason why.

"Great," I had thought, "we finally buy a farm, in the *sevens* no less, and I'm still shelling out over $500 a month for
Mickey's room and board!"

But when I walked into the barn I hadn't meant to kill
a swallow. I was genuinely taken with the nests full of babies and had profound respect for the courage of the adults
that protected them. It *had* occurred to me to scare off more
new nesters the same way I'd warded off the crows. Just fire a
warning shot.

An adult had perched on a rafter above my head enjoying
a rare break from the constant swooping. Without even aim-
ing I swung up my rifle and fired from the hip and the bird
dropped stone dead.

My surprise melted into abject guilt and a cloying sorrow
and self-loathing. Up close, the swallow's feathers were an exquisite tapestry of sapphire and cinnamon hues, to which the
greatest painter could never do justice. I hastily dug a little
hole near the barn, shoveled my victim off the concrete floor
and buried the corpse. No one need ever know, but I'd just
never do anything like that again. My God, how could I be
so awful? That I could make all the choices that life presents,
and take all the turns in its tortuous road, only to cross paths
with that innocent creature in such an unspeakable way. My
life, now, was only about that.

Judy pulled up a few minutes later and I helped her with
the groceries as she coaxed Brutus to step down from the
tailgate of the truck. Within forty-five seconds I confessed,
needing her help to carry my burden of shame and guilt.
If everything ended then, if her love died, I would have

understood. She was sad but kind of let me off the hook, I guess because she knew how terrible I felt.

From that day forward she never complained about the swallows and they are welcomed in our barn every spring like guests at a bed and breakfast. Her chalkboard by the tack room shouts *"April 18th-Swallows Arrive*!!" beneath the scrawled phone numbers of the vet and the ferrier. When a baby falls to the concrete of the barn floor, Judy ladders up to the nest and carefully places it next to its siblings. "Survival of the fittest" be damned. She's saved a dozen for the one I murdered.

When I got her a power washer that Christmas she returned it to the Home Depot. Judy keeps the swallow crap to a minimum though. She uses elbow grease, soap and water.

CHAPTER 18

"Gimmee my propers when I get home"—Otis Redding

THE THAW

WE KNEW PERFECTLY WELL WHY ROXANNE HAD TURNED SO much cooler to us than she had been the night she led our clandestine Foxglove tour.

Sure it was our "stalking" phase but really it was Rebecca who probably had a big problem with that. In order to be a good friend to her "best" friend, Roxanne couldn't be too friendly with us.

Throughout July her silver Lexus SUV would be headed to Fort Langley along Old Stone Road and Judy or I would be driving back to the Farm. There was an occasional small wave, sometimes not even that, so I, for one, stopped waving too. We'd never met Peter, who whisked past us in his moss colored Jaguar sedan, barely pausing at their automatic double gate.

Green Vanden Plas Jag. Country squire. Man of medicine. An *English* vascular surgeon, most likely. Probably with his own, even dimmer view of our post-purchase behavior.

"Shoddy form, what? Spotty judgment on their part and *most* improper I dare say. A nasty bit of bad luck to have them as neighbors, I should think!!" Peter had probably said to Roxanne.

But it had been a month for heaven's sake!

So where in hell was that renowned country hospitality? Shouldn't they have come over with a chicken casserole and fresh baked biscuits or raised us a new barn or something? Sure Roxanne and her sawbones hubby weren't kinfolk, but *hello*, we're talkin' neighbors here. When would they start being "right neighborly?" What if the river flooded? We shared the same river after all. Would we be sandbagging the Nicomekl elbow to elbow with Roxanne and Peter, mired in stony silence?

"Screw them," said Judy when I mentioned that Point Grey Road was Petticoat Junction on the warmth meter compared to these new neighbors of ours.

But one day Roxanne was driving toward me, as I was halfway down Old Stone Road, thinking about barbequed tenderloin for dinner. It was blazing hot in the valley so the Lexus was cruising topless for the drive back from my office. Sting was belting out "Brand New Day" through nine Mark Levinson speakers.

To my surprise, Roxanne stopped and lowered her window. There was a smile but no radiant, gum-snapping grin.

I shut Sting down and nodded to our neighbor whose blonde tresses looked freshly shorn.

"Hi Bob," the smile continued.

"You cut your hair," was my greeting.

"It's my summer look," she advised.

"Peter and I wanted to give you guys some space and time to get settled, you know, get adjusted to country life, but we'd like to have you over soon. I'll give Judy a call."

My response measured out the precise amount of warmth for which the situation called.

"Judy and I would like that Roxanne," I said, and we both drove on.

As I tooled down the driveway I could see Judy in cutoff jeans and a tank top, with her gloved hands on her hips surveying the chaotic tangle of the formal garden just north of the gatehouse and greenhouse. Crouching for a two-handed yank of a stubborn four-foot weed, she double tossed her long blonde hair over each shoulder.

Inside the house I poured two Mike's Hard Lemonade coolers over a dozen ice cubes and spiked hers with a further ounce of vodka, and mine with twice that amount of gin. Still in my business suit, I loosened my tie and sauntered back up the driveway. My bride was covered in dirt and sweat against the snowy backdrop of Golden Ears Mountain. Tanned getaway sticks emerged from baby-blue, hippie-flowered Doc Marten boots that she'd found on Carnaby Street on a London visit seventeen years before. Once her pride and joy, they were gardening boots now. They still looked good and so did she.

"*All day* pulling weeds," she advised.

"It shows," I said as I pulled a thorny rose twig from the back of her hair.

"Thanks," she said, "I think," she added.

I grabbed the Province from our mailbox on Old Stone Road and surveyed the garden for a chair with shade. Brutus had found it first and was curled beneath it, sleeping deep against the heat. Judy and I clinked glasses as I related my exchange with Roxanne.

"That's good," was all she said.

"I *knew* she wouldn't be able to stand it," I told Judy as I turned to the sports section, shoved my shades up on my brow and fumbled for my readers.

CHAPTER 19

"This land is your land; this land is my land"—Woody Guthrie

GOOD NEIGHBORS

MY INSTINCTS WERE EITHER HIGHLY TUNED, OR IT WAS JUST a lucky guess. Peter was about as English as it gets. Slim as a whippet, with a wisp of white hair, Peter had robbed the cradle when he married Roxanne over twenty years ago.

His long and brutal hours in the city were dictated by the sad state of the arteries of the populace. "A lot of them are smokers," he had commented. Emergency surgeries were a way of life for Peter. Most mornings the Jaguar purred through the double gate at 5:30, and only reappeared on Old Stone Road sixteen or seventeen hours later.

Judy and I, Roxanne and Peter were sharing some tasty hors d'ouvres and a Hawkes Bay chardonnay in their sunny back courtyard. Roxanne went in the house to check on dinner. She was in high spirits. The gum-snapping grin was back.

Within the first five minutes I'd broached the subject that was on all of our minds. I laughed about our many trips down Old Stone Road and Roxanne's dilemma in being caught between our blatant enthusiasm and Rebecca's righteous indignation.

"Yeah," she laughed, "we used to call you guys The Stalkers*!!*"

"We *were* stalkers," chirped Judy; "we called *ourselves* stalkers." Then she put on a distressed little girl voice and added, "We just couldn't help ourselves could we honey??"

Roxanne roared, the beige wad for all to see. While we were having no secrets I straight on asked her, "What's with the gum?"

"Nicorette!" she grinned, "I haven't had a cigarette in fifteen years!"

All this neighborly coming clean had sparked a bemused twinkle in Peter's eyes. "Actually, Roxy and I have been interested in your property for quite some time," he said. "If we had known it would sell at such a low price we would have made an offer ourselves. I'm not sure what we'd do with two houses, but it's such a unique place and you guys got a super deal."

Most of what I've seen of human nature would have had our new neighbor giving us the *bad* news. Telling us about our poisonous well that's dry most of the time anyway, and our locust swarms and our boll weevils; the leached soil and the sinkholes and the seventeen acres of dumped radioactive waste. Inside the house we'd find our dry rot and our carpenter ants and insulation levels below code. By contrast, Peter's positive candor won us over in an instant.

We mentioned that 224th Street was once called Old Stone Road according to the Lynch's, and this was news to Peter but it was information that pleased him. We all agreed to get a sign made to restore our dead end to its original and considerably more charming identity.

Peter was a hands-on farmer with his own tractor and truck and a lot of the essential equipment to which we hadn't given a single thought. Well, at least *I* hadn't. We'd noticed Peter spraying something on his orchard field just the day before, dressed in a moon suit with a tank harnessed over his shoulders. Judy had referred to him as "Rocket Man." Accurately sizing us up as a couple of greenhorns, Peter gave us a generous helping of advice.

Foxglove's old barn that frames the courtyard sheltered horses at one time, but had cramped stalls with low ceilings that could never accommodate noble beasts of the proportions of Mickey and Matt. The floors needed repair and so did the roof, but Judy had spent a day and a half sweeping out the old barn in a way that made it seem like she was expecting company. Judy is talented and vigorous with a broom in her hands and claims to enjoy sweeping. "Always have," she says. A handy value added in a wife.

"Sheep," she had said. "This would be perfect for sheep. Wouldn't it be cool to have sheep, honey, and we could have chickens over there." Judy had pointed to an old chicken run adjacent to an older coop.

Peter's brow furrowed a little when Judy described our resolve to become shepherds.

"What are you going to do about your fences?" he asked, finally spreading some crushed olive paste on a slice of baguette. They were very tangy and I was on my fourth, way ahead of my host.

"Fences?" Judy pondered.

"*We* had sheep, and if you don't have the right fencing they get into everything. Ruin your gardens. Get into the neighbors. Everywhere that you have fencing for horses has to be done again in wire mesh or your sheep will drive you mad."

I slurped some chardonnay and contemplated this news. I had been bemusedly onside when Judy first brought up sheep, but wire fencing sounded labor intensive and not just a little costly. And where were Peter's sheep now? Had this distinguished surgeon with the kindly blue eyes butchered them behind his *maison provençale*? What was for dinner after I polished off the olive paste and marinated mushrooms? Could that aroma wafting from the kitchen be lamb shank osso bucco?

"Dinner's ready babe!" announced Roxanne from the kitchen. She and Peter called each other "babe."

It was poached salmon.

CHAPTER 20

"Hey, you, get offa my cloud"—Jagger & Richards

"SOD OFF!!"

A FEW OF THE SMALL BUSINESSES IN FORT LANGLEY CARRIED a pad of identical colorful maps of the area. Visitors could simply tear off the top map and have a pretty good idea where the old Fort was, and how to find the other local tourist attractions.

Take 216th Street south for example and head towards the border of Washington State. About ten minutes from Langley you'd encounter Domaine de Chaberton Winery with medal winning vintages and a delightful bistro where the menu rivals anything you might find on Robson Street in Vancouver.

Redwoods Country Club and Belmont Golf Course are on the map too, each offering ample challenge and a scenic four-hour loop when you get a chance to tee it up. Redwoods has a muscular wooded front nine, emerging into Scottish style links that take you back to the clubhouse. Not so keen on the golf, Judy raves about the onion rings at Redwood's nine-teenth hole; huge, juicy and lightly battered, tempura style.

Another attraction is a dried hydrangea business called Everlasting Flowers. This, of course, had been Rebecca's enterprise, and a romantic black and white photo of Foxglove

Farm was prominent on the border of the map.

The business had grown over the years to the point where she held an annual fall fair that attracted a growing crowd of visitors, seeking a lazy, countrified Sunday afternoon. Foxglove Farm was actually a destination site for busloads of tourists throughout spring and summer who would pile out in the courtyard to walk the gardens and ogle the house.

Judy and I thought all of this was nice to hear about and I guess we were proud to know that our home had, at one time, commanded such interest. The map hasn't been updated though and we've only got ourselves to blame for that. We've never called to complain. I guess it must be number 267 on our *to do* list. As a result, we've experienced unwanted visitors to Foxglove, almost on a weekly basis.

We need to get the gate fixed. It's set up for automation, just like Roxanne's, but the motor's been long burned out and we weren't particularly unhappy with the bungee cord. Most times we'd just leave the gate open and trust the *Private Property* sign to deter trespassers. *Fix the Gate* is buried deep in the job jar. Well, once we called a Langley gate guy from the Yellow Pages, a time was set, and he never did show up. We weren't too concerned as the sign was clear that we weren't hankering for visitors.

Nonetheless, cars and the odd bus would ignore the sign and wind up in our courtyard. Mind you, the young couples who had heard that "*Legends of the Fall* was made here," never stepped out of their S.U.V.'s. Nor did the octogenarians venture to the courtyard from their buses. Brutus made sure of that. Woofing deeply in full stride to greet these sundry visitors, Brutus caused most trespasses to be only momentary.

"He's gentle," we'd say, but most unwanted company chose to take our word for it.

One hot summer afternoon in 2003, I was barbecuing a rack of baby back ribs that Judy had boiled first, so the meat would just drop off the bone. The barbecue overlooks the river at the back of the house and is stationed on an interlocking brick patio, a smaller mirror image of the courtyard at the front.

Judy and Brutus were toiling and snoring, respectively, in the garden by the gatehouse, several hundred yards from the exquisite aroma I was creating with charring pork and hickory sauce. My gin and tonic was strong, tall and frosty, and life was good.

My back was turned to the house as I moved the ribs to the upper rack and lowered the flame, but felt an eerie sense of not being alone. Then I remembered Hebes, Judy's latest acquisition. Hebes apparently was a niece of Neptune, our bearded, naked, God of the Sea, that had presided for a couple of years now by the pond at the front.

Hebes was better off than her stoic Uncle Neptune whose eight hundred pounds of exposed flesh was outdoors day and night, with no respite through rain, frost and visitations from migrant waterfowl. Hebes is about half Neptune's size, and came to Foxglove in what could pass for a concrete evening gown, and stands inside the Tuscan street sunroom with a view of the barbecue.

I shot Hebes a quick glance and saw that she had company.

A very old woman was in the sunroom, staring at me through the French panes. She was less than five feet tall and looked exactly like my Dad's mother, who has been quite dead for thirty-five years now. I *had* been quite sure that Nanna was peacefully resident in English soil, tucked beneath emerald Derbyshire sod.

"Foxgloves," she said through the open door. "Where do I get the foxgloves? I always get the foxgloves."

I took a belt of gin and tonic, then another, and ventured inside.

"I rang and rang and rang the doorbell but nobody answered," she complained. "I want the foxgloves, where do I get the foxgloves?"

"This isn't a flower business anymore, it's a private home," I said gesturing toward the front door.

"Who knows about the foxgloves?" she persisted.

"My wife might know," I said "She's gardening by the gate."

"Will she have the foxgloves?" she asked.

"I don't know, like I said, it's a private home now."

"It's a private home?" she asked as I opened the front door and saw a little old man behind the wheel of a compact car, waiting by the fountain.

"Yes it is," I confirmed, "and we value our privacy."

"I'm sorry," she said.

"It's okay, bye-bye now," smiling and waving to the old man as I gently shut the door.

I'd made an icy pitcher of sangria, with chunks of lemon and orange afloat. I poured Judy a glass and tore off a crispy back rib to give her a sample, then walked it up to the gatehouse garden. I was surprised to learn that she hadn't noticed the coming and going of the little car.

"Maybe it *was* your grandmother," she mused when she heard the story.

Then these minor annoyances took a darker turn.

One summer day while I was at my Vancouver office, a car

pulled past the *Private Property, No Trespassing* sign, came up the driveway and parked in the courtyard. The car was dirty and nondescript, and so was its lone occupant.

Brutus woofed deeply a few times and the man at the wheel thought better of getting out. His window was half open revealing a mullet and a Fu Manchu. Judy, alone, looked up from her weeding in the garden strip by the brick courtyard fence.

"Can I help you? You know this is private property."

"I'm with the fire prevention department just doing some inspections in this area. I'd heard how incredible this place is and just wanted to check it out."

"Well, like the sign says, it's a private home now," Judy heard herself say.

The dusty beige car made its exit, pausing for a minute by the gatehouse. Brutus trotted along beside, seeing him out.

Judy and I were getting used to these unwelcome visits though, and I hardly gave it a second thought when she told me she'd been a little "creeped out" by this one. Then he came back.

It was less than a week later. This time in a dirty paneled van, the kind with no windows on the back or side. Judy was in the barn, mucking stalls. I was at the office in the city.

The van went past the gate and up the five hundred foot drive. Instead of stopping in the courtyard it went past the fountain and the chapel and through the narrow arch of the old barn that holds the clock and then further, right up to the open doors of the new barn where Judy was just offering Mickey his daily carrot.

Judy moved quickly to the tack room in the barn and let Brutus out. He snapped into dutiful action, trotting and woofing his way out of the barn to inspect the intruder.

The mullet guy spoke through the van window.

"I just can't stop thinking about this place," he began.

"This is my nephew," he continued, pointing to a scruffy boy in the passenger seat that couldn't have been more than seven. Judy thought the boy looked frightened.

"There must be a lot of work around this place; gardening and other stuff. I thought it would be good for him to learn about work."

"I'm expecting a lot of people any minute," she fibbed. "They're filming a movie here, I'm sorry but he'd just be in the way."

The van had to back up through the arch so it could turn around in the courtyard. Brutus escorted it to the gate.

"Did you get the license plate?" I asked that evening.

"No, I should have, but the van was really dirty and I guess I was in shock that he was here again. I was scared."

A few days went by and I kept thinking about the creepy visits and found Langley Fire Prevention in the white pages. I left a voicemail and a fellow called me back.

"No sir, all of our employees have clearly marked trucks," he said and I flipped to Langley Police, before I even thanked him. "Plus they wear uniforms," he added.

The officer working the phones for the Langley Police wasn't a lot of help. She just took the description over the phone and said they would keep an eye on Old Stone Road.

Three-In-One Outfitters is a huge camping store toward the eastern side of Vancouver. They had tents and air mattresses and Coleman Stoves and lanterns for sale, and everything that a masochist might seek for a weekend in the woods.

I was there for pepper spray. A heard-it-all-before nod came from the man behind the counter, who seemed to be about my age. Oh yeah, they carried it.

"Would this be for four-legged bears or two-legged bears sir"?

"Definitely two-legged," I advised.

"Well this works good on city bears," he said as he put a sleek object that looked like a Mont Blanc fountain pen into my hand.

"I want to *level* this guy, not write him a letter. Is that all you've got??"

"It's just a one-shotter, but one's all it takes most times

for city bears. Different story for country bears; sometimes the one-shotter only pisses them off."

"Well I live in the country, show me something for country bears."

He nodded solemnly and reached under the counter, producing a canister that looked like a miniature fire extinguisher. "You're lookin' at a ten shotter," he said with some pride, "and the spray's more concentrated; this is your industrial strength, designed to discourage a grizzly."

"This would fend off a trespasser then, I suppose?"…No harm in being sure.

The man behind the counter lowered his chin and his eyes rolled up locking into mine. "Sir, one shot of this would incapacitate this entire store."

I glanced around me and saw about thirty would-be campers poking at sundry outdoor paraphernalia. There were all ages and both genders. A flaxen-haired brownie, in full uniform, held her grandmother's hand as they checked out a pup tent. I leaned into the counter and lowered my chin as he had, rolling up my eyes a few inches from his.

"Show me," I whispered and quickly added "just kidding."

"I'll take the one shotter and three of the ten shotters," I said, reaching for my credit card.

Of the canisters with ten shots, one went under our bed and one in a kitchen cabinet. Another was stationed in the new barn where Judy spends so much time. The creepy mullet guy hasn't been back; touch wood. But God help *him* if he ventured near Foxglove again. We'd have him peppered up like Jean-Claude's *bifteck au poivre* at "The Smoking Dog," our preferred bistro in Kitsilano.

The whereabouts of the Mont Blanc style one-shotter is a mystery for a couple of years now and that's a little disconcerting. I think it's lurking in a jar or a drawer somewhere, an imposter in a crowd of genuine writing implements.

"We'd better find it before *we* have grandchildren," I intend to tell Judy sometime.

CHAPTER 21

"How does it feel to be on your own?"—Bob Dylan

FRADY CAT

I WOULD GUESS BY NOW YOU PROBABLY SUSPECT HOW I FEEL about Judy, and on those days when I'm feeling okay about myself I think she probably loves me too. "Whatever love is," to quote Prince Charles, hardly an authority on the subject.

But Judy and I have never been one of those couples who rarely share a harsh word, and make a point of never going to bed mad. We've known couples like that and more often than not, after twenty or thirty years they arrange appointments with lawyers and amicably divvy up their stuff, including the bed to which they never retired in anger.

Carefully living non-lives, their gears have been spinning but never mesh. They don't engage. There's no interlock. It's not that I'm an advocate of thirty-two years of scrapping like cats and dogs. That comes with too much wear and tear.

But marriage is a simmering stew with a recipe as long as Shaq's shinbone. First you take a couple of gallons of transparent self-interest and add a pinch of insecurity. Chop and dice your own identity and chuck it in the bubbling cauldron. Thicken the broth with the irritating traits of one's in-laws and spice it up with divergent views on raising kids. Bring the pot to a screaming boil with two parts male menopause and a liberal dash of PMS. Flavor to taste with money worries and career crises and toilet bowls that need cleaning. Mop it all up with sourdough bread that's gone a little stale and then slather it with middle-age spread.

The genders need to approach mutual understanding as a mission with "live and let live," the guiding principle. If some-one drinks directly from the tap for example, after brushing his or her teeth, he or she probably has a good reason for doing so. Outside of a little alleged Colgate on the faucet, this might be seen as a crime with no victim. Neither should chronic failure to balance a joint chequing account result in a spousal over-reaction. There are, after all, worse things than abject financial disaster. So live and let live, I say.

The "toilet seat" issue that seems to be a bugbear in many marriages has not hit our charts as a top forty thing about which to fight. A savvy woman, with a flick of her wrist, en-joys comfortably dry seating. A *leave the seat down* advocate may well settle her unsuspecting buttocks on an icy oval of yellow piss, a greeting card from the man who loves her, but with much on his mind.

Occasionally the temptation to use a spouse's toothbrush needs to be resisted, particularly if the tempted party travels a lot, gets home late, and his or her luggage is still in his or her car or truck by the fountain in the courtyard. The probing carnal adventures of a thirty-three-year relationship notwith-standing, a mate's toothbrush remains sacrosanct. Character, after all, is defined by what we do when no one is watching.

The politics of marriage runs the whole gamut. You've got your dictatorships, which can be effective but over the long term somewhat brittle, given the way times and people change. Dictatorships can hurtle headlong into midlife revolutions and bloody coups. Then you've got your enlightened despots. The only problem there is that the despot's opinion of what constitutes enlightenment is basically the only one that counts. A lot of marriages survive for years under this system…well, at least until the kids are on their own.

The Wyf of Bath's husband in Chaucer's Canterbury Tales took a slightly wimpier approach. This fellow's Wyf was a genuine piece of work but his posture was that she was "sovereign through my strength." Yeah, sure; that was his story and he was sticking to it.

My take is that the Wyf of Bath herself was an absolute dictator or at best, an enlightened despot. Her old man was just kidding himself. Incidentally, my wyf shares an endearing feature with the Wyf of Bath. Both wyfs sport that comely front tooth space to which I referred in chapter two, the title of which I am certain is "The Gap."

Chaucer was quite emphatic that this space in the Wyf of Bath's grill was a good thing and the Husband of Bath was a lucky guy. Chaucer saw the gap as a hallmark of sensuality; something of which to *never* seek closure. Not that they had retainers and other "appliances" in the Fourteenth Century. *Do* gap-toothed wenches have a leg up when it comes to pleasing their man? You can draw your own conclusion, but for *my* part, I'm with Chaucer.

Our marriage has always been a parliamentary system of government like the kind we have in Canada and long favored by the Brits. There's a government, an opposition and a lot of bickering across the floor of the house. Kids are like the backbenchers.

With a majority the governing party, for argument's sake let's say the husband, can enact laws and carry them out with freewheeling confidence for the greater good of all. He can have a rotten day or even a bad year or two and just laugh it off because he has control; and control is what *everybody* wants; don't you think?

A minority has to earn its right to govern every day, with compromise its stock in trade. To keep control, control must be surrendered. Now that's precarious in my view; and you wonder why most marriages, and all governments, eventually fail.

For the first fourteen and a half years I ran things with a comfortable majority. Then somewhere around 1987 I found myself at the helm of a very slim minority regime where the tail would wag the dog more often than not.

In fact, it's *possible* that I haven't formed the government at all and have actually served many of the past seventeen years as the leader of the loyal opposition.

But Foxglove Farm put an end to any parliamentary debates and spirited or bitter exchanges as to the way things should be.

Foxglove was a special place where only serenity would govern.

So at the first sign of friction, Judy would simply pack Brutus in the Rover and head off to spend the night at Point Grey Road.

Solitude, once in a while, is not a bad thing in itself. Perhaps you're on a business trip where you're staying in a nice hotel. There might be a hot bath, a fluffy white robe, a fat newspaper, the latest *Golf Digest* and a menu of movies on TV. There's the possibility of high speed Internet for emails and maybe a chess battle; a well-stocked mini-bar and room service, or perhaps a super assorted Mr. Submarine with extra cheese and hot peppers.

Being alone at night on seventeen acres in an old gothic

house can be a different story.

In 1960 my dad was transferred from Calgary to London, Ontario. We rented an old two and a half-story house on Belgrave Avenue while my parents got to know the city and figured out where to buy. We'd lived in a sterile new Calgary subdivision prior to that and the old house on leafy Belgrave was a little bit creepy and one night my active nine year-old imagination got carried away. I came home from my friend Paul McKay's house at about eight in the evening and was surprised to find myself alone.

A week before I had seen a TV episode of *One Step Beyond* where the new owners of an old house can hear the faint laughter of children from the attic but can't find anyone there. They can hear it for about a minute every night of their first week in the place. At the end of the episode their kindly old parish priest pays them a welcoming visit with a view to blessing their home.

They mention the laughter, his face clouds, and then he haltingly reveals that three little kids died in that very house thirty years before. He'd handled the funeral. "A very nice service, but sad indeed. I still dream about those tiny white caskets."

It was something about a faulty gas line.

By eight-thirty all I could think of was that *One Step Beyond* show. By nine I was standing outside on Belgrave Avenue but starting to get cold. By ten I was sitting at the kitchen table with a butcher knife in my hand, quite certain I could hear the laughter of little children coming from upstairs. At midnight my parents came home to find me still at that table, butcher knife poised, with tears of rage and relief at their late arrival streaming down my face.

Left alone at the farm, without so much as even Brutus, that memory would return and every little sound in that one hundred year old house would be magnified. Whenever a train whistle or ambulance siren sounded in the distance, our coyotes would stoke up a discordant refrain from their blackberry den.

Flipping through the channels for diversion, I landed on *The Shining;* right at the part where Jack Nicholson's kid is tricycling down the hallway of the old hotel called *The Overlook,* and stops at Room 237. He looks up at that room number, pauses and for the time being moves on.

Then I changed the channel to Sportsnet and caught up on the latest scores and trade rumors. After twenty minutes of that I scrolled down the channels one more time and sure enough landed on *The Shining* again, having forgotten it was on. Remarkable, considering our satellite dish gives us a couple of hundred choices.

To make matters worse the kid was back in that same hallway, looking up from his trike. I'll be damned if he wasn't back at Room 237. This time the boy got off his bike and laid his hand on the door handle. Pausing for at least forty seconds he tried the knob and it turned. The door opened and he stepped into the room.

Quickly I switched back to Sportsnet, but was oblivious to the scores and standings and highlights and chatter. My mind was drawn into room 237 and the horror of its contents as I recalled the Stephen King novel. Empty; but then that sound; the squeaking rub of the old lady's rotting corpse against porcelain as it rose from the bathtub; her hands straight out in front of her to grasp the boy in a foul embrace.

I surfed the channels and wound up back at Sportsnet for

a few minutes. Then I headed for Point Grey Road, calling Judy en route to apologize. Damned if I remember what for.

A week later Roxanne was over for a glass of wine and to check out Judy's progress in her decorating plans. For some self-serving reason I shared *The Shining* story, maybe admiring my own willingness to be honest and vulnerable; a new age man of the new millennium.

"Well, you're just an old frady cat, that's all," Roxanne beamed through her snapping wad of nicorette.

As a footnote, in Stephen King's *The Shining*, the room with the corpse in the bathtub is number 217 *not* 237, as it was in Stanley Kubrick's film. While most of *The Shining* was shot in the U.K. the outdoor scenes were filmed in Oregon with "The Timberline Lodge" masquerading as the "Overlook." Apparently "The Timberline," while not having a Room 237 *does* have a Room 217, which would have been true to the book. Lodge management however, concerned that future guests would be afraid to stay in Room 217, successfully lobbied with Kubrick to have it changed.

So while Roxanne's "frady cat" assessment of her neighbor may be justified, it would seem that I have lots of company.

Christmas at Foxglove

Judy with Brutus, Matt and Mickey

CHAPTER 22

"The first cut is the deepest"—Cat Stevens

KNACKERED

THAT APRIL DAY WE BOUGHT BRUTUS IN CHILLIWACK HE was as much my dog as he was Judy's. For almost a week his welcomes and tail waggings were every bit as robust for me as they were for her. "Probably because his first owner was a male," Judy supposed.

But he soon fell under her spell. Not a waking moment would find them apart. When she trundled off to the barn to feed the horses or bring them in from pasture Brutus followed, even waking from the deepest sleep when he heard her hand on the doorknob. He'd make this trip several times a day despite being unceremoniously locked in the tack room. This extreme measure was deemed necessary owing to his habit of nipping at the heels of Matt, a couple of thousand pounds of chestnut gelding which had taken an immediate dislike to our Brutus. When directed to "be a good boy," Brutus would dutifully shuffle into the tack room on his own accord, never failing to start barking when the door was closed. "He *needs* to see me," explained Judy. He'd earn his freedom when Matt and Mickey were safely munching in their stalls.

Our master bedroom at Foxglove is a fireplaced, balconied room of ample proportions and soon became his boudoir too. An early to bed, late to rise kind of guy, Brutus actually stirs from his sleep in front of the TV in the library, woofs an announcement that he's turning in, and makes the trip upstairs to his blanket by Judy's side of the bed.

The deep and rhythmic jowl-flapping snoring begins early and stays for the duration. Whereas my alleged snoring can earn a quick trip to another bedroom that I call the "snoring room," Brutus is seldom banished there. Judy claims that I often revert to a particularly irritating snoring technique where I hold my breath while she has to guess if I'll ever exhale. She calls this my "Iron Lung." Brutus, apparently, doesn't feature the "Iron Lung" in his repertoire.

Even before adopting Brutus we had wind of the fact that the English Mastiff was notorious for farting. An American breeder's website discouraged whimsical purchasers who were unable to resist the English Mastiff's noble bearing and unconditional loyalty. *"Prospective owners of the English Mastiff must be prepared for constant drool and room clearing flatulence,"* was the stern caveat; fair warning for triflers.

But if this was reverse psychology it was a ploy that had its programmed effect on Judy and me. Whichever end of our Mastiff might offend, our collective response was "Lay on Mac Duff!"

Judy, always seeking improvement in Brutus's lot in life, switched him from dog food to cans of Puritan Beef Stew. Upon noticing my raised eyebrow she countered, "each can only costs a little bit more than Alpo, and he likes it *so* much better."

It seems to me that coincident with this upgrade in Brutus's diet, his gassiness became more frequent and noxious.

He'd taken to tightly wedging himself between the leather couch and the footstool that Judy and I shared, sleeping beneath our outstretched legs while we scanned the channels for something worth watching. Every ten or fifteen minutes, during Masterpiece Theatre or Hallmark's Hall of Fame he'd drop a silent bomb, and, nothing against the good folks at Puritan, but the putrid bouquet made me, for one, pine for his Alpo days.

On trips to Point Grey Road it would never occur to Judy to leave Brutus at the farm. He's been quite a hit with the dog walkers at Kitsilano Beach as well as in Langley, at locales as diverse as The Home Depot, Petsmart and Starbucks. All of our errands are run in the Rover because almost two hundred pounds of yellow drooling dog would be a sure fire way to devalue my roadster. Accordingly, it's Judy's navy blue 2000 Autobiography Series Range Rover, her latest "truck," which has taken on the permanent aroma of ripe pooch.

It was love at first sight when Judy met Brutus with his raw nose begging for her care. Otherwise a male dog probably would not have been her first choice. All of our dogs to that point had been females. After all, who wants a hundred and ninety pounds of red-blooded Anglo-Saxon mastiff seeking a frenzied tryst with one's thigh? Thankfully, Brutus never went a courtin' in that way, where a blushing surrender might be the only viable option for the target of his affection.

When he sat on his haunches his yellow coat would often ride up, exposing a good-sized pink shaft that gleamed ready and willing for action. The occasional appearance of this coral visitor was the source of some pride to me; an encouraging development for a big male dog which is loath to lift it's leg.

"There's nothing wrong with his hydraulics Jude!" I enthused.

One of my daughters though, witnessed this phenomenon and offered an "eeoooo!!!" of disgust that is the province of teenaged and pre-pubescent girls. This young woman, however, is in her mid twenties.

Considerably more worldly, but nonetheless insisting on a little decorum, Judy instructed Brutus to not "sit like that," and most times he would adjust his posture and we were able to bid adieu to this unwelcome appendage.

It had crossed my mind to pay a visit to "The Wack" and scout about to find a young lady Mastiff for Brutus, just to see if they might hit it off. Maybe we'd find him a fiancé, an apricot Brindle to add a dash of spice to the union; some likely lass who'd appreciate what he brought to the table.

But it wasn't to be. Plans were made; an appointment set.

Brutus's knackering was scheduled coincident with a long weekend trip to Palm Desert where we were guests of good friends at their hacienda at Rancho La Quinta.

He'd be all done when we got back. While we harbored mixed feelings, a last minute reprieve was just not in the cards. Judy was worried he'd run off womanizing if left in his natural state, or be drawn into the coyote pack for a good hamstringing.

By having him snipped while we were away there would be less chance he'd associate us with the neutering and any bad feelings that could crop up. We kind of felt like Mr. and Mrs. Pontius Pilate as we said our farewells to an unsuspecting Brutus at Judy's favorite veterinarian office at Alma and Tenth, then drove to the airport. Nonetheless we enjoyed a relaxing weekend of golf, shopping and dining out, and Brutus's pendulous testicles seldom entered our thoughts. Well, certainly not *my* thoughts; out of sight, out of mind.

The guilt only kicked in when we landed back at Vancouver International, jumped in the Rover and headed for the highway. "Maybe we should pick him up tomorrow or in a couple of days," I suggested as we approached the junction where a right turn headed southeast for Langley and a Vancouver sign pointed north.

"He's been there long enough." she said as I applied the brakes for a red light.

"I thought they had big cages," I recalled.

"Not that big," she said.

"You told me he liked it there," I persisted, "I thought the girls there were crazy about him."

"He likes the farm better; besides its thirty bucks a day," advised Judy.

"Maybe a dog that big needs more time to heal," I mused.

"Honey, you've got a flashing green," were Judy's last words on the subject.

I had expected a Brutus that felt betrayed, and acted sullen and resentful. But nothing of the kind!! Still in the vet's office, Brutus leapt off all fours, as his ecstasy at reuniting with Judy knew no bounds. He showered his trademark "hugs" on her, where he bows his massive head and pushes the furrows of his brow into the thigh of her blue jeans, all the while having his ears scuttled into disarray. He even broke from her once or twice to give me a little token love with those same hugs and a tail pounding like a metronome gone wild.

From the rear his landscape was a vastly altered terrain. Prune-like, an empty change purse wizened by financial disadvantage. But no mind, this was one happy dog. It was like we had done him a favor.

I guess you don't miss what you never had.

CHAPTER 23

"Shock the monkey"—Peter Gabriel

FIERCE CHIMPS & FIERCE PEOPLE

SHORTLY AFTER OUR OFFER WAS ACCEPTED AND LONG BEFORE possession, the movie people called. Judy handled all these conversations, being sovereign through my strength.

They understood we were the new owners of Foxglove Farm and wanted to confirm our interest in continuing Foxglove's long history as a location for Vancouver's booming film industry. Getting paid to have movie stars show off our property? Well…sounds okay…I guess.

Thirty years had flown by since Professor Yacowar's film course, Dramatic Media 295, but Judy and I had retained our passion for the movies. In the last decade, however, we didn't go to the theatre nearly so often, choosing to avoid the line-ups and the rambunctious youths in the audience who might catcall the screen or otherwise spoil our experience with their incessant and vacuous chatter. On a couple of occasions I have stood, mid-flick, turned and loudly advised pockets of these inconsiderate whippersnappers of our quirky preference to ac-tually hear the movie soundtrack. Back in the eighties I found it necessary to do this during *Ghostbusters* and was rewarded

136

with a smattering of applause from a dozen or so of my peers, like-minded crotchety geezers in training.

The evolution of big screens, flat screens, plasma screens and high definition was making it tougher to leave the couch. Woofed and tweeted surround sound certainly made it less tempting to check out the movie times, get in the car, try to find parking, get in the lineup, pay twenty–two bucks, have some pimply ticket ripping kid tell you to "enjoy your show," survive the popcorn line, then have a last minute pee, balance the popcorn and soft drinks on top of the urinal, occasionally wash your hands if time permitted, then find where your Judy's sitting in the dark at the front only to be rewarded with thirty minutes of advertisements and coming attractions and a sticky floor beneath your feet. There were these and a myriad of other compelling reasons to stay home, none more persuasive than a fridge full of icy Burrowing Owl, one of the Okanogan's superior whites. Showtime for us would be on our terms, usually ten past eight on weeknights, providing ample time after Final Jeopardy for a pit stop and a refill for those inclined.

There are only a couple of things I miss from the days when we'd actually "go to the show" a couple of times a week. Both involve messing with Judy's mind. First, whenever I'd find her in the darkness in the first or second row, I'd begin to devour my popcorn, focusing on the screen and basically ignoring her. After about three minutes of this I'd heroically produce a Kit Kat or chocolate caramel Rollo from my pocket and she'd know that she hadn't been forgotten. The other thing dates back to the early seventies when we were alone in a tiny Cineplex theatre in Toronto about to see *Breaker Morant*. Just before it started another couple sat in the row in front of us. The guy seemed nerdy and anal and it appeared to be their first date. "I've heard *good things* about this film" he told his companion with a tight, affected voice that said he might be an actuary in training, "and I *really, really* want you to enjoy it." Our skin crawling, Judy and I made eye contact and stifled a laugh. For the next three decades we basically couldn't go to a movie without me putting on the nerd voice and proclaiming "I've heard *good things* about this film, and I *really, really* want you to enjoy it," just about always receiving a hard punch to the arm and a "Would you *stop* it?!"

Judy's taste in cinema has evolved over the years and I've done my level best to keep pace. Our heroes were once Clint Eastwood and Charles Bronson pumping hot lead into villains in the bleak New Mexican desert or upstairs in some bawdy Wichita saloon. These days we'd much prefer to see Dame Judi Dench or Dame Maggie Smith use a timely bon mot to redden the face of a pompous guest in a drawing room at *Gosford Park*. We love our Anthony Hopkins, and, not wanting to be left behind, I'm trying to develop a taste for his role as a dutiful butler in *Remains of the Day* where absolutely nothing happens, as opposed to his Hannibal in the sequel to *The Silence of the Lambs* where much does.

Never a fan of gratuitous violence, Judy, nonetheless, has retained an open mind to a variety of genres. She actually appreciated Quentin Tarantino's brutally sadistic *Reservoir Dogs* and feels our son Dylan would be perfectly cast as Mr. Pink. Of course, the over-exposed Harvey Keitel was in *Reservoir Dogs,* and both Judy and I have wearied of his wallow in gore and the sight of his pasty bare ass. Not that I would prefer the sight of the unclad hindquarters of Dame Judi Dench.

When I coaxed Judy to see *Saving Private Ryan* we were both concerned about the unprecedented levels of graphic violence that had been mentioned in its reviews. "Well war *is* hell honey," was as persuasive as I got. The first half hour was overwhelming and I was concerned that it was all too much. Young boys shredded limb from limb, sitting ducks in their landing craft and on the beach, cannon fodder exchanged for a Normandy foothold; blood everywhere. "That film should be required viewing for anyone who benefits from democracy," was Judy's critique on the drive home to Kitsilano Beach. "The price that those kids paid...."

I wasn't able to convince her to see *The Passion,* but, feeling it was an important and controversial work, I had occasion to check it out myself when I was alone in Toronto. Missing lunch, I arrived at five at The Paramount conglomerate of theatres on Richmond Avenue in a state of ravenous hunger. Opting for the super jumbo barrel of popcorn, I ogled the vat of bubbling "golden topping," with which I intended to anoint my dinner. "Extra butter please, and layer it if you would be so kind," was my instruction to the young slack-jaw whose job it was to ensure that not one puffed kernel of that mountain of maize escaped the saturation of a yellow lube job. Later, down in the front row I was overwhelmed with a sheepish angst. I peeked over my shoulder in the nearly empty theatre, hoping, even though the odds were *in* my favor, that none of my business acquaintances were there to witness my pathetic presence. Alone, in the front, scooping handful after handful of that wet, greasy corn into my pie-hole, straw-slurping my quart of Pepsi right down to the ice; while they whipped and scourged the Son of God for a couple of hours, then spiked our savior to the cross. "You suffered and died to save the likes of me?" I whispered through the slickness of my oily lips.

My top five list of all time movie favorites hasn't changed much in thirty years and is unremarkable in that three have won the Oscar for best picture and the other two were nominated. *The Godfather* and *The Godfather Part II* are both in my top five owing to the richness of the textured detail and the depth and breadth of the memorable characters. *One Flew over the Cuckoo's Nest* presided at the pinnacle for twenty years beginning with its release in 1975. The Jack Nicholson vehicle still holds up well, with just a slivery hint of seeming dated. My favorite of the last decade is *The Sixth Sense,* at once deliciously creepy, romantic and satisfying. Buy the DVD and you get two movies for the price of one, the second screening offering the viewer an entirely different perspective, armed with the knowledge of the ending of the first. *The Sixth Sense* is a delight from which I abstain when I'm alone at night at the farm. My sleeper flick is Sidney Lumet's *The Verdict* which slips through the back door into my top five. I enjoyed the Paul Newman film on first viewing but never really had a craving to see it again; nor do I hanker to see it now. But in the early eighties, after it had its run on the big screen, *The Verdict* was on the movie channel almost daily for a year. Whenever I was surfing the choices on cable and landed on *The Verdict* in progress, I almost always watched it right to the end.

Braveheart gets honorable mention, surprisingly at the time, given its genre, another Best Picture recipient. The little boy, residing in the soul of we men folk, just can't resist the swashbuckling clash of good and evil, and the showers of flaming arrows and the vicarious joy of hand to hand combat from the safe comfort of an easy chair. For the women there's a kilted Mel Gibson still inspiring his oppressed followers during the disemboweling phase of being hung, drawn and quartered.

Perhaps a more worthy honorable mention should go to

Elizabeth with Cate Blanchett in the title role, simply the most powerful and elegant feminist statement ever put to film. In more than a few respects *Elizabeth* was a more convincing *Godfather III* and could have been subtitled *The Godmother.* Soaring above the "You go girl!" chauvinism of the joyriding *Thelma and Louise,* the virgin queen, like Vito Corleone, survived a perilous childhood to end up pulling all the strings. And like Michael Corleone, Elizabeth was not above resorting to something approaching fratricide if a sibling or cousin was disloyal. Mary Queen of Scots was her Fredo. But make no mistake, *Elizabeth* is about a great and courageous woman who takes names and kicks ass.

In stark contrast is the nasty and insulting little film, *Chocolat,* my choice as perhaps the most appalling movie of all time. Sugar-glazed in the cloying charm of a French village, the bitter taste of *Chocolat's* clumsy and manipulative core message fouls the palate for weeks after the end credits roll. And that message is that all men are either corrupt or insensitive, boorish louts, deserving the application of a skillet to the head, and we women have got to stick together. All men that is, with the exception of the longhaired, uncommitted gypsy, a Fabio clone that seems to have leapt from the cover of one of those exploitive romance novels and landed in the second half of this piece of crap. But bodice-ripping men like *this* are okay, don't you know; especially if they happen to be Johnny Depp. As repugnant as this artless pap is to my masculine sensibilities I am doubly offended on behalf of the women who can't taste the rotten center under its gooey chocolate cover.

Our fascination with the movies aside, a little Hollywood

revenue seemed timely indeed as the upkeep of Foxglove Farm was a bit of a drain on our resources. Our accountant frowns on expenses that can't be matched to income, so we welcomed interested filmmakers with open arms. Movie making at Foxglove was a going concern, all we had to do was carry on and hopefully enhance what Rebecca had started. I still harbored doubts that *Legends of the Fall* had been shot at Foxglove and, when Judy bought the DVD, we watched the film together and my suspicions were confirmed. Then we went to Deleted Scenes and I'll be damned if Brad Pitt wasn't sitting next to the fountain in our courtyard. Foxglove had been used as the French asylum where the young hunk was confined after scalping the Germans that killed his brother in a World War I firefight. "It was neat to find a French estate in Vancouver," explained the director, Edward Zwick, "but the script and the acting weren't that great, and neither was the directing." So the farm shots fell to the cutting room floor.

Our first gig was a one-day outside shoot titled *Spymate*, about a jet-setter private detective who happened to be a chimpanzee; not that there's anything wrong with that. They wanted to use our courtyard and east garden for a wedding scene. It portrayed a gathering of the top spies in the world. I'd forgotten that Judy had booked this and, when I came home from work on a summer Wednesday, I was surprised to see over a hundred people on our driveway and courtyard and an array of exotic cars. There were Lamborghinis, Ferraris, a James Bond BMW Z8, a Hummer and half a dozen more.

I worked my way through the throng, finding refuge in the house with a good stiff Johnny Walker Black over ice. Peering through the French windows of the pantry I could see everything about thirty feet from my discreet vantage point. They were filming a scene where a chimpanzee has to close the gull wing door from the cockpit of a yellow Lamborghini. He's dressed in a tuxedo and a frothy formal shirt with patent leather shoes and a glass of champagne in his hand. The monkey looks sharp and he looks like he knows it.

The scene isn't going well because it's a bit of a prima donna chimp that's extra-ornery today because apparently his shoes are too tight. His trainer is on the set doing everything he can to coax the star to cooperate long enough to get this scene "in the can." They've had over twenty takes and just can't get the chimp to gesture a toast with the champagne glass, smile and lower the gull wing door. Tempers are short all around.

Finally they bring in a backup monkey from Roxanne's place where a number of the movie's trailers are parked. He's in formal wear too and arrives with his trainer on the power golf cart that Peter and Roxanne use to get around their property.

Apparently there's yet another understudy if this primate doesn't work out. Disgraced, the first chimp is golf-carted back to his trailer, kicking off a patent leather shoe onto the driveway as he makes his exit. They get the second one into the Lamborghini. I notice the trainer is missing half of his nose, long ago scarred over; occupational hazard I suppose.

The new chimp isn't much more co-operative than his predecessor. I guess he's the second stringer for a reason. He drains his champagne before the director's ready for the toast. Another half hour gets shot with no success. I'm into my second Johnny Walker and pressing closer to the pantry window, transfixed by the ruins of the trainer's nose. What's left of it is red and bulbous, kind of inflamed like the ruddy backsides of his hairy pupils. Then, miraculously, the toast is perfect, the toothy smile happens and the Lamborghini door comes down right on cue.

"That's a wrap!" bawls the director as the trainer gets some tootsie rolls into the hands of his jubilant student, now screaming the way chimps can do. High fives abound in the courtyard. "Its Miller time!!" announces a thirsty security guy into his walkie-talkie. Then one of the cameramen explodes "*Jesus Christ*!! *He's* in the picture!!" He's pointing straight at me in the pantry window.

Judy and I watched the next twenty takes of the same scene, peeking from behind the barn. "It was an honest rookie mistake," I whispered, "anyway, how come with modern technology they can't just make me disappear?"

But we weren't rookies for long. Hot on the heels of Spymate we had a couple of TV series call to book Foxglove for shootings both inside and outside the house.

There was a *Mary Higgins Clark Mystery* where they filmed scenes in the kitchen, the courtyard and the barn. There was a three or four day *Smallville* episode where a young Superman scuffled with his nemesis, Lex Luther, in our ballroom, where a gun went off then fell hard on to the oak parquet. Not only did they repair the floor, but they painted the barn red for their story and repainted it earth-tone to suit Judy's taste. The barn had needed painting anyway and was a middling priority on our growing "to do" list.

Whenever a location scout came around Judy would have the place spotless and fires blazing at every hearth. She'd contracted with George the gardener whose company was called "The Yardman," and had a key employee named Mike. Mike was all long hair, shaggy beard, Export A's and chainsaw. Mike didn't say much but worked miracles with that Black and Decker. Judy's wish was his command as she had him tame the blackberries, trim right down to the river, clear the saplings that had sprouted in the riding ring, and then deal with the pond. With an opportunity for movie revenue Judy left nothing to chance, so she convinced Mike to put on some hip waders and trim every bulrush and reed, turning the pond from something wild into a gleaming feature that would have looked just fine at The Palace of Versailles.

"Poking around" an antique store, Judy found Neptune.

Neptune, our God of the Sea statue, is buck naked and tips the scales at close to half a ton. Modest, as gods go, the bearded deity conceals his naughty bits by curling his fish tail around from behind. There's an island in the middle of the pond preferred by nesting waterfowl and we thought Neptune would command the pond perfectly from there. Neptune's burly deliverymen rolled their eyes at that idea and left him on the grassy edge of the pond overlooking the courtyard. If we wanted him centered, we were on our own.

Judy's vision was always to restore Foxglove to the style it was in the forties by maximizing the groomed look, eventually even on the other side of the river. "They used to have formal gardens over there, everything was manicured," she had noted on the day she showed me the footings of an old bridge that she had uncovered.

The day when we moved in, the lawn at the back of the house was an alley of green sloping down to the river, maybe only seventy feet wide, encroached by brush, ground cover and weeds on each flank. You couldn't see the river on either side of the lawn. She let Mike in on her thinking, and in a week or two he and his chainsaw had it all opened up and we had grass seed blown in everywhere, leaving any precious acacia saplings standing.

A year later after a torrential rain was followed by blustery winds these young acacias would prove to be valuable successors to some of their aging relatives that had bordered the driveway for a hundred years. Six of the gorgeous old timers went down, one crashing through the glass of the greenhouse, adding insult to injury.

I had looked up at the short, skinny acacias that we had transplanted to replace their towering forefathers. "Oh well Jude, in eighty years we won't notice the difference," was the best I could do.

But all of Judy's planning and hard work was paying off. By the time we had a Stargate TV episode, she was asking for five thousand a day and was getting it, no problem. The jaws of the location scouts and directors dropped when they stepped out of their cars onto the brick courtyard. "Oh my God, this is fantastic!!" or something like that, was usually the opening gambit of their negotiation.

"We got a call from that site manager today," said Judy as I walked through the door on a Friday evening. "They're making a movie called *Fierce People* and it's with Diane Lane and Donald Sutherland. The director wants to come out on Monday to see the farm."

The director was Griffin Dunne who'd made quite a few good films and was an actor in the eighties and nineties. I checked the Internet and found that he'd had a major role in *An American Werewolf in London*. But Donald Sutherland and Diane Lane; Sutherland, the venerable Canadian thespian; *Mash, Eagle Has Landed, Eye of the Needle…. Ordinary People;* Keifer's Dad.

Oh, and Diane Lane, the hottest of commodities. A best actress Oscar nominee as Richard Gere's straying wife in *Unfaithful,* and very recent box office gold in *Under the Tuscan Sun*. Diane Lane probably commands ten or fifteen million a movie. Clicking on Yahoo, I found that Diane Lane has been

a professional actor since the age of six. Appearing in four
Francis Ford Coppola films, she's one of *The Godfather* director's favorite stars. The daughter of a 1957 Playboy centerfold
and a New York City acting coach, Diane Lane's stage career
includes a role opposite the legendary Sir Lawrence Olivier. A
multimillionaire since the age of eighteen, a solid professional
actress for over thirty years, and still only thirty-nine, a bona
fide superstar, and now there was a chance she was coming to
Foxglove Farm.

"So how'd it go?" I asked on Monday evening.

"They were here quite a long time," answered Judy. "They're
looking at one other place but the director really seemed to
like it."

"What's not to like?" was my response.

It turned out that *Fierce People* had a romantic angle
where Foxglove was short listed to be the guesthouse on the
Donald Sutherland character's property. They were using the
opulent buildings and grounds of Royal Roads College on
Vancouver Island for his digs. The leading lady was Diane
Lane and the story had her character and her teenage son
staying at our place if we were chosen. It was supposed to be
around 1970 in the old world splendor of The Hamptons or
Long Island on the eastern seaboard.

A couple of days later they were back with a set decorator
and Judy said they had done a lot of measuring, just about in
every room in the house. They even measured the chapel.

That night we spoke long distance with our son Dylan.

He's been an actor in the Shaw Festival in Niagara-on-the-
Lake for five years, ever since he crashed an audition in 1999
and got the part of Simon in *Lord of the Flies.* Just a year later
he had the title role in *Peter Pan,* and soon after that landed a
decent-sized part in a movie called *The Fraternity* with Treat

Williams, who once was *The Prince of the City.*

In the late summer of 2003 Dylan married Joanne Boland, an actress in the Global TV series, *Train 48* and a young and talented veteran of various films, having shared the screen with the likes of Diane Keaton and Mickey Rooney. Currently, Joanne plays Martha Stewart's assistant in the second segment of the made-for-TV movie where Martha gets in trouble and goes to jail. Cybil Shepherd, once again, is a marvelously bitchy Martha, staying in character, according to Joanne, even on their breaks. Dylan put Joanne on the phone when Judy told her that the *Fierce People* project was three and a half weeks of filming and we had no idea how much to ask.

"If they've been back twice and they're measuring, you can be sure they want your place; their mind is made up," was the voice of Joanne's experience. "With Diane Lane, that's a big budget picture, you wouldn't be out of line to ask for a hundred grand."

I was away on business when the offer came; forty-six thousand. Judy said "no way." They came back to her quickly at sixty-five thousand and that's when Judy played the husband card.

"My husband left strict instructions that we couldn't accept anything less than seventy-five thousand. It's just so disruptive and it's a disruption we don't really need."

Of course I'd never left Judy with "strict" instructions about anything since that evening when she tapped my shoulder at Brock University. As I left for the airport I *had* told her that the entire negotiation was up to her and I'd be okay with the result. I figured I could do worse than that. I called her from the King Edward Hotel that night in Toronto. "Eighty-two thousand," she said "seventy-five plus GST, and they're going to decorate two of the bedrooms and we get to approve the colors and materials; plus a ten thousand dollar damage deposit."

The movie people offered to stable Mickey and Matt somewhere else at their expense, but Judy was just as happy to leave them at Foxglove. Mickey, at almost thirty years might have been upset by the move and this way Judy would have an excuse to be there most days and keep her eye on things. Make sure there was no smoking in the barn. We sure didn't need that.

"Ten thousand doesn't go very far these days and that crew is going to be huge," she said, referring to the damage deposit.

A full week of set preparation was slated before the actors even stepped foot on Foxglove Farm. Carpenters framed a throwback kitchen inside our white kitchen with the Tuscan floor. Old magazines from the seventies were strewn around the library and a regiment of lead soldiers was deployed on the desk in my study. There was even a faint aroma of pipe tobacco that surprised me, but evoked a strange comfort within. I remember thinking that much of this period detail would never be noticed in the theatre but must nudge the actors into the right mindset, helping them submerge into their characters.

I was skeptical about the decorating of the master bedroom and the second bedroom upstairs. They wouldn't possibly wallpaper behind the armoires and headboards. No one in the theatre would be the wiser if they slapped up some cheap stuff just where it might show. But I was wrong. With a film that has a budget like *Fierce People* few expenses are spared. The rooms were done up lavishly and thoroughly by top notch pros and we had so much to do both inside and outside the house we were grateful for the freebie.

"Do you realize how much that wallpaper would be per roll?" Judy asked, knowing I hadn't the faintest idea. She then quoted some obscene figure that left me feeling quite favorably toward the film industry.

By the time they were ready to start shooting I was spending most of my time at Point Grey Road. The plasma screen at the farm had been masked over with cardboard and tape and the fridge was inoperative. Foxglove had no TV, no food, no beer and no cold white wine, but there was still the commute. My desk in the den, occupied by a legion of lead soldiers, offered no space for my emails and Internet chess games. Judy had not exaggerated in her negotiation ploy; this *was* disruptive.

But Point Grey Road proved to be a perfect change of pace, with the short drive to the office and the sounds and smells of the Pacific, sometimes lapping and sometimes crashing up to our shore. When we had bought Foxglove we had figured it would be primarily for weekends; but it turned out we had been spending thirteen days of each fortnight at the farm. We were hooked, junkies for the quiet privacy and the natural marvels that come with country land.

I was well entrenched at the townhouse when the movie stars arrived and never did see them. Judy only caught the odd glimpse of them, but kept me in the loop, updating me over the five o'clock chardonnay, with which I'd greet her at Point Grey's door.

"I saw Donald Sutherland today," she smiled as we relaxed at the wrought iron and glass table on our patio. The April westerly was whipping the flags on the masts at Kitsilano Yacht Club. "Totally white hair, pretty long, and he had a beard. He looked really cool. There was a scene where they had him drive an old black Cadillac convertible, right across our field. It looked like something out of the forties." A few days later Judy was in the garden by the gatehouse and a Jeep rumbled down our driveway on to Old Stone Road, headed for town. The petite auburn haired driver offered her a cheery wave and Judy was sure it was Diane Lane.

The filming went well and three and a half weeks later we had our farm back and some cash in the bank for our trouble. I was astounded that they hadn't worked weekends given the cost of mobilizing all that equipment and about two hundred crew. It must be a union thing. But on Saturdays and Sundays throughout April, Brutus and Judy and I had the place almost to our selves, albeit decked out for the seventies. The only sign of life from *Fierce People* was an aging security guard who never seemed to leave his van by the fountain and looked decidedly unfierce; not a fierce bone in his body.

"That old guy must be hooked up to a catheter Jude," I observed "and a colostomy bag too. He's been sitting there for eight hours!!" "He must be afraid of Brutus," was her analysis.

By the first of May Foxglove was back to normal with two mementos from the movie. There was a spectacular bouquet and vase that Judy placed in the square room that windowed onto the Tuscan sunroom. A note in the vase thanked us for our hospitality. On the desk in the library was a framed glossy photograph of Donald Sutherland and Diane Lane. There were handwritten messages, each with a signature. One extended best regards and warmest wishes. The other offered love.

CHAPTER 24

"A time to reap and a time to sow"—Ecclesiastes

A FARM FOR ALL SEASONS

EVERY SEASON OFFERED ITS OWN UNIQUE DELIGHTS AT Foxglove Farm.

The summers were hot and dry, most days absolutely cloudless. Few easterners realize that British Columbia's Lower Mainland, much maligned for its rain, can have stretches of summer drought where watering a lawn can be a fineable offence.

Foxglove was just far enough from the Pacific to enjoy several more degrees of Celsius for those who like it hot. Count Judy among them. This was keeping-up-with-the-weeds weather but she met the swelter head-on in cutoffs, tank top and baby oil. Her father is a Radford but her mother's a Sarrazzin and her French blood is dominant when it comes to sun worship, among a few other things. She'd pretty well go directly from white to tan, leaving the burning, peeling and double-digit sun block to those of us with Derbyshire ancestry.

Each evening we'd critique the sunset. Every one was different and we'd alternate our vantage points, moving to a new swath of Foxglove acreage, although the chairs in the garden by the gatehouse remained position "A."

I'd ice the white wine bottle in the freezer to sustain its chill through happy hour, guarded by the shade under one of the garden chairs to which Brutus had not laid prior claim.

Thousands of birds enjoyed their happy hour too, inexplicably gathering in one huge tree or another, twenty minutes before sunset. Not every evening, but as often as not.

When we could see this phenomenon happening Judy and I would top up our glasses and head from the gatehouse garden, as close as possible to the chosen tree for that sundown. One evening it would be the tall, dead pine lone in the center of Jessell's field. The next they might congregate on a sky-scraping fir on *our* land, just the other side of the river. Their gossip and celebration boiled into a swelling din that could top the racket of a Shanghai marketplace. Then, as one, seconds before final sundown, they stopped. Silence. Judy and I would do the countdown and before we reached ten, the sky would fold and crack with the sound of a bed sheet on a prairie clothesline as six thousand took wing.

We'd make eye contact, shake our heads in wonder, grab the bottle and head for the house, Brutus loping just ahead.

Summer was weeding time, nowhere more so than in the formal garden by the gatehouse. Judy attacked this task with a resolve that bordered on obsession. Weeds concealed the crushed French stone that covered the rail-bordered pathways when she first undertook the garden's restoration. We'd managed to live a combined one hundred years without a Dutch hoe but evidently we needed one now. Virtually every day a new flowering plant was recruited from Cedar Rim Nursery to swell the ranks of the citizenry of the flowerbeds, be they fragile peonies, hearty roses or towering foxgloves. Planting these was a pleasure, but the currency of the overgrown pathways and other weedy nooks was sweat and toil and nettled forearms. One Mothers' Day I gave Judy a cast metal sign that said *Garden of Weedin'* to go with a gift certificate from Cedar Rim and she planted it in the heart of her daily battlefield. A few days later we were sipping sauvignon blanc at sundown as I persuaded her to call it a day so we could head to the backyard to barbeque a couple of Tandoori chicken legs and a few Maui ribs. She agreed but yanked another sixty of the easier tall surface weeds in two or three minutes before she packed it in.

"Those ones fold like the 1940 French," I observed.

"Cheap tents," she concurred.

"There's really no end to it for you, is there?" came my rhetorical query.

"Nope, it just keeps coming at a girl," she said, adding, "I'm going to stencil a quotation on the beam or maybe the wall in the greenhouse and it's going to say "The Bitch Never Rests."

I gave that some thought.

"What do you think of that?" she asked.

"Its funny, it'll be great, very appropriate," was my reply.

"I'm glad you like it, so many gardeners put up these sucky little poems or slogans like *You are Now Entering Hyacinth Heaven* or some pretentious Latin motto."

"Oh, I see, well that one of yours will be perfect," I said.

"Really?" she asked.

"Well, probably not," I answered, carefully considering my next step through the minefield of this discussion.

"Why not??" She asked.

"Well what kind of husband would tolerate a sign on his property that calls his wife a bitch??" was my measured response.

"The sign's referring to Mother Nature!!!!" was Judy's clarification.

Autumn brought the harvest, although with the exception of the fruit trees Foxglove's crop was limited to the tiny spice garden that Judy started near the glass green house. Basil, rosemary, fennel, cilantro, sage and thyme are the homegrowns I can remember from what she told me. By 2004, around our third farm Thanksgiving, there was some talk of a pumpkin patch and even a full vegetable garden. Blackberries, relentless as always, were everywhere from August through October.

These are the days of the burn pile. Fir boughs and pinecones, golden maple leaves and blackberry canes mingle for a smoldering week with chestnut shells, pears and crabapples raked and barrowed from their fall from grace. Companies like Chanel could do worse than to bottle the soft, sweet fragrance of the autumn burn pile, steaming gently through a fine Scotch mist.

"We could live off the land, Jude," I said one fall day when I'd come home weary, caked in the grime of commerce.

"We *should* plant a cornfield over there," she said on another day when she was feeling even more ambitious than usual.

The local grain and feed merchants flaunted their gourds and pumpkins curbside through October and Judy would point out the biggest ones to me as Brutus, she and I stopped in to pick up hay and alfalfa and a couple of molasses licks for Mickey and Matt.

The best of these stores, Hometown Hay and Feed, was also the handiest, a three-minute drive down Glover Road, and besides having the "nicest hay" and rows of aromatic bridles and saddles, they also stocked several shelves of homemade pies. I can't comment on Judy's assessment of the hay but can personally vouch for the peach and rhubarb versions of these deep and flaky creations. The leathery aroma of the horse tack jockeyed with the scent of the fruit pies, vying for our senses. This year they expanded the store and still carry feed and hay and a wider assortment of horse gear. Sadly, with this progress, the pies are gone.

A profusion of dried corncobs with multi-colored kernels would attest to the fall bounty at Foxglove, adorning the worn front door from September through December, replaced then by a wreath, fashioned by Judy from the boughs of our own firs and bound with a red velvet bow.

Winter brings the gloom of rain but Christmas at the farm was a cheery and colorful antidote. The ballroom, with its baby grand and roaring fire was party central, and once a year I have to reacquaint myself with the chords to White Christmas, Good King Wenceslas and O Holy Night. For years I've put in yeoman's service at the keyboard, but for the past two Yules Dylan's wife, Joanne, has wrested the torch from my hands and is now the backbone of our family singsongs. She can actually read music without a three second *gap* between perception and execution, a competency that I had never quite acquired from piano lessons at age six. I still play O Holy Night, mind you, and Judy continues to easily hit the high C on the *vine* of *oh night divine!*

I sing bass while pounding out an upbeat *Goin' to the Chapel and We're Gonna Get Ma-aa-aa-ried* with my back to the ballroom and can hear the peels of laughter as Dylan and Harmony roll up the carpet and do an impromptu vaudeville-style brother and sister dance act, all the while belting out the lyrics.

"Jazz hands!! Jazz hands now!! Ya gotta *sell* it!!!" exhorts Dylan to his sister as the two of them perform a synchronized, bandy-limbed box-step number, using every square inch of the ballroom, circling their outstretched palms like Al Jolson.

Catching her breath, Harmony starts *The Chipmunk Christmas Song* in perfect chipmunk acapella with sister Taylor Blue. "I just want a hula-hoop," goes their munchkin voiced collaboration. Twenty-six and twenty-four now, they've mimicked Alvin and Leroy every Christmas since they were six and four.

Then the party really *does* spill into the chapel where a pious Jesus Loves Me in four part harmony takes a gospel turn and finally evolves into a hip-hop rap session of the same sweet hymn with irreverent daughter Harmony Sarah resolved to create the least pious verse and usually succeeding.

One year we had snow and, nicely liquored up, brothers Mark and Dylan, now thirty-one and twenty-nine, fashioned crude toboggans from the cardboard boxes that had encased our gifts. Egg-nogged wives and sisters looking on, they went rollicking down the backyard hill, doing their best to dodge heaps of semi-frozen mastiff dung, and to ignore Judy's prediction that they'd both end up in the river.

Around mid-November Judy frets to me daily, "I haven't even begun my Christmas baking yet!" getting herself gumptioned up to start producing her annual quota of tourtieres and sugar pies, both further hallmarks of her Quebecois roots. Every year I get a rise out of her, maintaining the sugar pie's sole purpose is to keep the flies off more worthy pies that may be cooling on a shared window sill. She never fails to take the bait, emphasizing the differences between her very French sugar pies and the southern based shoo-fly pie which, according to Judy, indeed functions as a decoy on the sills of Dixie double-wides.

As a young wife, Judy cooked the hell out of the Christmas

turkey, drying the bird to the point where you could barely swallow. She caught on quickly though and for about thirty years now nothing compares to the golden perfection of our Christmas feast.

She insists on a fresh bird from the butcher, and organic, I suppose these days, but frankly I can't tell the difference. Whether Christmas dinner is fresh or a frozen butterball it's always heavenly and crammed with the most basic stuffing, heavy on the onions and sage.

Spring is a farm season of glory and wonder. New blooms emerge in February and one after another, explode like a firework competition, each outdoing the other. Crocuses precede daffodils followed by lilac and forsythia, quince, magnolias, rhododendrons and azaleas. And let's not forget the forget-me-nots; or indeed the foxgloves.

In May of our third spring wildflowers were everywhere like dabs of paint by Monet. There were tens of thousands of these lanky blue and white visitors woven through the high grass of the pastures, lining the meandering Nicomekl and overrunning the chicken run. A prolific laburnum droops fragrant clusters of yellow and dominates the balcony off our bedroom. All the fruit and nut trees flower in turn and finally the Acacias with their tiny white petals, destined to eventually come snowing down in June.

February can be the finest month, frigid sub-zero mornings warming to seventeen Celsius by three in the afternoon. Brilliant sunshine warms the frosted courtyard but doesn't quite reach the fountain where a solid rink of ice reveals three years of loose change; silver and copper wishes held in frozen aspic. These sweet February days often see Judy unclogging the icy hose when she fills the buckets for Mickey and Matt in the morning. By two she's gardening sleeveless and thinking about shorts.

Suddenly the snow-capped Golden Ear Mountain peaks seem right in your face, well beyond Jessell's field to the north and flanked by Mount Robbie Read; bleached white by day, all apricot rose by dusk, a northern mirror for the late winter sunset.

Two years back, George, the "The Yard Man" gardener, had a bad day. Each side of the driveway sports hundreds of daffodils that sprout early green between the Acacia trunks. That spring, George, or maybe his new protégé lawn cutter, sheered them flush to the grass before they ever had a chance to bloom. The daffodils, rightfully offended, boycotted Foxglove Farm the following year as well. The vigorous sprouts that have emerged this early spring give us reason to hope that the daffodils are willing, at last, to forgive and forget. Time will soon tell.

CHAPTER 25

"Hey, Teacher, Leave Those Kids Alone"—Pink Floyd

NOGURU

MUCH OF THE TIME, MY VIEW OF THIS SEASONAL REVOLUTION was through the checkered panes of the windows of my den.

Once, it had been the dining room for Alma Ziegler back in the forties, before the addition of the copper-domed dining room, into which the kitchen flows today. Alma was the sister of Austrian blue-blood Fritz Ziegler, honorary Ambassador for Monaco to the Americas, First Grand Prior of The Sovereign Order of St. John and a resident of Fort Langley. A choclatier, Fritz Ziegler had moved to Vancouver at age nine and joined the family business in 1923. Interred during the war, he was released on the condition that he not live in Vancouver and relocated to Fort Langley where he built The Ziegler Castle. This imposing structure, created in the style of King Ludwig of Bavaria, overlooks Glover Road to this day and is more museum than family home.

The fact that Alma never married couldn't be attributed to her appearance. Apparently quite a looker, Alma actually had an affair with William Randolph Hearst and Foxglove Farm, during Alma's lifetime, boasted quite a number of artifacts from The Hearst Castle in San Luis Obispo. The two remaining white pillars in the ballroom reportedly came from Hearst, but an informed source, which knew Alma, told us that there were actually ten pillars at one time.

Our "informed source" was the venerable Lucille Johnstone who visited us at Foxglove towards the end of 2003. Lucille was head of St. John's Ambulance for BC and the Yukon, as well as Chair of The Fraser River Discovery Centre, an interactive theme attraction in New Westminster that celebrates the history of the mighty Fraser.

Lucille had been referred to me for my charitable fundraising specialty. We expected Lucille on a Saturday afternoon and, returning from golf, I stopped at The Fort Langley Liquor Store.

Knowing Lucille was almost eighty, I got it in my head to offer her a glass of the finest sipping sherry, one of the few strong beverages we never have on hand. "I won't spend over a hundred bucks," I had promised Judy. The Fort Langley Liquor Store manager heard my request and with a shrug produced the only sherry they stocked and rang it up for $14.95.

Lucille arrived in her little car and had a devil of a time getting out. I extended my hand but she insisted on going it alone.

About four-foot-ten and broad as she was tall, Lucille walked with a cane and doddered from the courtyard into Foxglove with the warmest of greetings and we stationed her on the couch in the library. Brilliant, sharp and analytic, despite her age, we could soon see why Lucille was so highly regarded.

A member of The Order of BC, and one of Canada's first female Certified Management Accountants, Lucille, was renowned as Chief Financial Officer, for turning around the fortunes of RIV-TOW, the barge and tug concern. She was affectionately known as "Tug Boat Annie." Now a passionate leader in charitable circles, Lucille is listed with the likes of Jimmy Pattison in "B.C.'s Top Thirty Business Legends."

I asked her if she would join Judy and me in a glass of sherry, sounding like we drank it all the time. "Anything wet," said Lucille. "*Actually* I prefer martinis, but sherry will be fine."

"Where'd your pillars go?" she asked and proceeded to fill us in about Alma Ziegler and William Randolph Hearst.

When Judy mentioned her ongoing renovation of the gatehouse, Lucille jumped in.

"You mean Shorty's cabin!"

"Shorty?" Judy asked.

"Shorty was my handyman back in the fifties," began Lucille, "But Shorty was an alcoholic; a hopeless drunk. *I* had a farm; fifty acres near here at the time, but I had to give him the sack when he set fire to the place. Not on purpose mind you, but you know what I mean. Probably smoked in bed. But other than the booze, Shorty was a good man and I felt sorry for him, so I spoke with Alma and she took him on."

Lucille paused and twinkled a smile and sipped her sherry.

"That's why we call it Shorty's cabin. He lived there for years but he damn near burned it down too...."At least a couple of times!!" she added with a cackle.

"Did Alma die here," I asked, "*in* the house?"

"No," Lucille said.

I resisted the urge to plant a sherry soaked kiss on our guest.

Lucille's eyes became pensive. "There was some burning going on in the field," she recollected. "Things got out of control some. Shorty was in his cabin, sleeping one off, I think.

Alma ran up the drive to roust him up. She had a heart attack, but she died at Langley Memorial, a few days after, I seem to recall."

Sadly, Lucille was hospitalized herself a few months back and dropped eighty pounds in a few weeks. She called me from hospital regarding her insurance and predicted that she might die before too long. As usual, she was right.

Nancy Ziegler, Fritz's widow and a great-granddaughter of Canada's fifth Prime Minister, Sir Mackenzie Bowell, invited Judy and me over to the castle for an afternoon tour with white wine and strawberry shortcake when we first bought Foxglove. We knew Mrs. Ziegler's health wasn't great and wouldn't have been surprised if we had felt like a couple of Pips visiting Miss Havisham. But on the contrary, while she struggled physically, her mind and spirit were vibrant and her welcome was warm indeed. Mrs. Ziegler herself was our personal tour guide, weaving us through suits of armor, European artifacts and an immense and priceless stained glass exhibit, created in Europe centuries ago by a renowned artisan. Word has it that the stained glass at the Ziegler Castle has a twin that resides in the Smithsonian Institute.

She had a few pictures of Foxglove Farm and showed us an old black and white photograph of the whole family gathered for a formal dinner in my den. There was a pretty blonde in forties garb and she confirmed my hunch that it was Alma.

By 2002 when we were "so buying" that place, Rebecca had relegated that room to storage duty for her dried hydrangea arrangements. Judy transformed the den into a special haven, painting the mid blue wainscoting an antique black and wallpapering above it herself. She found an earth-toned French toile that was just right, equal parts elegance and masculinity. Three classic prints lend weight and history. A black and white World War I scene entitled *Tipperary* shows weary British troops singing while they march through high mud in front of a horse drawn war wagon. Behind my desk a victorious Duke of Wellington surveys the Waterloo battle-field in *A Hero and His Horse*. Between the leaded paned win-dows a blacksmith never seems to finish the job of *Shoeing the Bay Mare*. A weathered, leather golf bag holds a couple of wooden-shafted clubs and is propped in a corner along with my pellet rifle.

Hooked on the lamp on my desk is a key to Room 210, attached to a cumbersome brass bar that says "Royal Golf Hotel—Dornoch." The heavy piece of brass, ostensibly, was a manifestation of Scottish angst, that some blackguard might pinch their stuff. Back in 1997, after fourteen rounds at Royal Dornoch in eight days, I hadn't discovered it in my luggage until I had flown from Inverness to Heathrow and was looking for aspirins in the wake of too much Glenmorangie. I didn't mean to steal it, honest. But it *has* been nearly eight years and I haven't mailed it back.

The other thing on the wall is my fish. In 1985, buzz-ing with six Heineken, I'd somehow landed a ten-and-a-half pound rainbow trout at Babine Lake, north of Smithers. Thrilled then, blushing now, I admit it was on hardware, a willow leaf lure and a worm, the line neglected, the monster trout dancing on the surface over a hundred yards behind the boat piloted by the guide and owner of Tukki Lodge, who, while piloting and guiding, was skunking me out of twenty dollars at crib. Dave Hooper was a multi-tasker.

I wanted to donate the lunker to Tukki Lodge for the last-ing acclaim of a brass plaque and to avoid the taxidermy bill but there was no room at the inn. Hooper pointed out that the lodge's dining area already had an eleven-pound rainbow on the trophy wall, where an Arctic Char and the heads of mountain sheep, elk, and wolverines kibitzed, poker-faced, at our nightly card game. So my fish got stuffed by a local expert who skunked me for another three hundred.

Defying all odds, that fish is mounted today in my Foxglove study. The fins are tattered and two decades have otherwise taken their toll. But who am I to talk? Other than being twenty years dead, the trout's certainly holding up better than I am.

If his re-emergence had been my idea, rest assured that the aging rainbow would still be attic fodder or garage fodder, locales where he has resided for a couple of decades. Save for one undignified appearance around the neck of my yellow nor'wester for a late eighties Halloween bash, my trout had been of no fixed address. "Don't get too attached to him!" is my morning self-admonishment with the steaming French pressed coffee that I take in the den.

I'd made that mistake with my desks. A submissive benefactor of Judy's antique quests I'm now on my third one in three years. Just when I'd get really comfortable with the old old desk, a new old one would appear and I'd hear about the rationale behind what, I was assured, was both a bargain and an upgrade.

My current desk is one that might well have been Peter's if Roxanne had been on her toes at Cloverdale Antiques. That is another story, but in that, I have no complaint.

I spend most of my time at that desk on my compact but powerful, Sony Vaio computer. It's about two and a half pounds and travels well.

Foxglove Farm has neither cable TV nor high speed Internet but somehow we manage. A Bell Express-Vu two-foot dish is stationed a hundred feet up a cedar that shades the house. Great reception, in the absence of gale force winds. The Sunday Football package brings me instant access to every NFL game and Judy is seldom without options for her gardening, cooking and renovation shows.

I actually don't mind the dial up Internet. Bank balances and business emails are, in fact, too readily available on the high speed, broadband access. There's something comforting about the scratchy, discordant dial tone searching for a connection. Most news is bad and with dial-up it can only reach you after going through due process. And even then, mercifully, connections are fragile and negative tidings can evaporate into thin air. Sort of like a Dear John letter in a mailbag on the Lusitania, long soggy on the ocean floor; undelivered heartache, blurred by time and by brine.

The dial-up serves well enough for Internet chess.

I enrolled in the Internet Chess Club about five years ago.

My won-loss record is currently 2,641 wins and 2,586 losses. 191 of my games have been drawn. Having a life, I set a fifteen-minute limit on each match. My handle is "Noguru." "No method, no teacher, no guru" being a recurring theme in the compositions of Van Morrison, the prolific Irish musician, well beloved by both Judy and me. My password is eric.

My father taught me the game when I was six. He'd beat me every time but I kept playing, regardless, motivated by the incentive of winning whatever car he happened to be driving at the time. Beat Dad just once and I'd be the proud six-year-old owner of a beige '56 Volkswagen, and subsequently a two-tone 57 Ford Fairlane, and then an orange 1959 Dodge Desoto that boasted the largest pair of tailfins in automotive history.

We always played with a chess set that I was led to believe was pure ivory and hand carved. Losing all those games, I nonetheless felt honored to even touch the pieces, whether they were from white-tusked beasts or the even more exotic black. The rooks, as if to dramatize the set's authenticity, were actually elephants, blanketed, with a Bengal rider astride.

When I was seven or eight, my dad suffered a concentration lapse and I skewered his rook after forking his queen with my bishop. He wailed in some treble octave to my mother like a newly widowed Yemenite but with a Derbyshire accent, "He's beaten me, Jean!! He's beaten me!!!" Five minutes later he turned over the keys to the family car.

"Don't be so silly Eric!!!" intervened Mom, not really grasping that a deal's a deal. Ten minutes after, he persuaded me to accept the ivory chess set in lieu of the Ford, and threw in the heavy wooden board that had, so recently, been the scene of my inaugural victory. A week later, I beat my brother John too. He chucked the checkmating white rook at my gloating head, and ducking, I saw the castle crash against the *Schubert* piano bench, upon which we both suffered weekly lessons from a stooped, seventy-six year old hair-bun named Mrs. Stephens. The elephant's ivory trunk snapped off as if it were plastic. That's just what it was, of course, and the three of us battled with that synthetic set of mine for another thirty years. By the time they shot J.F.K. all of the rooks were trunkless.

At age seven I nervously wandered into the chess club at Calgary's Glendale School and somehow managed to hold my own. Most of the kids were eleven or twelve and a few of them were good strategists for their age. The vice-principal, Mr. Skanch, was a player and had persuaded the Calgary Herald to do an article on the chess club and its young membership.

I remember being matched against a ten-year-old girl named Laura who was kicking my butt. She had me trapped and badly down in material. The honorable thing would be to resign, given the hopelessness of my plight.

"A gentleman would resign," my Dad always said when *he* had me in dire straits, as he usually did when I was trying to win the family automobile.

Mr. Skanch brought the reporter and cameraman over and surveying the board, they assessed my dilemma. Then the vice-principal rearranged the pieces so I had Laura in a stranglehold and the cameraman got his shot.

"Seven Year Old Chess Whiz!!" was the headline, with a story that I was undefeated and "Bobby regularly beats students five years his senior." My mother still keeps the now jaundiced Herald clipping in that same Schubert piano bench; me in a plaid flannel shirt, checkmating queen in hand, in the act of pouncing; Laura looking perplexed and helpless to defend.

I guess I should have spoken up, but in 1957 they were still strapping kids and who wants to piss off your vice-principal?? I had been sent to see this same Skanch only the week before, charged with the very strappable offence of kicking snow in the lineup that was required when the bell signaled the end of our morning recess. It should be understood that snow had been kicked at me first; it was *my* retaliation that had not escaped the notice of the vigilant teacher whose duty it was to monitor our frigid fifteen minute break.

As a first time offender I had dodged a strapping that morning, but Skanch saw fit to show me exactly what I could look forward to if I was to kick snow on another occasion. From his desk drawer he extracted a foot and a half of flat leather, two inches wide. Curiously it was two-tone, red and black, very much like Brutus's nose before Judy got him fixed up. Most cars were two-tone in 1957 and I can only guess that this jaunty style was also the informed choice for the up-to-date corporal punisher. Confronted with this sleek, striped threat, my eyes grew wide but, miraculously, remained dry.

But Skanch was a chess player and his *show the kid the strap* gambit was an effective strategy. There'd be no more trouble from me. Well, at least not until just past the afternoon recess of the same day.

Brenda Goodyson's desk was next to mine, near the back of our grade three classroom. Brenda had long dark hair that usually sported a good-sized silk or velvet bow. Her pretty face had lost a few baby teeth whose successors had yet to sprout, leaving Brenda with a gap. Brenda was always dressed as if she was going to a birthday party directly after class and her finery was never finer than on that same day that I had kicked snow. A white, lace full-skirted dress, complete with crinoline and puffed sleeves, matched white lacy ankle socks, with pink trim, emerging from patent leather Mary-Jane's. The bow in her hair was pink velvet on that winter afternoon.

Brenda liked to tease me and had sneered at the dismal state of my little starter set crayon box where the few crayons that I had left were broken nubs. Brenda was proud of *her* crayon box, the Crayola Deluxe Edition, boasting no fewer than one hundred and forty-four crayons. Her pristine array of Crayolas had nuances of every shade, right down to several options for *white*. The colors were in perfect order and each of the twelve dozen looked back at you from its place in the box, a multi-racial audience in a packed opera house. Early in the term, lured by a smile, I had asked to borrow a red and her blunt refusal blew me away. She'd been waiting, a hunter in a duck blind.

While not particularly skillful at teasing, Brenda was persistent. She'd whisper my name one syllable at a time while wagging her index finger in my face, "*Baw-Bee-Trow-Bridge, Baw-Bee-Trow-Bridge,*" repeating this cadence several hundred times if the opportunity was there. Our young teacher was a demure lady in her rookie semester and never seemed to notice Brenda's obsession with torturing me in the back row.

While Brenda *was* pretty, I had long since decided that I for one felt no attraction. "*Handsome is as handsome does,*" my mother used to say. Brenda's flaw was not so much her teasing, but her habit of eating her boogers.

Beautifully turned out every day, if overdressed, Brenda would regularly extract whatever she could from her pert nose with a delicate index finger, and then hold it up for inspection. Satisfied, she'd roll her prize between finger and thumb, stick out her tongue through her toothless gap, and make a deposit upon the pinkness of her young taste buds. On this day I'd caught her in the act, and we made eye contact. Its owner unconcerned, that same pink tongue re-emerged through the gap and pointed in my direction. Then she wagged her ballpoint in my face, hissing another round of *Baw-Bee-Trow-Bridges.*

But *I* had a pen too, a gift occasioned by my seventh birthday. It was a Parker and it was a fountain pen with a full cartridge. Wanting no more than to mimic my frilly antagonist, I shook it hard, wagging at Brenda as she had at me.

Brenda's geography notebook was the recipient of the first splash. And what a beautiful Hilroy it *had been*, with flawless turquoise printing, carefully traced maps and the multicolored underlined headings, courtesy of her Crayola Deluxe Edition. But it was the lacy white dress and crinoline and even the pink velvet bow that took the brunt of the contents of my leaky Parker, and in a matter of seconds the Goodyson girl was indistinguishable from a Rorschach test.

Hand pumping the air while she wailed, Brenda summoned the teacher in an instant. "Bobby Trowbridge!!" gasped our young instructress, "you go straight to the office and report what you've done to Mrs. Lovegrove!!"

For a dangerous second I weighed a response like, "But I haven't done anything *to Mrs. Lovegrove,*" then thought better of adding insolence to my compounding list of crimes. Perhaps kicking snow and ink-soaking that nasty little nose-picker would be enough for one day.

Mrs. Lovegrove was Glendale's elderly principal; quite a posting for a woman in 1957. The pupils respected Mrs. Lovegrove and thought she was okay, albeit long in the tooth, but something like this would land squarely on the turf of Vice-Principal Skanch; the same Skanch who had previewed his two-tone strap to a snow kicker only a few hours back.

Doomed, I shuffled out of the classroom and headed slowly toward the office. I'd only gone fifty or sixty feet down the hall, one classroom removed from the scene of the bluing of Brenda Goodyson. There was a fire hose and an ax in a glass case that was built into the wall and it was there that I stopped. Turning my eyes to that case, I read, "In an Emergency Break Glass." For the next twenty-five minutes, I stared at that hose and ax, counting the folds in the hose over and over.

Thinking you could give a kid a damn good strapping in twenty-five minutes; I skulked back to class and sat. Brenda was gone, excused, I suppose, for a tearful cleanup. Most of the pupils peeked in my direction, seeking redness of the eyes or of the palms. Few things relieved the tedium of a dusty hour of social studies as much as rubbernecking the wreck of a freshly strapped classmate.

Forty-seven years have passed and I never heard another word about this bit of bad business. Maybe the young teacher, hearing nothing from Mrs. Lovegrove or Mr. Skanch, was too timid to broach the subject with her seniors. Or maybe she was just a beautiful soul who, fed up with nasal excavations in her classroom's rear rank, decided to take a *laissez-faire* approach.

Maybe I should have kept my counsel for another twenty years. Mrs. Lovegrove's got to be gone, but old man Skanch could still be spry at eighty-five; these days he might have a personal trainer, and maybe he's still got that two-tone strap.

I unburdened my conscience by telling my parents about the injustice to Laura that same evening of her shafting at the chess club, but neither seemed the least bit concerned. Triumph and acclaim, whether bogus or genuine, is something we want, I suppose, for our loin fruit. I just hope that Laura's therapy went well and that she grew up to become a litigation lawyer.

My passion for chess exists in spite of the fact that it's an anti-social pastime that brings out the worst in people. Chess is about one ego asserting its will on another; two naked intellects colliding. There are no excuses and luck plays no part.

At bridge, arguably the other game with a claim to greatness, you can blame your partner or the shuffled fortune of the deal. Bridge proponents would maintain that the cards equal out over thousands of hands, or they may point to the contrived equality of duplicate bridge where, in an evening, everyone eventually gets the same cards. Nonetheless, you'll never hear chess players ask, "So who dealt this mess?"

Chess is like the model of democracy envisioned by the

architects of America's constitution. Sixteen pieces each, of which fifteen are *men* and one is a woman. Both sides are created equal but one has to move first, and yes, that would be white. As the game progresses a skillful black can seize the initiative and punish his white adversary and the Queen, once liberated from the confines of the rear rank, can wreak mayhem all over the board.

"I don't know why you play when it just makes you so upset," said Judy in the door of the den, Brutus looking on. "Come on and help us bring in the horses. Then we can watch the sun go down."

I had just annihilated some stranger named Knighty-Knight on the Internet after he or she had asked for a *takeback* claiming a slip of his or her mouse. I wasn't buying the mouse slip story. The blunder, in my view, wasn't a physical faux pas as much as it was the consequence of a greedy plot to molest my Queen; an impetuous gaffe with ill intent.

In any event, I never ask for takebacks and seldom give them. Like golf's mulligans, they cause the integrity of the game to break down. Children, I suppose, can be Internet Chess Club members. Takebacks are for kids.

The bitter loser had sent me a text message.

"Well they shouldn't have called me a "butt jockey" I said as we headed for the barn.

"What on earth is a butt jockey?" Judy asked.

Before I could say "I'm not sure you want to know," she spoke first.

"That's disgusting!!"

"Just an immature, sore, bloody loser!" was my summation.

"A gentleman would have resigned."

CHAPTER 26

"Just look over your shoulder; I'll be there"—The Four Tops

SEMPER FIDELIS

THE CRUEL WIND OFF LAKE ONTARIO SNARLED UP YONGE Street where the movie lineup for *Bananas* was bouncing on the spot, pounding a hug on itself to keep warm. It was winter, 1973.

Judy and I took our place at the back of the line and I wrapped an arm around her shoulders.

⇝

In February 2004 we sold our insurance brokerage to our investment fund dealer and part of the deal had me staying on to run the business. Half the cash was up front, the balance spread over the life of my contract. These kinds of contracts usually don't work out. An entrepreneur who sells his business and continues on contract may be employed, but in his heart he feels *occupied*. Occupied like Holland in 1940.

My card says President but for the first time in eight years I actually have a boss that isn't my banker. The Chairman of our company is the C.E.O. and I'm the C.O.O. That's Chief Operating Officer, a nice title that comes without genuine control. And control is what you need, don't you think?

They didn't ask me to move to Toronto. Tacitly they tolerated insurance headquarters in Vancouver, while their epicenter was King and Bay with a key subsidiary in suburban Markham.

And while most contracts don't work out, mine is five years. To flesh out the value of our mid-life's work we need to hang on for half a decade. I kind of like the chairman who was really the guy that bought us, on behalf of his firm, over a year of due diligence, where you can get to know a person. He doesn't know much about my business but he's a quick study and remembers his commitments. So far so good.

If they had asked us to move east we probably would have declined. But my sense is I need to be in Toronto most of the time at least for three years to get fair value from the sale of our business. So Judy and I started looking, first on the web and then in person, even before the business sold, and there was a slick, Victorian brownstone in Yorkville that caught our eye. On chic Hazelton, it was a short stroll from Yorkville Avenue where the Riverboat coffee house had been a landmark in the late sixties. Joni Mitchell and Bruce Cockburn had played The Riverboat as virtual unknowns and the few blocks north of Bloor between Yonge and Avenue Road became Toronto's answer to Haight-Ashbury in San Francisco.

Capitalism slapped Yorkville silly over the next thirty years and free love gave way to high priced fashion boutiques, higher priced art shops and the party 'til you puke excesses of The Toronto Film Festival. World-wide, fest-wise there was Venice, Cannes and now *Toronto* just a two minute stroll from the black, lacquered front door of that sandblasted brownstone. Hell, we *had* to get us some of that! After all, we were Yacowar disciples from Dramatic Media 295.

Our first official "date" was a concert at the Riverboat

on Yorkville Avenue, a week after Judy tapped my shoulder. She'd worn a short, purple dress with little elephants all over it and chocolate suede thigh-high boots. The Brock women's volleyball team was competing in a tournament at the University of Toronto, and the squad was staying at the glitzy Royal York Hotel, long before the Royal York sold its soul to the Fairmont chain.

We saw Murray McLaughlin's gig and as we walked down Yonge St. to the Royal York I couldn't get his *Farmers Song* out of my head.

"Straw Hat and Old Dirty Hanky, Moppin' his Face like a Shoe. Thanks for the Meal, here's a Song that is Real, from the Kid from the City to You."

There, now it's stuck in your head. Well, that is if you're over fifty.

This farmer's in Yorkville right now and alone. I've got a cheap chardonnay on the go to wash down a pizza that I've learned to order online. Judy flew back to Vancouver a couple of days ago after we survived our first cruise; seven days with six ports on the Caribbean. It was a floating business conference, a perk from one of the insurance companies. She had to get back to Foxglove to see to the horses and release poor Brutus from the vet's. He's not sick; it's just that the kennels don't have a cage that's super-sized. Apparently this vet does.

Flying home from Puerto Rico we vowed to never cruise again, though we weren't seasick and we had a pretty good time.

I had some nice casino wins and Judy belted out *Summertime* with Pablo Rodriguez, the ship's guitar player, who could make his Stratocaster weep like Clapton. Pablo's gig was to play each night at sunset in an outdoor bar on the stern, starting just as the ship left port. Our gig was to drink

Margaritas.

A lot of our business acquaintances were on the cruise and Judy put up some token resistance to taking the mike and singing on the deck. Any coyness was soon overcome by our usual ritual of my persuasion abetted by several ounces of tequila. After a couple of slushy Jose Cuervo Golds, her Bess done be ready to please her Porgy.

I asked him to play it in her key, slow and sexy in E Minor, and Pablo grabbed his spare electric axe and shoved it in my hand. It was a nice solid Gibson. I chunked out the chords and he shook his ponytail with delight and respect as Judy howled the blues like an alley cat in heat. His blues leads on his Strat made time stand still, wailing over the frothy sea. His riffs, at once savage and tender, poured straight from his soul to ours, bypassing fingers and frets.

Janice Joplin would have approved.

The crowd around us chanted "Judeee!! Judeee!!"

It was only the last couple of days where we 'fessed up to each other. "It's all just too much isn't it? And it's a bit like camping with no leisurely bath. And we're on the ship's agenda, not ours. And so much bloody food and drink. And all those islands look the same. And they're all rotten to the core with their history of slavery. How can these islands be anything but dysfunctional?? Just like America."

The low point came when I turned to Judy at poolside and said, "Well it's happened. We're on a cruise and the band is playing The Macarena."

⤳

As far as being drawn to Toronto goes, it's not just the business. You see, three out of our four kids are in Toronto.

And don't forget what Lori Bogen had to say about

Vancouver, Toronto, Schwarzennegger and Danny DeVito.

Our elder son, Mark, is a computer graphics guy in Vancouver, creating special effects for movies. Mark was married, right in our chapel, to Akane, a terrific young woman. Speaking virtually no English a couple of years ago, Akane is rapidly becoming fluent thanks to repeated viewings of *The Simpsons* and the *Austin Powers* trilogy of comedies. The other day in her apartment elevator she charmed a neighbor by saying "Don't go freaky-deeky Dutch on me Fat Bastard!!" Her name is Japanese for sunset. Mark and Akane are west coasters all the way.

Back East there's Dylan the actor married to Joanne the actor. The word actress has fallen into a mild disfavor these days, the calling transcending gender.

And there's a daughter who's a piece of work named Harmony Trowbridge, a brilliant singer-songwriter well known in the Bohemian haunts of Queen Street West. Don't take the word of a proud daddy. Check out quotes on her website where a half dozen respected names from the Canadian music scene pay homage.

Then there's our baby Taylor Blue; a hostess at the trendy Drake Hotel on Dundas West at night, a budding actress when she's not meeting, greeting and seating. She enjoyed glowing reviews as a "deliciously sultry" Audrey in *As You Like It* this past summer and her updated resume caught the eye of The Shaw Festival in time for the 2006 season. Twenty-five, but looking fifteen, Taylor's been cast as one of the girls from Salem whose fabrications jumpstart the witch hunt in *The Crucible*.

These kids are fun to visit and it's always a thrill to see them perform. With these various motivations we bought that semi-detached Victorian on Hazelton Avenue, in the heart of

Yorkville, in June of 2004. Elegant, built in 1883 with a recent renovation, pool, and steps from the Four Seasons, The Park Hyatt and Sassafraz, a hot spot bistro where the stars hang out. Stars like Russell Crowe and Orlando Bloom. Big mortgage; enough said.

Lately I'm here in Yorkville more often than not.

These days I've got two Lexus roadsters, two sets of Callaway clubs and three toothbrushes. When I fly to Toronto nobody travels lighter. This two-pound Sony Vaio notebook is all I carry. No waiting at the luggage carousel. And I can't recall ever being so goddamned miserable. I wonder why.

That theatre on Yonge St. is still there just south of Bloor St. thirty-two years later. The other day I walked by it and remembered that frigid night in the *Bananas* lineup. Despite Professor Yacowar's opinion of my essay, I'd remained a staunch Woody Allen fan. This of course was well before Woody betrayed his wife, Mia Farrow, an actress I'd admired in my boyhood when she was Allison Mackenzie on *Peyton Place*. She was a longhaired girl next door until she cut it Auschwitz-style, birthed the devil's kid in *Rosemary's Baby* and married Frank Sinatra. "Old Blue Eyes" was fifty and Mia just twenty.

Mia's mother, veteran actress Maureen O'Sullivan, upon hearing their plans said, "Frank should be marrying me!"

"I've got Scotch that's older than Mia Farrow!" was the quote from Sinatra's *Rat Pack* crony, Dean Martin.

I'd seen *Bananas* before and loved it. I couldn't wait to get the reaction of my young bride to the bizarre humor therein. She laughed in some of the parts and much later she told me she thought it was brilliantly funny; but emerging from the theatre, she was as icy as the wind from the lake.

"What's the matter?" I asked.

"You know."

I didn't know at all and I said so.

Driving home in the Austin Mini Cooper she finally let me have it.

"Those blondes," she said.

"What blondes?"

"Those two blondes."

"What two blondes?'

"Those two blondes in the lineup outside the theatre. I saw you looking at them."

By all that is holy; by the lives of my children and their children; by my dear aged mother and my departed Dad, I have never seen those blondes. Not then, not since, not ever. It was kind of neat that my young wife worried like that, but I'm happy to say she doesn't worry now and hasn't for a long time. Nor should she.

I've always believed in a "great ledger sheet in the sky," where you enter debits and credits every day. You can expect no more back than the sum that you deposit. I guess that's spirituality, or maybe it's just The Golden Rule, sort of like religion without all the bullshit; or maybe it's only accounting. Whatever, but I square things with checkout girls when they fork over too much change.

Once I was sharing part of my philosophy on business recruiting with a fellow executive to whom I had just been introduced by a friend at an industry cocktail reception. I mentioned my bias, all else being equal, towards hiring candidates, who, against the odds these days, hang in and work on their marriages and spare me the cliché of having "this new lady friend." I said, as recruiters, we should ask ourselves, "what kind of bloody conceit must we have to expect business loyalty from someone who couldn't even be loyal to their choice as a life mate?" The fellow sauntered off to the bar and my friend put his hand on my shoulder. "Jack's working on his *fourth* marriage," he said.

At any rate I've always had a mantra where I've claimed to be married for x number of years, "without so much as flirting with a bank teller." Most people think I'm kidding but essentially I'm not.

It's just that you only have one chance to get things right. Life is more like golf than tennis. No mulligan; no second serve.

And though I guess you could argue that time is linear, and that was then and this is now, something that occurred once is every bit as true as something that happens today. I can still see the arc of that perfect spiral. I may be fifty-four, but I remember the fragrant huddle and the scarlets and ambers blazing in the backdrop of a certain autumn day.

CHAPTER 27

"I'm drunk again and I'm rarely sober"—Van Morrison

SLEEPING AROUND

MAYBE IT WAS THE STRESS OF SELLING THE BUSINESS. AFTER all, the negotiation ebbed and flowed, sputtered and stalled and started up again over the best part of a year. By the time we got the cheque, I was weary; bone tired from lawyers' fees and rumors spread by competitors, and the earnest questions posed by our own employees.

More likely it was the wine. Roxanne makes nicorette-snapping eye contact when she pours and it's really hard to say no, or even to say *when*, while you're focused on her perky banter. She pours Chardonnay with abandon, saturating her guests; assuming consent rather than asking whether a topping up is in order. The perfect hostess, come to think of it.

But facts are facts and truth is truth. Remorse and best intentions of a warning shot aside, that barn swallow is dead; deep in a dirt nap for over two years now.

Then in September of 2004, I slept with another woman.

In August Judy had a voicemail to call the *Fierce People* location manager. We thought the movie was going to be released to the theatres soon and maybe he was calling as a courtesy, just to give us a heads up; or invite us to the premiere. They had been so pleasant, even that wouldn't have come as a surprise. After Judy called back she had a new deal in hand and shared the details when I came home from work. Apparently one scene needed re-shooting and they wanted the farm for just one day in September. I guess they had other projects on the go during the week because they requested a Saturday. Disruption would be minimal; they wouldn't be coming inside the house at all. The crew was setting up in the courtyard and maybe the barn.

"Five thousand; I figured you'd be fine with that," she said.

I was fine with that.

That Saturday came and I snuggled Judy's cheek as she slept. "Play well sweetie," she murmured.

It was 6:10 and the days were starting to get a little shorter. My tee time in the city was 7:58 and I could get there in plenty of time to work on my swing and hone my short game. Shaughnessy has a superb practice range and my game needed a ton of work. My handicap was still twelve, but I was on a losing streak, and we play for a few bucks. My partner might be Avery, after we toss up the balls, and he could get a little acerbic if I didn't hold up my end. Or worse, he could be my opponent, when he was even more caustic if he had the upper hand.

Avery looks a bit like a dog and admits to being called "Dog" in high school forty years back. Furthermore he loves dogs and is an approved name on Brutus's very short list of babysitters.

Or I could have Howard. He's the fellow who missed his putt when the coyote ate the squirrel. Howard had his own swing problems, but anytime I was his partner he took a keen interest in my game. He'd noticed my stress level over the months when I was selling the business. Howard was born in Hawaii from Portuguese ancestry and claimed to be descendent from Hawaiian royalty. Retiring early, Howard had been a C.F.O of a major corporation following service as a Captain in the U.S. Army. Howard is a hands-on kind of guy.

"Relax Bobby," was his unsolicited advice, offered through an affable grin, his arm around my neck, my personal space violated, "just try to relax."

I felt that *trying* to relax was the ultimate oxymoron for verbs. It was kind of like *working on* goofing off.

A few weeks back I had tried to relax as my partner Howard cold topped his drive on the first hole about a third of the way to the lady's tee.

"He's doing the hat-dance," Avery whispered to his partner, Tony, but loud enough for all of us to hear. The "hat-dance" is Avery's term for Howard's tendency to bail out with his left foot when he tries to swing too hard. When partnered with Howard, Avery would quietly but urgently alert him to the problem, advising a smoother pass at the ball. On days when Howard was his opponent, Avery would celebrate the appearance of the "hat dance," to the point of humming the first bar of *La Cucaracha*.

Howard and I actually won money that day and my heroics could only be compared to the R.A.F. in 1940. Never was so much owed to so few.

Howard did the hat dance for eighteen holes but could see that I was a one man wrecking crew. By the thirteenth he knew that Avery and Tony were forking over the cash that day.

"I want a pup out of you boy!!!" Howard roared when I sank a twelve footer to birdie fifteen.

That September Saturday of the Fierce People re-shoot it was drizzling and I grabbed a Seattle's Best coffee and some gas at the Chevron. I stuck the coffee in the bird's eye maple cup holder of the Lexus and blasted off westward. Rain doesn't deter us at Shaughnessy. It's like going to war. You can't choose a perfect day to land at Normandy. You suck it up, you dress for it, and you take that beach.

I was lucky to be partnered with Tony on that Saturday. Tony's the best golfer in our group, with the build and grace of Fred Astaire although he's always looking for a little more distance. "Get fat Tony," was my advice. Tony lived on coffee and Belmont Lights that weren't like smoking at all.

I've never smoked much but the year we sold the business I'd taken to having four or five of Avery's Rothmans during our Saturday round. Taking up smoking at fifty-four. Brilliant. The deal was always the same. If I bummed even one smoke that day Avery's first pint of beer went on my account at the nineteenth hole. Avery had done the math.

In his early sixties, Tony's silver hair frames a gaunt leathery face that spent eleven years selling liquor in Perth, Australia. We call him "The Fox." Drizzle had turned to rain as Tony saved par from the sand on eighteen. Tony looked more like a drowned rat than a fox but was grinning as he carded seventy-nine and extended his hand for a power shake.

"Thanks pardsy!" said Tony, ever the gentleman. I hadn't played well and he'd carried me all day. Avery trudged ahead of us through the rain to the clubhouse; his shoulders a little slumped. "Nice sandy, Fox," he offered wearily without turning around. "And Bobby, I don't mind telling you that you're lucky you had a partner," he couldn't help adding.

After a hot shower we gathered over a Moosehead Lager at the nineteenth hole to settle up. Avery's first pint went on my account. The Fox had a coffee and stepped outside for a Belmont. Howard avoided the hat dance and played very well, certainly better than his partner Avery, and scored quite a bit better than me. That day, however, belonged to The Fox. As always, when Howard pays, his normally congenial face was contorted in genuine pain.

"Relax Howard," I said as I made change for his fifty, "Just try to relax."

The ride back to the farm was a slow one for a Saturday afternoon. There was a fender bender on Highway 1 and its participants were pulled over, exchanging pleasantries between raindrops.

It wasn't until I turned onto Old Stone Road that I remembered *Fierce People*. The caravan of white trailers stretched from our gatehouse halfway to the BEVO greenhouse complex. At that moment they were actually filming in our driveway. I could see the brilliant white light through the drizzle which had been downgraded to a fine Scotch mist. Security people bounced up to confront me as I drove right up to the gate. They knew my Lexus by now, but even Foxglove's owner can't do an impromptu cameo. I'd learned that hard lesson at the pantry window in *Spymate*.

With a certain smug satisfaction I ignored them and turned left to Roxanne's gate and entered her code as the wrought iron bowed open in welcome. The Lexus meandered slowly through the orchard, past the barn and pastures where her horses idled away. Reaching the crushed stone courtyard I parked right next to Judy's navy Rover. Brutus stirred a little from his backseat slumber and I could hear him sigh through the open window as he slumped back to sleep.

There were about fifty people at the lively afternoon gathering. I can't remember what the occasion was but it might have been someone's birthday or maybe a going away party for one of Peter's medical colleagues; but Peter wasn't there. Probably a vascular S.O.S. had torn him away. Or had he gone to England? Seems to me there were health challenges in his family overseas. I'm certain Roxanne explained his absence then and with Peter gone, Roxanne did double duty, stepping up the pace of the hospitality. The food, the people, and the wine were all good and in plentiful supply.

As usual I made sure I got my share and then some. This was great!! It was an antidote to the dampness of the Scotch mist and the displaced feeling you get when Hollywood takes over your world. If it were just the director and the actors it'd be one thing; but who are those two hundred other people, the hangers-on, with their tattoos and their Styrofoam coffee cups and walkie-talkies and their looks of self-importance as they crushed out their smokes on our courtyard brick?? I don't know what a key grip and a best boy are, but you can be sure they posture like the next coming of Martin Scorsese.

After three hours of revelry Roxanne's party started to disband. Judy and I had to park a hundred yards down Old Stone Road where there were gaps between the trailers. Judy and Brutus went straight into the gatehouse, which was her current project. She was in the process of tarting up Shorty's cabin, and I could hear Mozart's *Air on a G String* as she carefully closed the door to avoid trapping Brutus's tail. An old ghetto blaster played CBC in Shorty's cabin, twenty-four seven.

Judy had stripped the ceiling back to the original wood

and squeezed a claw foot tub into the tiny bathroom. A crystal chandelier now blazed where a raw bulb had dangled. Gold fleur-de-lis wallpaper had been carefully chosen, and she'd found a fifties fridge for a retro touch and a chunky McClary stove from the same era for the little kitchen. The only thing missing in the kitchen was Harriett Nelson in a housedress and pumps, fixing Ozzie liver and onions for supper.

Just about every evening for a few weeks we'd stroll up the driveway with a chilly glass of Russian River chardonnay and wind up in the old gatehouse, where we'd take turns chipping at plaster to expose the brick of the woodstove chimney. In no particular hurry, we'd hammer and chisel about four inches of rough, red brick per happy hour, while getting up to speed on each other's day, savoring Jurgen Goethe's *Disc Drive* on the ghetto blaster. I guess this labor was, contrary to our deal, *lifting a finger,* but somehow the buttery Sonoma Cutrer made it a labor of love.

"We can turn it into a Carmel cottage," was Judy's vision for the gatehouse, even back when it was still Rebecca's office. Carmel, California had long rivaled Cannes on the French Riviera as a place where my wife could see herself fitting in quite nicely. Carmel's okay with me too; just a little eight-iron from the links at Pebble Beach and a civilized day trip from the vineyards of Napa Valley. Starter cottages, I seem to recall though, command *from* a million-and-a-half U.S.

I walked on past the gatehouse, toting my laptop, and paused in the drizzle at the top of the driveway. The lights, cameras and action hadn't budged an inch in three hours; still halfway down the driveway. Tedious business, making movies.

Fuelled by a quart of Roxanne's white wine, I just walked down that driveway as if I owned the place, fully expecting to be gang tackled by a pack of security goons. But they were wet and weary too, and everybody was on a break, more concerned with hot coffee and sticky buns from the catering truck. I got a few sideways looks, but I made it to the courtyard and the worn front door.

With the rainy day, any commitment to stay outside the house was long forgotten. About twenty of the crew were in the entrance hall and flowed into the kitchen. No one was in my den but a few folks blocked the double French doors, and at any rate the handles were bound together by masking tape. A scrawled sign on the door of the den said *OFF LIMITS.*

I had hoped to dial up the Internet for an afternoon chess game, but could see that there was slim chance of that happening.

The crowd was a little thinner in the library, but half a dozen souls were in profound discussion there about some aspect of the lighting. I pressed on, ignoring everyone and quite happy to be ignored. Finally reaching the ballroom I stepped down on to the oak parquet where the ramp had once been. I was alone at last, although a Louis Vuitton bag was on one of the settees, looking quite at home in the Frenchness of the ballroom décor.

Judy's touch had worked wonders on that cavernous room over our two years at Foxglove. Parts of the floor and ceiling had been restored and the walls were painted a light apple green. Three arched French doors led to the back lawn and the thick white lacquer on their trim contrasted perfectly with the new paint job on the walls. A slick, black baby grand commanded one corner, and next to it, a recess in the wall housed a larger than life concrete bust of Ludwig von Beethoven. I'd found Beethoven at Thomas Hobbs' Kerrisdale store on Mothers Day 2003.

There were tapestries on the walls and a big gilt-framed mirror over the fireplace. It's the kind of room where Marie Antoinette might have had the brainstorm that the peasants should eat cake. I sank in the goose down of the cream, silk couch nearest the fireplace, kicked off my shoes and looked through the French doors to the back lawn. The drizzle had just stopped and a few of the crew were enjoying their break under an old apple tree just outside of the ballroom. One of the guys picked a couple of the apples, buffed one on his plaid sleeve and handed it to his female crewmate.

Legs straight out and dozy from the afternoon wine, I looked up at the light green walls where they met the ceiling. "Crown moldings," I thought. "What a difference heavy white crown moldings would make to this room." I'd mentioned it once before to Judy and I knew she agreed. Both for the ceiling and the floor, multi-layered moldings would add so much to what was already a stunning room. It would be the finishing touch; maybe with the five thousand we were getting for today's re-shoot.

At that moment, two young blondes strolled into my private haven. Probably mid-twenties, they were tall and both wore jeans and jean jackets. They could have been sisters. The taller one was showing the ballroom to the other and they nodded in friendly deference when they saw me on the couch.

"You have really done an amazing job with this place," smiled the taller young woman, "even more so since we were here in April; you've really turned it into something fantastic. This room's incredible."

"It's my wife," I said, honesty being the best policy. "She's really worked hard at it and she's the one with the vision." They took one more admiring look around and headed back to the library leaving me in solitude.

"Probably wondering why they don't make men like me anymore," I speculated through my Chardonnay haze.

Another fifteen minutes passed and I was almost asleep. Then Dornoch jumped up beside me. Dornoch is our special cat, a male tabby that had roamed Shaughnessy Golf Course for several years, defying the odds by surviving the coyotes. He'd probably belonged to someone who lived adjacent to the links, but over time he'd become the resident golf course cat. Gregarious with the membership, you might return to your power cart from the green and find Dornoch curled up in the driver's seat. He'd disappear, for six months sometimes, and we'd all just assume that the coyotes got him. Then he'd magically re-appear and rub up against you like he'd never been gone.

After we bought Foxglove I kidded with the assistant pros in the golf shop that the unnamed tabby would be a perfect addition to the farm.

"There might be a chance for that," one of them said;

"A couple of older lady members are put off by his hunting; most of the members love him though." Later I found that Dornoch had taken down birds and even squirrels in full view of some of Shaughnessy's membership. Sounded like a farm cat to me.

The next day I'd bought a vented, black polyester carrying cage from the pet store on Dunbar. Forty-nine ninety-nine well spent; Dornoch was coming home.

Prior to my round I gave one of the pros the cage and told him I'd pull up in the Lexus right after my shower, four and a half hours later, and spirit him away. It had to be all hush-hush; most of the members saw the tabby as a fixture at the club.

The deal was done and the black bag was in the passenger seat and its content was meowing incessantly. As I pulled onto Highway 10, I unzipped the bag a little, just enough to get my hand inside. I wanted to comfort my prize with a little petting to go along with my soft verbal assurances. But Dornoch's an irrepressible spirit, and burst his head and then his shoulders through the little opening. It was like childbirth, or so I can imagine.

Then began a ride from hell. Dornoch perched on my shoulder, then on the windshield and by the accelerator and finally under the brake at 110 kilometers per hour. Somehow I managed to pull over in heavy traffic and got the cat back in the bag.

When we arrived at Foxglove, Judy wasn't disappointed. I'd been singing the glossy tabby's praises for at least two years. Brutus was onside from the start, delighted with a little four-legged male companionship. Zhu Zhu bolted for cover. The chubby part Persian spent Dornoch's first week at Foxglove under our bed. "She was in the same spot for two weeks when we brought Brutus home," Judy reminded me.

The ancient Yum Yum was another story. She gave the male tabby one look; I guess it was a Siamese evil eye. Dornoch ran from the frail matriarch like he'd seen a banshee. He found shelter in the rhododendrons. I was sure we'd lost him as he was gone for over two hours; but finally he emerged and Judy locked him inside the house for the time being. That day we named him Dornoch after the village in northern Scotland, home of Royal Dornoch, the greatest golf course in the world.

Like all of the best cats, Dornoch ended his affectionate ballroom visit on his terms. Just when he could see how very welcome he was, he pounced onto the parquet floor and sauntered slowly into the library.

Twenty minutes later I was more than half asleep. I could hear murmuring from the library and could see Dornoch stretching and purring as a small hand rubbed the treacle fur up his spine. "Dornoch's won someone over," I smiled to myself.

The hand's owner rose from her seat, just out of my view through the door to the library. Then she stepped down into the ballroom. She was petite, with shoulder-length auburn hair. Her floral dress was below the knee, and over it she wore a brown velvet jacket.

"You must be the owner," she observed as she moved across the room to the loveseat across from my couch, about fifteen feet away. "That's right," I confirmed her hunch, bracing myself for another stream of accolades about our decorating.

She clutched the Louis Vuitton bag and I hoped her visit would be a short one. I'd had just about enough of the Fierce People crew and I was eager for our routines to get back to normal.

To my surprise she put the bag on the floor and sat on the loveseat, then fluffed the pillow and lay her auburn head upon it. She kicked off her sandals and drew her legs up in a near fetal position. She pulled the hem of her floral dress over her tiny, scarlet lacquered toes and closed her eyes.

Cheeky, I thought. Bold as brass. Then it registered.

"You've got to be Diane Lane."

"Yep," she said, not bothering to open her eyes.

"You've come a long way for one day," said I, demonstrating a swift grasp of the obvious.

Her eyes opened a little. "Yes, but everyone here is so

nice."

Ninety seconds passed.

"Is it okay if I just sit here?" I asked.

"Of course," she smiled, "is it okay if I just lie here?"

"Of course," I echoed.

She seemed to fall straight to sleep and after about ten minutes I joined her in slumber. I fought it off as long as I could, not wanting Diane Lane to hear my Iron Lung.

After about half an hour my Blackberry rang in my shirt pocket. It was Judy.

"*Where are you?*" she quite rightly asked.

"In the ballroom," I said, "sleeping with Diane Lane."

"Oh, I figured you were up to no good.

Honey, it's almost six. We should probably start thinking about heading back to the city."

"I really hope she's discreet," I said.

CHAPTER 28

"Life used to be so hard"—Crosby, Stills & Nash

"CIGGY-POO??"

Selling the business and turning right around and buying an expensive house in Yorkville brings to mind our calamitous year in the log cabin. I know that I turned forty there so it must have been 1989-1990.

We'd sold Pine Crescent for almost one point four million and had slithered out from under the oppressive weight of that $618,000 mortgage. Judy actually sold it; she had her real estate license in the late eighties.

Don and Shirley helped to sell Pine Crescent too. You remember Don, our asthmatic lawyer with the pet allergies, and Shirley his wife. They're the couple that used to have to sit in the rows up front with us when we went to the movies. They were married in our backyard in 1989 and Judy really had the place all decked out. Cut flowers everywhere, the elaborate gardens trimmed to perfection, a big white wedding tent in case it rained; Pachabel's Canon on the stereo, ready for Shirley's walk down the aisle.

The Symphony Designer people were smitten. Every year the Vancouver Symphony would buy an old Shaughnessy mansion and have a different designer redo every room. The

designers would donate their services and The Symphony
would charge for tours of the finished product. Then they'd
sell the house for a profit that helped keep the Symphony sol-
vent for another year.

3790 Pine Crescent had been for sale for a few months
and we even had one irritating offer for $910,000, to which
we didn't respond. Some low-baller giving us a taste of our
own medicine.

But when The Symphony Designer lady ogled our place a
few hours before the wedding she had an offer in our hands
the next day. There was no commission to pay and the handsome but sniffling groom gave us his usual discount on the
legal work.

Pine Crescent had seventeen rooms so no less than seventeen designers set about trying to outdo one another. Judy and
I paid ten bucks each a couple of months later just for a tour of
our own house. That's okay, it was for the Symphony.

By that time we were in the log cabin.

We'd been aware of the charming, narrow lanes of Caulfield Cove for a few years. Tiddley Cove, the locals called it,
a small swath of old England in West Vancouver, muscled
down against the sea by the North Shore Mountains.

Next to Tiddley Cove is Lighthouse Park, where an aging lighthouse does its best to prevent Alaskan cruise ships
and freighters from Japan from floundering in the fog on
the rocky shoals of West Vancouver. Tiddley Cove has street
names like Pilot House Road and The Highway and Dog-
wood Lane. Housing is eclectic; slick but generally tasteful
new construction bellies up to quaint English style cottages
and more substantial estates.

It was on Pilot House Road where we found the log
cabin.

Perched at the back of a third of an acre, the log cabin embodied two small levels of undeniable charm.

We were taking a lot of Sunday drives after selling Pine Crescent, really having no idea where the eleven of us should next reside. That's Judy and I, Mark, Dylan, Harmony, Taylor, Steisha, Liberty, Yum Yum, Mozart and Archimedes.

Mozart and Archimedes were a couple of budgies that kept Liberty and Yum Yum occupied. Then a spry five-year old, Yum Yum, posed a genuine daily threat to the feathered members of our clan.

Properties seldom had "for sale" signs in Tiddley Cove, but there was a ReMax sign by the hedge of that log dwelling and it said "Open House." Inside we met Heinz.

Our kids pride themselves on their "gaydar" where they instantly perceive another person's sexual orientation. Given their show business careers I'm sure that skill has been further honed. I think they inherited their "gaydar" from their mother.

A few years back Judy and I had lunch with the new artistic director of an arts group that had asked me to serve on their board. Driving home I said, "You know, I kind of wonder if he's gay; not that it matters."

"You think?!" came her response soaked in a little benign sarcasm.

But even my "gaydar" screen had Heinz as a flashing blip.

Very German, very dapper, and oh so gay, Heinz eyed us suspiciously as we were enchanted by the magic world inside his little home. He was short, slim and slicked-back blonde.

Cozy and rustic with just a hint of pot pourri, Heinz's haven juxtaposed Indian rugs with non-stop whimsy touches. A hewn log balcony off the main floor gave outlook over the narrow cove with its government dock. Above the living room was a small loft with a very low ceiling. The one-room first floor flowed into a kitchen that oozed macramé charm and stepped out the back door to where Pilot House Road was an old narrow lane.

Downstairs there was one bedroom with a stone fireplace and more ocean view down the sloping lawn. A vinyl accordion divider was there to turn the one bedroom into two tiny ones until we built our addition. We'd be sharing with Harmony and Taylor. I flashed a wink in Judy's direction. "It's a damn good thing that neither one of us are screamers," I whispered. "Well, at least to the best of my knowledge," I added, and got elbowed in the ribs.

Heinz and his partner Bob had a bottle of red wine on the go and we couldn't bring ourselves to leave. He was asking $695,000 and after the brutal load of Pine Crescent it just all seemed so manageable and yet so bold. For once, we could actually pay cash.

Seeing we were serious, Heinz let us know he didn't really want to sell. They were happy there, but the open house was an easy way to get to meet prospects. Heinz was a realtor.

Judy asked him whether he'd let it go for $600,000 and he looked wounded to the core. She asked about $650,000 and he looked sulky and offended as he lit a cigarette. He said something about full price and we huddled for a second and offered $685,000; not a penny more. Heinz burst into tears as he exhaled and we knew we'd found our new home. Half an hour later we'd helped Heinz and Bob through another bottle of merlot. Heinz had mellowed out beautifully in the interim. "Ciggy-poo Bobby?" he offered and I accepted. We were wheeling and dealing West Vancouver style.

Within twenty-four hours we had engaged local architect Brian Hart. We wanted three more bedrooms and a family room and we wanted them fast; a couple of more toilets and showers too. We were determined to build on in entire sympathy to what was already there. Word was that the log home went up in 1912.

Short, bearded and hobbit-like, Brian had won a few awards for design. In a province that favors west coast contemporary, Brian was like us. He liked old things. He was confident he could create the space we sorely needed and stay true to the heritage of our unique little find.

A year later we wrote Brian a cheque in final payment for services rendered. Just under thirteen thousand and not a sliver of the log cabin had been changed since the day that Heinz wept in response to our offer. No hammer was ever raised and there was no shrill buzzing of power saws in idyllic Tiddley Cove.

We had the Anglican Church to thank for that.

CHAPTER 29

"You can stand me up at the gates of hell; I won't back down"
—TomPetty

CHURCH AND STATE

THE DAY WE BOUGHT THE LOG CABIN, ST. FRANCIS IN THE Woods was a big part of its appeal. This was even in spite of my ambivalence towards organized religion. Like our old friend Woody Allen said, "I'm not convinced there's an afterlife, but I'm taking a change of underwear just in case." Maybe it was time to give "god fearin'" another chance.

Right across the lane to the west, tucked just out of sight, indeed *in the woods,* the church was a sought after site for weddings, reportedly booked as far as five years ahead. It would seem that these betrothed weren't in any sort of hurry at all, unlike Judy and me in 1972. We would have got hitched on the hot tarmac of a Wal-Mart parking lot; we didn't have to wait half a decade for nuptials in the woods and by the sea.

But Harmony and Taylor were eleven and nine. We could book their St.Francis in the Woods ceremonies right now and let the girls grow into them.

Within a month though, the three weddings per Saturday and the two services on Sundays were taking their toll on us, the church's most immediate neighbor. Parking was at a premium and the eager St. Francis flock thought nothing of leaving their cars bumper to bumper on our property. Granted, they were just outside our laurel hedge, but their tires gouged cruelly into our turf leaving a muddy trench, a wound you could be sure they'd re-open the following weekend.

"Maybe we should call Drake's Towing," was my suggestion to Judy one Sabbath morning.

A little further up the mountain behind us was the rectory. It was the kind of cheap and tacky bi-level that British Columbians call a "B.C. Box." It was more nondescript than ugly but it really had no place among the properties that comprised Tiddley Cove. Happily, we couldn't see much of it as it was tucked in the trees on the other side of Pilot House Road. Furthermore, with the ocean to eyeball, we weren't spending much time looking back up the mountain. The rectory was a rental property, where the frugal board of St. Francis sheltered their minister.

The Church was very curious about our building plans. Maybe they got wind of things by neighborly word of mouth, or they might have even knocked on our door and asked. Judy would remember; I'll ask her.

Regardless, it soon was evident that we couldn't touch a shingle on our home without the approval of our local chapter of The Church of England. Any alterations to property within fifteen feet from the road required a variance permit in West Vancouver, a precious certificate that could only be obtained with the approval of all of our neighbors, of which St. Francis was the most immediate and beyond doubt, the most annoying. Our other neighbors were supportive of our plan and relieved to hear that the historic log home was to be spared the indignity of the wrecker's ball.

(After about a year at Foxglove Farm, I observed a monklike statue in the flower garden that surrounds the chapel, behind the boxwood hedge at the front of the house. Fielding my inquiries, Judy informed me that this was St.Francis, the patron saint of animals, and the concrete holy man had been half-price at some place that sold things like that. I'm almost certain she told me that this was neither St. Francis of Assisi nor the despicable St. Francis in the Woods, whom caused us so much consternation back in 1989. For all I know this trio may well be the same damn saint, but on the infrequent occasions I make reference to the statue, I call him "St. Francis in the Flowerbed.")

The log cabin was at the very back of the sloping one-third acre. There was a brass spike driven flush to the pavement of Pilot House Road, more than halfway across the lane, towards the rectory.

"That's our property line," I pointed out to Judy, "we own two-thirds of Pilot House Road."

This righteous entitlement only served to inflame her resolve to build whatever the hell we wanted. So did the growing restlessness of our seven other cabin mates. After six weeks our regard for the church had ebbed to its lowest point since that petulant minister in Barrie had flung holy water at baby Taylor. We could see the full St. Francis board coming and going for tea at the rectory, where, collective tongue a-clucking, they'd point at our place and imagine our demonic intentions from the rector's balcony.

"I'll bet the good reverend serves egg salad sandwiches with the crusts cut off," I commented to Judy, whose frustration was well past boiling point. One bedroom and one bathroom for the six of us was pretty much the way things were as summer rolled into fall.

"At least you've only got one toilet bowl to scrub," I dared to say, trying for a laugh that was not forthcoming.

The boys shared a bed in the tiny loft. Not an ideal circumstance for two young teenagers. On more than a few occasions one or the other lad would forget the proximity of the ceiling, sitting up in bed, only to suffer a good noggin conking by a stout hewn log.

We could hear them muttering to each other on school nights as we watched David Letterman or Cheers a few feet below them, and they could hear our wine-soaked tirades against The Municipality of West Vancouver, The Anglican Church of Canada and, occasionally, each other. Remember, this was 1989; back in the years where I hadn't totally learned that arguing with my wife was akin to sticking a knitting needle in my eyeball. My stupid years.

The usually cheerful Dylan was in full rebellion, bussing for four hours to Tsawwassen on weekends and sleeping over at friends from his years at Cliff Drive Elementary.

Finally, the Municipality of West Vancouver was ready to hear our appeal for a variance permit. Council was meeting and we were an item of business on their evening agenda. The local Cable TV channel televised all the council meetings, so, avoiding any kind of power look, I wore an earth-tone jacket and a woodsy tie; the garb of a sensitive team player.

We arrived punctually with Brian Hart in tow to explain just how modest our expansion was going to be and how sympathetic to the heritage dwelling and how unobtrusive to anyone's view. We were building our bedrooms and family room down the slope of the hill, tucked nicely out of the sight of our good neighbors further up the mountain. Nothing huge, nothing modern; just more logs.

The cameras were rolling as Brian stepped up to the mike to state our case and his appearance couldn't have been less threatening to the council. With his brown corduroy suit, woolly beard, shaggy hair and granny glasses, Brian looked like he could build a hobbit dwelling right into the side of our green hill, like Bilbo Baggins.

Judy and I exchanged encouraging glances as Brian emphasized that we wouldn't be exceeding twenty-seven-hundred square feet, just roomy enough for a family of six. A few of the council were nodding towards Brian from their panel style table and to each other, in apparent sympathy with our humble expansion plans.

Just when things looked rosy, an alderwoman grabbed a mike to say her piece. I'd seen her with a teacup in her hand on the balcony of the rectory; in her fifties, with cropped sandy hair. We knew she had a waterfront place too; a great location with a massive, gray stucco house, devoid of charm. We saw it everyday as we drove up Marine Drive, to and from Tiddley Cove.

"I'm worried about our little rectory," she began. "I'm on the Board of the Church and the view from the rectory *is* going to be affected, not a lot, but we've talked it over and there you go.

Our position is that these people should go back to the drawing board and modify their blueprints."

Brian Hart turned to us and shrugged.

Judy shot from her chair and beat me to the microphone.

"This is simply not true," she began, "that rectory doesn't even have a view and even if it did, our plans aren't going to affect it at all. We're just trying to build something that's true to the original and have enough space for our family."

The alderwoman jumped back in.

"We're just saying that your plan, *as it is*, doesn't work for St. Francis." She sat up straighter in her chair, took off her reading glasses and zeroed in on Judy. "Get your Mr. Hart here to rework the drawings into something acceptable to the church. We'd be glad to suggest some guidelines."

Judy, flushed with rage, countered, "Our architect fees are quite enough now, thank you very much!! And we have no intention of building our home to please the church!"

And then the words that scorched my soul before she stormed back to her seat.

"We're not millionaires, you know!!!"

The alderwoman began cooing platitudes into her mike; offering us a little friendly advice.

"We have a big family too and we have a big house. Way too big, actually," she added with a dry, little chuckle. "When you've got a big family it's even harder to keep a large house clean and organized. It's probably better for your kids and your whole family if you build something smaller. Take my word for it."

Judy looked murderous. This time I beat her to the mike.

"We've heard the alderwoman's advice," I began gently, fixated on her smiling face under the short sandy thatch, "concerning a couple of matters." She nodded her assent.

"And I am certain that the councilwoman's generous advice on both architecture and raising a family are well meaning," I added quietly. She nodded again and her smile broadened a touch. The TV cameras zoomed in.

"But while I am certain that her advice on each of these matters is well meaning; I want to let council know that it amounts to condescending crap, and is totally, utterly and absolutely unappreciated."

The smile crashed into a "harrumph!!! Well, I have never!" she blustered, rising half out of her seat before slumping back into dumbfounded, head-shaking silence.

I wasn't finished and wrapped my hand around the mike.

"Council should know that we've got enough building envelope on that lot to put up 6,000 square feet," I said, "and we can do it without your precious variance permit. We can tear that old log cabin down and build a monster home right in the middle of our lot; and that's exactly what we're going to do."

I turned on my heel and sat down beside Judy, but she was on the rise.

"Let's get the hell out of here honey!" she said, full voice.

As we drove back to Tiddley Cove along Marine Drive we were laughing out loud to the point of tears.

"I just wish you hadn't said we weren't millionaires," I said, wiping an eye.

"Billionaires would have been okay."

CHAPTER 30

"It takes two, baby"—Marvin Gaye

"LET US ABSORB YOUR STRESS"

In case you thought I was bluffing, well...I wasn't.

We had Brian Hart scrap the blueprint of the modest log addition and get straight to work on designing something stupendously large. Something that was certain to obliterate any hope of a view from that shabby, little rectory.

We decided on a mariner theme loosely echoing The Beaconsfield Inn, a massive arts and crafts bed and breakfast that Brian had long admired in Victoria. We pictured a white four-story mansion with sea blue shutters. The blueprint called for more angles and decks than that Caribbean cruise ship to which I referred a few chapters back. We'd have a mortgage again, but hey, why not enjoy now? At the risk of repeating myself, it's a nuclear age; we could all be vaporized on the weekend.

The wild card was the kids. Dreadfully unhappy don't you know; hating their schools, missing their friends; in fact pining for everything about Vancouver's Westside on their preferred south shore of The Burrard Inlet. Living in Tiddley Cove also meant that Judy had a long daily trek to her horse in Southlands. She boarded Boozer there but still personally mucked his stall; and the links at Shaughnessy were a bit of a journey for me.

One Sunday I had a gin and tonic after my round and headed back towards The Lions Gate Bridge and the blueprints that Judy would be studying on our pine table at Caulfield Cove.

At Angus and Nanton a white Dutch Colonial had an *Open House* sign. I knew the realtor and I slammed to a halt. The property had been over a million; then $895,000. It had just dropped that day to $795,000. The owner, the C.E.O. of the Zodiac raft company, was moving to Annapolis, Maryland since the U.S. Army had started to insist on buying products that were made in America.

I called Judy from the phone in the house. "You've really got to see this place," I said. "It's the heart of Shaughnessy; a cross-hall Dutch Colonial, wonderful inlaid hardwood floors; light oak with dark oak trim. We can just move right in. There's nothing to be done. The kids are going to be ecstatic. I love West Van honey, but we're just beating our heads against the wall. Oh; it's got a sunroom off the master bedroom, and there's a fireplace in the sunroom! Do you realize we've been a year now without our own bedroom?!"

Judy arrived in half an hour. She still had her real estate ticket and talked directly to the owner with the listing realtor in attendance. Having just dropped to $795,000 they were looking for a quick sale. They had to move; but the price was firm.

"You have an absolutely beautiful home," she smiled, "but we're going to have to hope we can sell ours. Our best offer, our only offer is $725, 000," she said, "but that's clean, no conditions, no subject to sale, no subject to financing. Let us absorb your stress."

We had no idea how true that would be.

Be careful what you ask for, so the old adage goes, you just might get it.

CHAPTER 31

"Help me, I think I'm falling"— Joni Mitchell

TAKING A BATH

THE NEXT DAY, AUGUST 2ND, 1990, SADDAM HUSSEIN INVADED Kuwait. For the economy, already in an uneasy malaise, that was just enough bad news to bring on a plummeting tailspin.

The log cabin on Pilot House Road had a For Sale sign again, but no takers were forthcoming. Sales of West Vancouver homes in general crashed to a halt. We listed, hoping for a small profit; then dropped it again and again and again while settling into the Dutch Colonial. No longer contending with the bottlenecks merging onto Lion's Gate Bridge; now we were up to our teeth in bridge financing.

In agony, we accepted $475,000 just a year after Heinz offered me a "ciggy-poo." A $210,000 bath in just twelve months since he burst into tears at our offer.

The buyer was a neighbor from just up the mountain. Her place kind of overlooked ours. We knew her socially and she was a pretty nice lady. Still I had to fight the feeling that she and her new man were like vultures, biding their time with a bird's eye view of our suffering.

I guess you could say that she absorbed our stress.

So what docs the rectory have to look at now after all

the fretting and forelock tugging? We understand that the church had some input into the new building plans for the addition to what was once our little log treasure by the sea in Tiddley Cove. We drove by our cozy home a year or two after selling just to check things out. One could use adjectives like sprawling and modern and unsympathetic. If provoked, one could modify the new construction with words like garish, or obtrusive or ill-advised. With a scotch or two one might call it a hideous, fucking abortion. But one will merely say that the church got just what it deserved and it wasn't exactly to our taste. But the once log cabin was listed in 2004 for around two-point-four million and they probably got it. "Chaque a son gout," as the French would say.

"If Heinz were us, this would really give him something to cry about," I remarked to Judy back in 1990 as we signed the paperwork that let it go for a song.

CHAPTER 32

"Why??"—Annie Lennox

DOUBLE JEOPARDY

"Don't let me lose you," I said to Judy as we sat side by side on the leather couch in the library. I was back in B.C. for four or five days, then off to Toronto again next week.

She had a white wine and I was sipping a ten-year-old Glenmorangie with just one little ice cube to open up the flavor. We'd ordered Indian food and I'd picked it up in Langley. The ruins of our butter chicken, saffron rice and stuffed Nam bread waited clean up in the farm kitchen; but first there was Jeopardy.

A Duraflame log burned in the fireplace beneath the plasma screen.

"We should really get a cord of wood delivered Jude," I said. The piles of firewood that we had inherited at Foxglove were in a leaky shed at the back of the old barn. They were old, wet and un-split and Judy had recently had them hauled away. I thought they'd dry eventually and we could pay Mike to split them, but she was concerned that mice or worse might set up shop.

She nodded, petting Dornoch who would actually join us on the leather couch if Judy folded a blanket next to her. Very picky, our Dornoch. Brutus sighed and stretched in the glow of the Duraflame.

"THIS IS JEOPARDY!!!" announced Johnny Gilbert over the theme music.

Word on the Internet was that Ken Jennings was supposed to lose this week, having amassed over two and a half million cash over several months. He was growing on us despite his know-it-all intellect and, okay, a smile that was a little ferrety and you know how Judy feels about rodents.

"I think we might actually miss him Jude."

We never did like to miss our nightly fix of the numbing comfort of Jeopardy. We both try to get the right answer first and have a ritual of saying "Good for you," or "Good for you honey," when the other succeeds. In the event of a tie, I usually say "Good for us."

Occasionally I'd be half right by giving an answer like "Portrait of an Artist," while Ken Jennings would properly phrase it as a question. "What is 'A Portrait of the Artist as a Young Man,' Alex?"

"I would give that to you honey," Judy would say.

"Oh shut the hell up Alex!!" Judy hisses when Alex Trebek pontificates about the question, all the while holding it in his hand, or rolls his R's with a highland brogue if the question refers to Robbie Burns.

The category was "Nineteenth and Twentieth Century Wits."

"Oh shit, it's not Bertrand Russell!!" I agonized; "it's not George Bernard Shaw"; it's right on the tip of my freaking tongue!!"

"Who is Oscar Wilde, Alex?" that ferret Jennings beat me to the punch. "I would give that to you honey," said Judy.

The category was U.S. Presidents. Judy and I fare pretty

well on the presidents from Franklin Delano Roosevelt to the present time. One or both of us can usually come through when it's a question of Truman, Ike, JFK, LBJ, Nixon, Ford (although his abbreviated term in office can make Gerry forgettable), Carter, Reagan, Bubba Clinton, or either one of the two Bushes. Pre-World War II, its hit and miss for me, nailing the odd Woodrow Wilson, or Warren Harding; but I pretty well have to go way back to the Washington's, Lincolns and Franklins for any kind of relaxed comfort with the category.

Judy takes a different approach, responding "Who is Taft?" to any presidential answer that may pre-date the Great Depression. She's come up with "Taft" for quite a number of years now, her rationale being that sooner or later the corpulent Chief Executive has to be the question.

"*What* are *you wearing* tonight Alex?!" she'd demand of the screen when the Jeopardy host wore one of his beige on beige on beige on beige suit and tie and shirt and puff combos.

"He looks like a bowl of cream of wheat," I'd agree.

"A proud example of Canadian fashion sense," she'd add, referring to Trebek's Sudbury roots.

"*EXCUSE ME* you're cutting into Double Jeopardy!!" She snarls at Alex when he lingers too long on the introductions, chatting up a contestant about the most interesting experience they've had as a claims adjuster from Des Moines, Iowa.

The category was Presidential Wives.

"*This* First Lady was the *first* First Lady to have a driver's license," came the answer from Alex.

"Who is Mrs. Taft?" came the question from Judy.

We could hear the ratcheting croak of the pheasant, from just beyond the riding ring, his favorite spot. Dornoch hopped off the couch, needing to explore the ballroom.

"How could you lose me? You could never lose me," she said.

"By being blind," was my reply.

"What is, shut up, Alex??" Judy posed the question to the screen.

CHAPTER 33

"I wish I had a river I could skate away on"—Joni Mitchell

IT'S COMING ON CHRISTMAS

"I'M GOING TO TRY TO SEE HARMONY ON SATURDAY NIGHT," I said, as I made sure I had my laptop power cord before heading to the airport. "I think the tour stops at The Stratford Festival Theatre and that'll be a great venue. The acoustics should be stunning. Sunday she's in Hamilton."

"You're not coming home for the weekend??!" Judy asked. "You're *choosing* to be there??"

It took me twenty-five minutes to find my Ontario Lexus at Pearson's Terminal 3 Parking Lot. I'd flown Jets-Go for ninety-nine bucks and even though I'd written 3B on the ticket that gets tucked into a special spot in my briefcase, I hadn't recorded which level on 3B. When I finally found it, it cost $125 just to bail my car out.

Winter had arrived and I confessed to myself that I'd forgotten how really nasty that could be. It seemed that the Great Lakes region had been denied the boon of global warming, since we moved west in 1982.

"There'll be snow but it won't stay," I'd misinformed Judy

when we offered on the Hazelton brownstone. "In the heart of the big city, it won't be that different from Vancouver."

I was half right. There *was* snow, but the first flake to fall on December 3 was the last one to melt in mid April. Snow doesn't melt at sixteen below zero; Celsius or Fahrenheit. Out of principle, I refused to buy my first toe rubbers and snow tires since the demise of disco. I chopped ice and snow off my windshield with the side of my bare right hand, unwilling to buy a plastic scraper and certainly not gloves. Gone was the trendy charm of the al fresca cafes and, with them, the parade of beautiful people. Yorkville in winter had all the panache of a Siberian gulag. My convertible could have been any make or model, a white hump, curbed for weeks on Hazelton Avenue. I took cabs and rode the metro. One ungodly cold day on the crowded subway I was standing, packed tight with the other poor, lost souls jostling for balance and position. Daydreaming, I could see Foxglove Farm and Judy, and the luxuriant green fairways of Shaughnessy Golf and Country Club. I wondered whether a newcomer was being inducted into my slot in my foursome there. A golf foursome is like that gnarly old bitch, Mother Nature; neither tolerates a void. I was jolted out of this dream by the nightmare of a young lady who called me "sir," and was prepared to surrender her seat. Declining, I made a note to myself to check out Grecian Formula or Just for Men or better still, get my ass over to Vidal Sassoon on Avenue Road for a cut and color.

On the occasion of that early December trip Yorkville had been preening itself for a month and was ready for Christmas. The old streetlights were adorned with fir boughs and velvet ribbons. Tomorrow I'd go for a walk and check things out.

Just as I expected, the red brick house on Hazelton had done absolutely nothing to clean itself up while I'd been back in Vancouver. Two panzerotti pizza boxes were in the fridge, one with a hardened, lonely slice of double bacon, double mushroom and double mozzarella pepperoni pizza. The other was just empty from two weeks back. There were two Styrofoam containers of hot and sour soup left over from Dylan's visit last week. The shrimp therein had tasted somewhat suspect on the night when we picked it up at The Pink Pearl on Avenue Road. Maybe a week in the fridge would have it freshened up by now.

"I might call Rent-A-Wife this time," I'd told Judy at the farm. Rent-A-Wife's menu of services was left by the phone in Hazelton's immaculate kitchen when we took possession in June. Apparently a Toronto institution, they'd clean your house, shampoo your rugs, run errands and organize your sock drawer. They were proud of the fact that they counted Goldie Hawn and Mel Gibson among their clients. "If you get to thinking about calling Rent-A-Wife for something more than cleaning, be sure to call me first," Judy advised with just enough smile.

With the three hour difference, I dozed past nine and was down a pint of Americano by the time I wheeled into one of Yorkville's three Starbucks where snowy folks stamped their boots then lined up for pumpkin or egg-nog lattes and an earful of Diana Krall. Straight, black java in hand I strolled south on Belair and merged into a ruddy-faced river of overcoats on Bloor that was blinking and grinning through fat, wet flakes. Williams of Sonoma and The Pottery Barn were just opening and the crowd spilled in from the blizzard. Holt Renfrew left nothing to chance, posting a jovial, come-hither doorman who would engage with the better dressed side walkers as far away as the curb. Past Yonge, in front of The Bay, the sausage vendor had already fired up his grill, luring

a short queue of would be brunchers. Inside the Bay a matching pair of young blonde models, six feet tall in their heels,
strolled self-consciously from their lingerie headquarters
through the other main floor departments, clad in not much
more than garter belts, stockings and little tops and chatting
only to each other about who knows what.

Back on Bloor, snow had turned to sideways rain.

Vancouverites know squat about snow unless it beckons
from the slopes of Whistler or Blackcomb, Grouse or Cy-
press. The first dump of the year, if we happen to get a dump
that year, always takes us by surprise and, as a rule, para-
lyzes both commerce and education. Cars are abandoned in
ditches; workers and students and teachers hunker down at
home, savoring their righteous truancy. C.E.O.'s, lawyers and
stockbrokers rediscover why they despise Regis, Judge Judy
and Dr. Phil. Life takes a time out; after all, it's snowing.

Torontonians know squat about rain, or at least about umbrella etiquette. At the corner of Bay and Bloor I waited in the
tight, packed crowd for a light to change next to a bulimic
looking woman in a chartreuse, cashmere wrap, brandishing
her open umbrella like a premenstrual Mary Poppins. Yak-
king on her cell phone, she hadn't noticed that her rain gear
had established a beachhead in the corner of my eye. "Aren't
you going to say 'Out vile jelly!!?'" I asked. "Fuck off!" she
hissed then said "Oh, just some asshole," into her phone, leaving me with a feeling that it had been quite some time since
she'd read King Lear.

This very minute I'm in The Boar's Head in Stratford Ontario,
I've got one of a line of tightly crowded, little round tables and
a seat on a long cushioned bench that looks out at a cheery,

well stocked bar. I've got a double Chivas Regal on ice and it's twenty to six. The pub keeper asks me if I want dinner and I say maybe later. I allowed six hours for the eighty minute drive from Yorkville, and I'm not really sure why, although I took a few side roads to get reacquainted with rural Ontario.

Before I left I cleaned the house for half an hour. I haven't called "Rent-A-Wife" yet but probably will before Judy decides to visit Toronto, mainly to shampoo the carpets.

Stratford is what you might anticipate. Lights dazzling on the shops for the season, but by five those shops are all closed. Light snow dusting and classier houses than you expect from a Southwestern Ontario town of thirty thousand. Probably owing to the Festival. The Bard pumps a lot of dough into this little town. The river's bank is where the upscale houses seem to be and, sure enough, it's The Avon. I wonder what came first, the name of the river, the name of the town or The Shakespearian Festival. Big time chicken and egg enigma.

I saw those spiffy houses on the river about an hour ago, when I made certain I knew where I was going at eight. The Stratford Festival Center was all lit up, presiding over the Avon. When Harmony's performing I'm usually early and never late. She was in the middle of a seventeen-stop Ontario Christmas tour for Vinyl Café. Stuart MacLean had discovered her in a little Queen Street club called Holy Joe's back in the spring, and had become an instant fan of her songwriting and engaging delivery.

The last time I was in Stratford, and the only time, I was with Judy in 1972. Brock arranged a bus trip. We either saw *As You like It* or *Twelfth Night* or *A Midsummer Night's Dream* or something like that. I love Shakespeare for his tragedies but, with the exception of *The Merchant of Venice*, a lot of the comedies strike me as being all the same; and with all due respect, not so damn funny. The tragedies are cleansing for the soul of the reader, climaxing as they invariably do with a jolly good enema of human life. The comedies are cluttered with mistaken identities, cross-dressing, saccharin endings with double weddings and characters too dumb to figure out the obvious. Sort of like a fifteenth century *I Love Lucy,* where a penciled mustache would have a star-struck, boot-licking Ricky Ricardo convinced, for half an hour, that his zany red-headed spouse was actually David Niven. The nuptials of The Bard's comedic characters give one pause; a scary thought to imagine them breeding. I'd become a quick fan of the comedies too if they were rewritten to likewise slaughter off these thick folks; but then again, at one time I had no taste for caviar, sushi, and raw oysters. Hell, I even had to develop an appreciation for Scotch.

I signal for the barmaid. She replenishes my Chivas and I order some dinner, settling on a sizzling shepherd's pie.

So I figure I'm the guy with the problem, not William Shakespeare. As far as the comedies go, when the student is ready, the teacher appears. So sleep easy your Bardness.

All's well that ends well.

Four hours later, reading glasses perched low, I poked Judy's number into my Blackberry, scanning the dark ribbon of Highway 7 while I steered with my knees.

"I'm on the highway between Stratford and Kitchener."

"Be careful," she said.

"You would have been so proud. She started the show off with *I'll be home for Christmas.* It was restrained and sophisticated. She looked great. She wore this long black dress. The band was so tight and professional. Every note was perfect and she enunciated so crisply. Her phrasing was superb; like Ella Fitzgerald meets Diana Krall."

"That is so great, I envy you," said Harmony's mom.

"And Stuart McLean was fantastic, so funny; there's one Christmas story you're gonna really love…"

"Don't tell me!" she cut me off, not wanting the story spoiled. Long a fan of *The Vinyl Café,* Judy was coming to see the Toronto show at the University of Toronto's Convocation Hall on December 18th.

"It probably killed her not to do her own stuff," I said. "You know how she hates to do covers."

Harmony had just released her first CD to extremely encouraging reviews. *Amoraphobe* is a half dozen of her original tunes steeped in poignancy and urban angst. Toronto's entertainment scene publication *NOW* had given *Amoraphobe* an NNNN rating; their equivalent to four stars, and the reviewer wound it up with a promise that, "she can floor you with her loveliness!" For perspective, in the same issue, *NOW* had awarded best selling artists *Boyz 2 Men* just an NN rating for their new disc.

Judy said "But she'd be thrilled to do Joni Mitchell. She'd feel that was an honor."

"Yeah, they took a break and that's how she kicked off the second half. It was 'I Wish I Had a River I Could Skate Away On.' You know. It starts, "It's coming on Christmas; they're cutting down trees."

I was singing this into my Blackberry, as I slowed down on Highway 7 for the little town of Shakespeare.

"Judy, I am telling you it was so soulful, so exquisite."

There was this kid named Owen Pallett who's a hell of a violin player, a virtuoso who played a solo and sings a bit like David Bowie. He laid these incredible high harmonies on her lead vocal. We actually heard him once when we saw her at *C'EST WHAT,* remember? But Jude, on this number she really let her soul shine through the way you know she can. She had her hands curled halfway into fists and that look she gets on her face, and it was so passionate, when she sang, "I made my baby cry."

Emerging from Shakespeare I booted the Ontario Lexus up to highway speed.

"The audience loved it, sustained applause, there must have been five or six hundred there. I hope Joni Mitchell hears it. I honestly think she'd be so impressed. It's a generation since that song you know; although that cokehead Robert Downey Jr. did it last year; crap compared to this."

"She probably will, it's the CBC," said Judy.

I guess Judy figures that Joni listens to the CBC these days. She's probably right. We do.

"Or maybe someone will tell her about it," I said.

"What are the roads like?" Judy changed the subject; probably time to check on the horses I thought.

"It's not snowing but it could."

"Well you be careful," she said.

"I'll call you when I get to Yorkville," I promised.

I called her when I got there but got voicemail. I left a message that I'd call tomorrow.

Sunday Football starts at 10 a.m. on the west coast, but in Toronto I had until one to get ready. Past nine I grabbed a five shot Venti Americano at Starbucks and slowly window-shopped my way past a five thousand dollar cashmere over-coat at Stavros to The Bay where I bought a few mundane necessities. Socks and underwear, those kinds of things.

"I know you're just doing your job," I said to the sales clerk as I laid down cash. His nametag said "Jameer."

"But no, this won't be on my Bay card today; I don't have a Bay card; and no, I don't want to apply for a Bay card."

The blast of Starbuck caffeine was kicking in.

"And no, I don't want any HBC Rewards points; and, Jameer, I know it's not your fault, but please pass on to management that I would like to simply buy some socks and underwear and get the hell out of here. Tell them to charge less, get the transaction over with; no Reward Points, no Bay card, no Air Miles. Just take my cash and get me back on the street."

"Have a nice day sir!" smiled Jameer as I headed for the Bloor Street exit.

"Don't tell me what to do," I muttered, just out of earshot.

The LCBO on Yonge was open at 11. I stocked up with vodka and Mott's Clamato and lemons and the Bloody Caesars numbed the pain as I switched from channel to channel. Both my teams, the Seattle Seahawks and Detroit Lions were self-destructing, dropping passes that Judy could have caught, missing chip-shot field goals, taking bonehead penalties and coughing up the ball on punt returns. Doing their damnedest to stumble out of playoff contention. Another season down the drain. And I was lonely.

CHAPTER 34

"Just let the cowboy ride"—Bob Segar

AGAINST THE WIND

THERE ARE JUST A FEW THINGS THAT JUDY AND I REMEMBER from Psychology 190 from our days at Brock.

There's Mazlov's pyramid of needs, where our species needs food and shelter before worrying about love and self-esteem. Pretty obvious Mazlov…you guys got away with murder. So you figure romance was the farthest thing from a Neanderthal's thoughts when he was running to escape the jaws of a saber-tooth tiger.

There's the theory of intermittent reinforcement whereby a rat that is rewarded for ringing a bell gets a food pellet. If the reward is occasionally withheld, the rat rings the bell with more frequency and vigor than if it got the pellet every time. Women since Eve possess an innate understanding of this principle.

There was Pavlov's Dog, which, upon getting fed coincident with a ringing bell, would salivate. Over time, just the bell would kick-start the drool even if there was no Alpo or Dr. Ballard's in the general vicinity. Trowbridge's Dog, you might well guess, needs neither food nor bell to get his juices flowing.

Then there's the notion of Thanatos Urge, a condition from which Judy thinks I suffer. Loosely translated, it's a death wish.

She first got this idea, solely based on the fact that I used to run out of gas.

Like most women, Judy fills her tank while it's a third to halfway full. A quarter tank is tantamount to emptiness for my wife. Better safe than sorry.

Like a lot of males, I don't fill up until I'm running on fumes. Until you've actually run out, how would you ever assess the accuracy of your gas gage? Judy's appreciation of my theory bottomed out in 1976 when our Pontiac Grand Prix was immobilized from a lack of fuel with cranky toddlers in the back, at the Columbia Ice Fields in Alberta, halfway between Jasper and Banff. I dusted off my old hitchhiking skills from the sixties and had that gas pig on the road again within seventy minutes, amid a chorus of "told you so's."

Not too long after we met I shared my recurring dream with Judy; a dream I had as a child and a teen. I'm walking along a path, several feet from a ledge of a steep cliff, or a mountainside. There's no guardrail at the ledge, but I take a few steps towards it so I can look straight down into the abyss. The ledge crumbles, and I fall, saving myself by grabbing a root of a bush, a foot or two from the top. I struggle to pull myself up; its touch and go for a few desperate moments, but somehow I get back on the path. I resume walking and after a minute or two, I look over towards the edge of the cliff. After another minute I'm drawn to the edge and I fall again. Then I wake up with that delicious relief that accompanies emergence from a nightmare.

A few months ago, my son Dylan shared the details of his nightly dream that has haunted him for years. He's doing something routine and mundane, totally convinced that he's awake. Usually he's brushing his teeth, then looks up and sees the reflection in the mirror is a hideous hag or creepy old lady. He wakes up, sometimes screaming.

"I've got a story that's even scarier Dyl," I told him when he confided in me. "I'm brushing my teeth and I look up, and in the mirror I'll be damned if there isn't an old man. What's really terrifying is that *I* know I'm not dreaming!"

But my falling off the cliff dream had Judy convinced that I had a deeply entrenched Thanatos Urge even before Nixon resigned.

I shared a couple of other secrets with her that served to further validate her theory. One was when I was nineteen and shared a quart of rum with Jack Fisher at my parents' eighth floor apartment near High Park on Toronto's west side. Jack had been our band's drummer and our plan, with my parents vacationing in Derbyshire, was to get smashed, check out Doug Kershaw's Cajun fiddle at The Colonial Tavern on Yonge Street and maybe find some women. Thanatos Urge kicking in, I butted my cigarette on the balcony, grabbed the railing with two hands and vaulted both legs over it and dangled for five seconds over High Park Avenue. Then I vaulted back and we headed to the subway to catch Kershaw.

I probably shouldn't have told Judy about driving on the 401 in 1969 in my Triumph TR 250, closing my eyes at a hundred and seventeen miles per hour. I know it was 117 because that's as fast as that TR 250 would go. I told her my record for driving blind was six seconds, but truth be known, it was probably only three; four tops. And I only did it twice.

But her Thanatos Urge theory might still hold water.

I certainly hope not; but who would take up smoking at fifty-four?

And who would choose ice and snow and smog and obscene financial commitments and The Don Valley Parkway over Foxglove Farm? Even part time. And who'd opt to be away from the copper haired girl?

Who knows why we do things? If life is a veil of tears, maybe you try to keep the wind hard on your face; keep moving; leaning into the gale. "Still Runnin' against the Wind," like the Bobby Segar song. "Just let the cowboy ride."

Golf can teach us about life, provided the student is ready to learn. Learn about the trade-off between risk and reward and the value of patience; to never give up and to let the game come to you; to cheat at all is to cheat yourself and the paradox that the easiest swing often results in the longest drive.

In 1985 Judy and I vacationed in Maui with Don and Shirley, a few years before they got hitched in our backyard. Don was recovering a from a slo-pitch injury, a broken femur, and only golfed once, then hung around the pool all week with the girls. So I teed it up every morning at seven with a lumberyard owner from New England who had joined Don and me on that first day. He'd brought his girlfriend to Maui and she wasn't a golfer. Greg was close to my thirty-five years and we played to about the same handicap.

We loved everything about the sweeping palm-lined fairways of the Wailea Blue Course. Wailea offered breathtaking ocean vistas, and undulating, four-putt greens until you figured out that they all break toward the Pacific. The friendly, courteous staff made us feel like longtime members and seventy-five bucks covered green fees and a power cart. These days you'd be looking at close to three hundred. We had some terrific matches there and each day we'd be joined by other pairs of guys who raved about the brand new McKenna course, or Kapalua, or The Plantation Golf Club; tracks that we just had to try; fellows who urged us to forsake Wailea for something different.

My partner from New Hampshire grinned at my response, and his hand flew up, smacking mine in a high five.

"Thanks all the same guys, but we just figure that when you stumble on paradise, your first responsibility is to recognize it!"

CHAPTER 35

"We can't return. We can only look behind from where we came"—Joni Mitchell

HOT GRANNY

"Now I can die!" beamed the portly, old Englishman as the applause got its second wind, cranking up a bit the way ovations can. This was one of the standing variety, befitting a valedictorian address that avoided the usual bromides. There was no grasping the torch; no seizing the moment; no greening the planet. There was no rallying call to a new generation of leaders. There *was* a light hearted thesis that life was like the grand old game of baseball and the crowd had bought it. The seventeen-year-old valedictorian loved baseball.

He might well have hated the game. As a young player he was short of confidence and muscle tone and had kind of twitched at the ball when he was at the plate. When the valedictorian was nine or ten, Coach Zaretsky paid his mom a courtesy call. The coach hadn't really kicked the boy off the squad; he was just putting him back with another team of younger kids. The lad would have more fun there.

The coach, though, saw fit to reinstate the boy the very next day. Swallowing his pride seemed preferable to swallowing his balls, freshly torn from his scrotum and shoved down his throat. As fate would have it the youngster twitched at a fastball the next day with the bases loaded with Zaretsky disciples. The horsehide collided with the twitching aluminum bat and the slow roller eluded the pitcher. Then it got past the second baseman and the daydreaming centerfielder, who for this batter was playing shallow indeed, while sucking on the rawhide of his glove. Official scoring could have called it a four-base error. Popular opinion with the kids on the team and the folks in the stands was that it was a grand slam; a game winner. The hero had been high-fived and hugged and cheered beyond his parents' dreams; but not his dreams.

The valedictorian built on this triumph to become a pretty good player; not a great player but a gutsy catcher and team leader. A few years later he'd routinely flip off his mask and scuttle in the dust of the backstop at Elm Park to grab a passed ball or wild pitch and dive to the plate to tag a runner out. He was about passion and willpower and a quiet pride.

Those qualities served him well on the high school wrestling team. By then he was a hundred and ten pounds of chiseled sinew; a grappler that couldn't be pinned and wouldn't be denied. "What's wrong with being lean Dad?" he smiled at his stocky his old man who had thought that the boy could use a few pounds. The speaker's wrestling prowess had been one contributing factor to another honor he'd received just thirty minutes before he took the podium.

The young orator had given his folks the heads-up that he was chosen to give the valedictory message and that had caused the old Englishman and his old wife to undertake a rare trip to the city to claim front row seats to get a good look at their grandson. Half-an-hour before the standing ovation the valedictorian had been named "Outstanding Boy" of the graduating class. It wasn't his style to mention the possibil-

ity of that. That's part of what made him outstanding. He'd
inherited his humility from his mother. He was quietly effective. Labeled "outstanding" at anything, his dad would
have hired a skywriter.

Hearing this announced, the old lady had jammed her
right elbow into the doughy girth of the old man and her left
prodded the meaty ribs of her middle-aged son. She had stood
first. Her son and his wife and their two teenaged daughters
followed suit. Then the old man pushed himself up with his
cane to make it half-a-dozen. The middle aged son peaked
over his shoulder to confirm his suspicion that he was front
and centre in a six-person standing ovation. About five hundred souls made eye contact, applauding but seated.

"He was outstanding," the son whispered through the long
hair of his wife who was glowing and fragrant with a dash of
Obsession…"We're just standing."

The old man died but not until he'd doddered around
for another seven years, breaking the valedictorian's heart by
falling off his perch on November thirtieth, the young man's
twenty-fourth birthday, one shared with another old Englishman who doddered and died, Sir Winston Churchill. Most
of the old man's doddering was in his White Rock garden,
a profusion of vegetables, berries and flowers, all in delightful disorder. Horticultural chaos; an English thing. Bold art
must be shared, so he was both tour guide and lecturer for
unsuspecting visitors who he would shepherd through the
raspberries and trellised sweet peas and red runner beans,
flourishing in the wild little patch behind his B.C. Box. His
keenest student was the wife of his son, who one day would
have seventeen acres of her own soil for tilling, weeding and
planting. But by the time she stuck a trowel in the dirt of
her gatehouse garden, the old man was boxed and horizontal

in Victory Gardens within earshot of the drone of traffic on King George Highway. There would be no reciprocal tour. A misprint on his headstone sentenced him to an eternity of sod busting; "Till We Meet Again."

I'd always thought that congestive heart failure was a pretty good way to go. Certainly it must be preferable to a "jammer"; cardiac arrest, with the shooting pain up the arm, the panic and the sweats, the nausea and the sensation of an elephant standing on your chest; then the bug-eyed gasping for air, like a ling cod on a sun-baked pier. Those paddles and the sirens just meant for you; this time wailing just for you. This was your day and you wore that shirt and those pants; the fear of death exceeded only by the fear of recovery.

Congestive heart failure; that's the ticket. Sign me up for some of that. Probably just slip away in your sleep. Ah, but not so.

Most people fear death by drowning, second only to burning alive. Congestive heart failure amounts to drowning slowly. I had a taste of a quick drowning when I was eleven when I inhaled half a lungful of Lake Erie. There was a rented cottage at Point Pelee, with a friendly young couple renting a similar cottage next door. The man, probably in his thirties, was a strong swimmer and took me way out on a huge tractor inner tube to bounce on the waves. Then his woman appeared on the porch and, without a word, he dove off the tube and swam for shore. I figured he was hungry; horny only occurred to me about three years later. The undertow had tugged that tire about sixty yards down the shoreline from our cottage and about seventy yards out. Growing concerned, I struggled to wrap my left arm around the bloated tube and tried paddling to shore with my right. The waves were two-and-a-half footers and the first or second one knocked the tube from my hand. I went under and emerged choking and saw the tube was six feet away. I swam and stretched to just touch it when the next wave hit. Sixteen feet away now and I knew that I was going to die. I was never a strong swimmer, and the waves and the undertow had been quietly waiting; biding their time for easy pickings.

Crippled with panic, I thrashed for shore knowing it was hopeless. My one reflection was that I was eleven and had much unfinished business; and still more business that hadn't even been started. Who knows by what chance a doughy middle-aged Englishman would emerge from our cottage at that moment, sit for a second then bolt down the steep stairs. He waded towards me until the waves were putting him under. He wasn't a swimmer at all and manufactured a comical sidestroke that day to give me hope then meet me halfway. "I've got you boy!!" he shouted, "I've got you!!" Then I coughed and puked and cried on the hot beach, amid the reek of slim, dead smelt.

When the old Englishman drowned in 1999 I couldn't return the favor. He drowned slowly, fighting for breath for the best part of two years. If he'd been an old Packard or Studebaker some car buff would have jacked him up on concrete blocks and built him a shiny new engine. A transplant would have saved him but new hearts don't grow on trees; not if you're going on eighty-one and just plain bone weary.

On two occasions my mom had to call the fire department to extract him from the bathtub in their White Rock bungalow. The young firemen laughed at the sight and so did he and so did she. Then he was bedded in the Peace Arch Hospital where, all cleaned up and feeling better, he twinkled over his cheaters at Judy and me when we trekked from Vancouver for a visit. "Dying's inconvenient for everyone!" was his greeting.

He was in and out of Peace Arch a couple of times, finally settling in to die. Peace Arch Hospital has five or six floors with the highest being palliative care. Folks up there don't come out through the front door. I came to call this floor the "Stairway to Heaven."

Dad started on the first floor and it didn't take him long to wear out his welcome. A couple of the nurses were hard-ass shrews, ignoring his complaints and brooking none of his sarcasm, but one young Filipino woman was all kindness and good humor. Promoted to the third floor, he wandered the hallway with his walker, bellowing "*BORING*!!!" In my assessment it wasn't so much dementia as it was the real Eric coming to the surface, his governor removed by his illness and circumstance and medication; but maybe that's just what dementia is.

By the time he was on the "Stairway to Heaven" floor the slow drowning had him in a stranglehold. His walker hadn't made the trip upstairs. He wouldn't be needing that. They'd suck water from his lungs from time to time for temporary relief; but very soon the drowning returned and each breath sounded like a straw slurping the last of a milkshake. One evening I brought him a soft Dairy Queen cone and he crushed his face into it like a baby, a welcome change from grey pureed pears and the other crap that he was generally refusing. The Filipino nurse from the first floor was at his bedside that night, holding his hand. Her twelve hour shift had ended ninety minutes back.

Two weeks before he died he showed some rare improvement and asked for his harmonica, which he called a mouth organ. He spent some precious breath playing The Rose, Judy's go-to number when she wins Karaoke contests. He fashioned a big finish with some hand vibrato and a trill, his intravenous tubes dancing along. That was the last time he played.

Ten days later he was in a coma and the family had been visiting for an hour. We thought the spirit had gone ahead, just waiting for the carcass, until Judy took his hand and whispered, "Dad? I know you can hear me Dad." She softly began to sing *"Some say love, it is a river that drowns the tender reed."* The old man stirred a little and with the faintest of smiles, murmured along to The Rose for a few lines, his parched lips barely moving. I thought of looking around the room for his mouth organ.

I was at Shaughnessy when he died, co-hosting a lunch for new members. I got the message from Judy as my sizzling curried seafood hot pot arrived at the table. It looked and smelled delicious.

I arrived at palliative care in half an hour. His eyes were closed but his mouth frozen open and twisted to the right side, having struggled for one last breath. His face was a contorted mask like the heads in the chamber of horrors at Madame Tussaud's in London. His flesh was cold like a bone-in ham that had done an overnighter in the fridge. I kissed an icy cheek and felt the stubble grain of his beard. My cheek had been rubbed by that stubble long ago and it had made me laugh. One time it had made one of our babies cry. Grandpa was shocked and had been so sorry. The stubble's still alive I thought, still growing. Already there was a faint death smell. You get a whiff of the death smell when you're a little late.

I don't care what the death certificate said. That old man drowned.

And he died because he could.

Last night I was in Toronto while Judy saw to things at the farm.

The night before I was at Dylan and Joanne's for pizza, wings and an exceptional bottle of Amarone that Dylan and I polished off without Jo's usual assistance. "Naw, really Dad, I'm *good*," she smiled when I insisted.

The Canucks were on the tube and kicked the dog piss out of the Minnesota Wild. At the end of the first period Judy called, and Dyl and Jo picked that time to let us know we were going to have our first grandchild. I hugged Joanne and high-fived my son. "Looks like you've hit another homer Dyl," I beamed.

Back at my place I watched the White Sox take on the Astros in the longest World Series game in history, fourteen innings. Jet lag and the Amarone and Lafroaig single malt had knocked me out though, and I was oblivious to the game by the seventh inning stretch. At five a.m. an infomercial woke me up moaning.

That day I thought about things a lot; especially the news from the night before. What superb parents Joanne and Dylan would be. The bump she would soon have and the renewal of it all. What you might do differently if they gave you a parental mulligan; a fresh start with the benefit of experience. I thought of how young we had been. I pictured a nineteen-year old wife in her little McKinnon tartan kilt on that cold day at Brock University when Professor Yacowar stepped in dog shit.

At three that afternoon my Motorola had a text message from Judy.

"Hi Grandpa…Love Grandma."

I was happy to get the message and typed one back.

"Do grannies still wear knee socks?"

"All the time," the response came back in forty seconds.

"You'll be one hot granny!" I shot back.

"Thanks Grandpa from Grandma, x o x o."

I text mailed back; "Dyl proudly confided that this was their first attempt. I just had to tell him that he and his three siblings were the results of us not trying at all."

"You're still the champ, Tarzan," was her text response.

"Just a couple of sport-fuckers," I typed and re-read it; paused, then closed my eyes and plunged the send key.

It took less than a minute for my phone to beep.

"Too Far—Thanatos Boy!!"

"Touché!!" I typed and sent.

CHAPTER 36

"A ramblin' gamblin' man"—Bob Segar

BELLAGIO BOB AND BUDDY BRUCE

LONG BEFORE WE BOUGHT FOXGLOVE FARM, JUDY HAD MADE quite a number of journeys to Cloverdale. Upon our move to the country, these trips became more frequent.

Cloverdale is a down to earth, western kind of town on Highway 10, about fifteen minutes west of Langley. Every May there's a Cloverdale Stampede, with a fairground and rodeo, along the lines of its better-known counterpart in Calgary. Cloverdale boasts more than a few tack and saddlery shops that cater to both western and English riders.

Judy's Cloverdale junkets were solo, save for Brutus, and their mission was to prowl for old furniture and tapestries. There is no shortage of antique shops in Cloverdale and their pricing, word has it, can be more flexible than what you might find on Main Street in Vancouver.

Every couple of weeks I'd notice that some aspect inside Foxglove was different. Dining room chairs and tables would come and go or be reshuffled into that square tearoom where I'd thought of putting a chess table. Large, beveled mirrors would be there one day and absent the next. On other occasions heavy antiques would appear in the ballroom, only to be gone a week later. Judy's a "worker ant" in the sense that she can lift objects three times her weight, and prefers to do so without my help.

Now, if my assistance came without my questions, she would undoubtedly seek it more often.

This desk was on approval. That table's gone to consignment. This tapestry was on the lay-away plan. Those dining room chairs from the past three weeks just didn't work. Sometimes, when I asked her to elaborate, I suspected she might be weary of getting the third degree.

Once I accompanied Judy to a Cloverdale antique store and the owner and staff called out "JUDY!!" as she walked in the door. It was like "NORM!!" rolling into Cheers for a couple of pints. Inside, a lot of items looked familiar and I realized that I'd sat in that chair, or slept in that bed over there, or wiped my feet on that Persian runner.

Roxanne was in hysterics when she told me about finding the perfect partner's desk for Peter's study at the Cloverdale Antique Mall. Then she noticed a little yellow tag on one of the brass drawer handles. Hoping the price had been further marked down, Roxy took a look. The tag said "*HOLD*—for Judy Trowbridge," and Peter's desk remains an ideal centerpiece in my Foxglove den; a stump, one could say, that had been pissed on.

So Judy's trips to Cloverdale weren't for the rodeo although in recent years she's taken quite a shine to professional bull riding, televised on ESPN. Her interest in the PBRA (Professional Bull Riding Association) came as a bit of a shock to me as it had grown to a fanatic level before I was aware of it at all. By the time she came out of the closet she knew the top dozen riders, had her personal favorites and was even better acquainted with the bulls. Just when you think you know a person.

"Oh, I love this next bull honey! This is "Dictator," I've never seen anybody stay on him!" she enthused one day in front of the plasma screen. "That is one big bull!!"

I've mentioned Judy's bias for big things and the massive "Dictator" certainly filled the bill. I watched as Dictator dislodged his cowpoke in about three seconds and gored his rectum with a deft horn insertion. "Wooooooeeeeeee!!! Now that cowboy just got his oil checked!!" squealed Don Gay, the PBRA's resident color man.

My wife is a woman whose passions include antiques, estate jewelry, dressage, interior design, formal gardening, historical biographies and classical music. She can hold her own with a Globe and Mail cryptic crossword. She ably creates on canvas with oils and pastels. She sings along commendably on Saturday afternoons to many of the great operatic arias on CBC and harmonizes on the duets. She has a dovecote and is in the market for her first dove. To say the least, Judy's zeal for the PBRA came as a genuine surprise.

"I told Jackie we were in Judy Trowbridge country," Brian Tattrie had said around 1992.

Our friends Brian and Jackie had just returned from a road trip where they had visited Martha's Vineyard, Cape Cod, and Hyannis Port. Brian had personified the sophisticated clapboard and shingle charm of the eastern seaboard with a woman who likes to see cowboys get bucked.

I hadn't had a clue. Could my spouse be harboring any other embryonic interests since our move to the country? Would our weekends soon be spent at tractor pulls and cockfights? Was she already subbing in some Wednesday morning ten-pin league in Langley, to cheers of "Lotsa wood Judester!!

Now make that spare, girlfriend!!" having left only the seven-pin standing?? Did she have her eye on her own fourteen-pound fuscia ball and a polyester shirt that has *Jude* embroidered on the sleeve?

Bruce Allen's a big fan of bull riding too. In October, 2001, Judy and I took in the PBRA Championships in Las Vegas with Bruce and his woman Katy-Anne, a professional photographer. While I was lukewarm to the idea of bull riding, any excuse to hop on a plane to Vegas was fine with me, and how sweet it was that it was Judy's idea. Oh, to hear the snap of the down card against cool, green felt and the ratcheting spin of a nearby roulette wheel and the cries of "WHO'S YOUR DADDY??!!!" when some lucky prick hits his number. Just one more time, let me take a deep, greedy breath of that piped-in casino oxygen, the elixir of The Strip. Bull riding? No worries. For a spousal initiation of a Vegas junket, I'd tolerate a three day exposition of Limoges china or Faberge eggs at some sterile Vegas convention centre, feigning interest for as much as a full half hour before starting to pout.

Bruce Allen, of course, is the manager of Brian Adams, Anne Murray and Martina McBride and is a gruff and larger-than-life Vancouver personality. With Bruce's connections he secured terrific seats for the four of us.

Judy had boarded Mickey at Bruce's barn in Southlands for years and had bought her first Range Rover from him.

Every two years Brian Adams presented Bruce with a new car and around 1996 it was a black Corvette. Bruce's forest green, long wheelbase Rover became expendable and Judy was ready with an offer. It only had about 60,000 kilometers on the odometer and Bruce let it go for $24,000. A Range Rover had always been Judy's dream ride and she did

242

the deal for the price of a Toyota Corolla. "Get it checked out, if it needs any work, just send me the bill," was Bruce's generous proposal.

Range Rovers *can* need work.

Once around 1992 we were in bed in that Angus Drive Dutch Colonial and I was just drifting off to sleep, glad to see the end of a less than stellar day.

"I want to get a Range Rover," Judy announced from her pillow.

"I'd get you a divorce before I'd get you a Range Rover," came the empty threat from my pillow.

I hadn't forgotten all the problems and expense that were the hallmark of British Leyland products. I recalled our Austin Mini-Cooper woes from our days at Brock and the adage that "those who ignore history are doomed to repeat it." British Leyland's electrical system was by the Lucas Company and a car buff acquaintance of mine had referred to Lucas as "The Prince of Darkness."

The green Range Rover is parked now on Hazelton Avenue, shipped to Yorkville this year to deal with an Ontario phenomenon they call winter. The navy blue one, the 2000 Autobiography, is parked near the fountain in the brick courtyard of Foxglove Farm. It's currently peeking back at me between the winter rhododendrons through the window of my den.

The atmosphere in Las Vegas was surreal in October 2001. American jingoism, already flourishing in the bull riding world, had been further enflamed just three weeks prior by Bin Laden. The popular singer Jewel, herself the main squeeze of a bull-riding champ, offered a soft, dewy Star Spangled Banner and then the grounds of the arena were ignited into Old Glory itself, fiery stars and stripes flaming red, white and blue. After that the bulls bucked and the cowboys rode.

The highlight for me was the Gentleman Jack bourbon cocktails that seem to be the beverage of choice of bull-riding aficionados. That and Bud of course.

I got to know Bruce Allen a little on that trip, although I don't think he got my name right more than once or twice. I guess Bob can be a tough one. When Bruce learned that I was on the Board of the Vancouver Opera and had installed a program of planned giving, and had sponsored a production of "The Magic Flute," he grimaced.

"I hate opera," he began.

"When we promote a rock concert, sometimes people go so far as to camp out to get wristbands for the chance to buy a ticket. We never look for charity because people want our product because it's good. If Opera is so great how come they have to be constantly begging for handouts?"

Awaiting a table for dinner while Katy-Anne and Judy went browsing, Bruce and I had a crisp bottle of Chablis with a few dozen raw malpeques at The Hard Rock's oyster bar. He asked me about my work and then he talked a bit about his efforts to resurrect Anne Murray's career. He was more than a little derisive toward her previous management and their direction for the once barefoot Maritime songstress, whose laid back style had struck pop gold with *Snowbird*.

Apparently they had tried to take her wholesome image uptown and sparkle her up with some Vegas-style glitter. "I'm telling you Bill, fishnets would've been next. They were just about to have poor Annie high kicking, for fuck's sake!!" was Bruce's take.

After dinner, Bruce and Katy-Anne, Judy and I cheered on the Arizona Diamondbacks as they vanquished the favored and hated Yankees in the final World Series game in the sports bar at The Hard Rock Hotel and Casino. The "Big Unit," Randy Johnson, was the ace of the Diamondback staff then, but sadly, typically, has just signed a contract with the Yankees for 2005.

Bruce always stays at the Hard Rock Hotel but on our bull-riding trip, Judy convinced Katy Anne and him to join us at Bellagio's.

We'd been to Vegas a half dozen times over the past fifteen years and Judy harbored a pronounced distaste for much of what goes on there. Bellagio's changed that.

She'd never been much of a fan of the casinos and didn't care for my enthusiasm for gambling. Not that I was any kind of high roller, but if I was winning at craps or blackjack she'd want me to quit while I was ahead. Judy would actually encourage me to turn over my hard earned stacks of chips and growing wads of bills into her custody, consolidating our gains and leaving me to forge ahead under-funded.

In a gardening sense, she probably felt she was pruning me back to stimulate further growth; but as a gambler, as a warrior of the green felt, *I felt* she wanted to send me against the Viet Cong with a BB gun.

On occasions where I'd lost a quick five hundred dollars she'd always notice my furtive slink over to the cash machine. She'd invariably be stationed at a two-bit slot outside my peripheral vision, but somehow always knew how I stood.

"It's in your blood, you know," she'd remind me, referring to my paternal grandfather.

Edgar Trowbridge had been a very competent tailor of fine clothing in Derbyshire, England. Papa was a sweet and gentle man, extending credit to his clientele throughout the dirty thirties, but couldn't resist the horses and as a result lost his business, the family home and the respect of my father, Eric, along the way. Apparently things bottomed out when my dad threw a pound of butter at his dad in the kitchen of the home in question, or perhaps it was the kitchen of the government subsidized council home to which they were relegated in the wake of the aforementioned disgrace. These being depression years, not even an ounce of butter was thrown lightly.

So Judy may have had a point, but a trip to Bellagio's in 1998 softened her position somewhat.

I had a half dozen new business partners at the time and meeting in Las Vegas was cheaper and decidedly more fun than gathering per usual in Toronto. The partners converged on the desert from Newfoundland, Nova Scotia, the Prairies and Ontario. Most of them stayed at Bally's but we were on our own in terms of choosing accommodation.

We flew in from Vancouver and booked into Bellagio's, the latest new hotel, which had recently trumped the extravagant Mirage, just down the strip. Bellagio's doors had opened only the previous day.

As part of a grand opening incentive our first two nights were $89 and the third was $125. We have since stayed at Hotel De Russie near the Spanish Steps in Rome for over five times that tariff. De Russie is the newly and exquisitely renovated five-star hotel that had been Mussolini's headquarters during World War II, but the elegance and style of Bellagio's compared favorably.

Everything felt great at Bellagio's. Sinatra's vocals greeted us at check-in with *I've Got You Under My Skin*. The casino was soaked in Tony Bennett tunes and a Dean Martin disc crooned *Volare* as we enjoyed linguini vongole with a suitable Brunello in one of the superb Bellagio ristorantes. Our room was slick and huge and fabulous, beige Italian marble with a sheen of rose. Rolled fluffy towels at the foot of the shower and bath. Our sumptuous surroundings had us in fine spirits and then there was a quick jackpot win at the slots.

My business meeting was at nine in the morning at Bally's.

I showered at six forty-five, leaving Judy in blissful slumber. By seven a hostess had brought my morning espresso to one of Bellagio's video poker machines. The casino was nearly empty; just a few diehards and me. Mel Torme was singing *I'll be Seeing You.*

Around seven-fifteen I drew the Jack, Queen and King of Clubs, having held the Ace and Ten. Bells went off, the place lit up, attendants flocked over and I had turned a five dollar investment into forty-three hundred U.S. greenbacks.

They withheld tax of thirty percent but, still elated, I rousted a groggy Judy with the house phone, wanting her to elevator down to see the Royal Flush before they re-set the machine. She put on her face and indulged me. Everybody loves a winner.

Wallet bulging, I rolled into Bally's and met with my partners.

That night, freewheeling with Bellagio's money, I hit the blackjack table hard. By two a.m. Judy came over and, all smiles, ordered me to bed, but the cocktail waitress had talked me into a Chivas that was on its way. And the rest of my table was a fun sextet from Dallas, a couple of the women dripping diamonds. We were all winning and pumped and getting a little louder.

The three couples had started calling me *Canada* and we were in a "zone." Riding two straight hours of fabulous cards and a couple of dealers prone to busting, the Texans couldn't imagine changing even one thing at that table. I hung in there and won another two grand, bringing the day to $8,500.

I'd finished that Scotch by then and the dealer was shuffling one more shoe. The group from Dallas was working on me anew. Then Judy played a trump card of her own, sidling close and whispering in my ear.

"*Canada*, you just stay put! We're a team here!!

Never y'all mind that little girl!!" exhorted my new friends from Texas.

Fifteen minutes later Judy and I were in our king-sized bed and our stack of cash and chips was locked in the safe in our closet. She had made me an offer I couldn't refuse.

Three years later, remembering these good times and the bargain rates we had enjoyed, Judy convinced Bruce Allen to cancel his Hard Rock Hotel reservations and join us at Bellagio's.

To her dismay the first two nights were quoted at $325 and Monday was $199, U.S. of course. Calling from Pt. Grey Road, Judy sprang into action and summoned Bellagio management to the phone.

"Don't you have gamblers' rates?" she wanted to know.

"My husband's a big gambler; you should have special rates for us based on how much he bets. Check your records; he won a jackpot at Bellagio's when you opened in 1998."

I was relieved when she stopped short of telling Bellagio's about Papa Edgar Trowbridge having to dodge a pound of butter during the depression. Nonetheless, while she was pleading our case I couldn't help but coach her a little. "Tell them it's in my blood!" I said and got shushed for my trouble. Bellagio's made no promises but suggested that maybe something could be arranged when we checked in.

A few days later we were at the front desk under the incredible colors of the glass petal ceiling that sets Bellagio's lobby apart. Bobby Darin was piped in, singing "Across the Sea."

It took Judy about twenty minutes to penetrate about five levels of management, after dismissing the blank stares of the clerks behind the desk. I was relieved that she refrained from referring to me as a "big gambler" again in the presence of people who probably knew one when they saw one.

Then we were ushered into another room where an executive type was most cordial and issued four cards, two each. One was for the tables, the other for the slots. "If you wager at least two hundred dollars an hour during your stay, your visit will be complimentary," said the impeccably groomed young manager.

"Hell, my husband here'll have that covered in the first five minutes!" Judy said without a word of a lie.

"Welcome back to Bellagio's folks! Good Luck!!" said the nice young man.

I inspected my two V.I.P. cards, bursting with pride, finally having made the big time. Judy chucked hers in her purse.

"You!" she said, grabbing my elbow, pointing to the acres of noisy slots and crowded tables. "Get to work!!"

It did feel exactly like work. The furtive, guilty feeling was replaced by an onerous responsibility and the burden of legitimacy. Not only did I have two V.I.P. cards, I had a spousal mandate and an hourly objective.

I found a blackjack table and being sure to bet my quota, went through my initial five hundred dollar grubstake in less than half an hour. I didn't win one hand. To tourniquet the cash hemorrhage I withdrew just three hundred from the bank machine and headed for the slots. I found the same video poker machine that had been so generous in 1998, hoping lightning would strike twice. Three years, though, had hardened that slot into a jaded, stingy son of a bitch and I was soon down eight hundred.

This was simply not fun, and mercifully it was time to head out to catch the bull riding.

"These are incredible seats Bruce," I enthused as I brought Judy, Katy-Anne and him a tray of drinks to the second row from the concession at the UNLV arena, "but I'd really like to pay for ours."

Bruce snorted a laugh. "Oh don't worry Bill, you're paying for them! My office is sending you an invoice." They did and the invoice was almost twelve hundred for the two day championship. And even at that price, we didn't see one cowpoke get his oil checked.

But no matter. Lightning *can* strike twice. This time my morning royal flush was in diamonds and came before breakfast the next day. About three machines down from the 1998 bonanza. At $4,600 U.S. it seemed like Vegas jackpots were indexed to the cost of living.

That night Bruce and I had a lot of laughs gambling side by side and we both won a few thousand at blackjack. He may have called me "Bob."

Our Bellagio bill came to $171 for incidentals. Three weeks later they sent us a check in that amount to Point Grey Road. We put the reimbursement towards Bruce's invoice that had arrived just the day before.

CHAPTER 37

"Hear the mighty engines roar"—Gordon Lightfoot

T.O. AND FRO

MORE AND MORE COMMITTED TO TORONTO IN A BUSINESS sense, I was back at Foxglove for a precious weekend. It was mid January 2005, after Judy and I had spent Christmas in Yorkville to see how that felt.

Brutus came east for Christmas too; his airfare forty bucks each way and his super-sized cage a three hundred dollar capital expenditure. Judy, in an effort to be a good role model, spent quite a bit of time behind bars herself prior to his maiden flight. Curling up in the back of the cage in the farm kitchen, she coaxed and cajoled him to join her in what was rather cozy confinement.

"Come on Brutus! Get in Brutus's house with mommy!"

Reluctant at first, Brutus put a paw followed by his head into the cage from wherein Judy beckoned from her fetal position. Then he'd withdraw and turn to me, the heavy folds of his brow wrinkled, in some kind of canine search for sanity. All I could do was shrug.

But his was no ordinary love. This was love and devotion in an unconditional bundle. There never was a doubt that Brutus would join Judy in that cage, and within a minute they were cellmates. Apparently Judy had done the same at Petsmart prior to buying the cage. She had crawled in to check out the merchandise from the end customer's point of view. It was the biggest they had but still pretty cramped for an English mastiff. She wanted to be sure.

"I should just lock that door and put both of you on the special luggage conveyor belt," was my observation. "Think of the airfare we'd save."

"Very funny," she countered, "I just want him to get used to the idea. I'm not sure whether to put his blanket in there; it's going to be cold in the belly of the plane, but he needs room to move around a little."

"Just like *we* do, flying economy," was my voice of reason.

They both got out of the cage and I peeled a foot long cord of drool off the back of her turtleneck.

Two weeks prior to Christmas, Brutus was in that cage, attracting a small crowd of fans at Vancouver International, mellowed by a sedative, the administering of which saw Judy's arm disappear to the elbow.

"Otherwise he'll just spit it out," she had noted. By the time we'd exchanged an aching adieu at the special cargo door, he'd won over a few of the airport personnel and I offered a little reassurance.

"He's in good hands, honey, don't worry, he'll be fine."

I was the second last passenger to board, as Mr. and Mrs. Trowbridge were subject to a final paging. Judy's nose was pressed to the airport window, watching the luggage get fork-lifted into the abdomen of the 767. "I think I might have seen him; it was hard to tell," she said after jogging to join me.

On the runway awaiting takeoff we could hear repeated slamming and rocking in the fuselage right below seats 23 K and H where we were settling in. "That's him," fretted Judy,

"I guarantee you that's him."

I hoped it *was* Brutus, preferring that to some lethal mechanical malfunction, but I kept that thought to myself.

Brutus finally did bust out of his cage, but not until he arrived at the luggage carousel at Pearson Airport about five minutes before we did. Certainly untold havoc could have resulted from one hundred and eighty pounds of jet-lagged, yellow mammal bounding unrestrained around shiny new Terminal 1. Thankfully this crisis was averted when a courageous and savvy dog lover in his late thirties collared our groggy canine and locked him in his Petsmart clink forthwith.

Disassembling his cage required the laborious removal of about thirty screws that secured Brutus' ceiling to his floor, a tedious task that I shared with Judy. Brutus, still logy from the dope, supervised, dangling tongue on full display. Assembled, the cage was too big for any limo that might whisk the three of us to our Yorkville Christmas.

A cavalcade of big dog lovers who seemed to sense that she, rather than I, was the one to ask about Brutus, constantly interrupted Judy's share of the unscrewing. Most insisted upon referring to him as a "Bull" mastiff, a misnomer apparently tantamount to referring to a medium rare chateaubriand as pot roast.

"He's an *English* mastiff," Judy corrected, "The snout on the Bull mastiff isn't as long."(The longer snouted mastiff is the nobler breed, I knew she was thinking.)

"How much does he weigh?" a youngish blonde needed to know. I suspected she was referring to Brutus but sucked in my gut nonetheless and carried on unscrewing.

"About 175," Judy responded "He's only three."

"Oh! Just a puppy!" came back the blonde. "How big will he get?"

"Some of the males can fill out to 250 pounds," said Judy.

Feeling invisible and having recently filled out to 205, I exhaled and began to remove the screws on Judy's side of the cage.

About another half-dozen Brutus fans gathered around Judy and she fielded their questions like a presidential press secretary.

It fell to me to deal with the overflow.

"We've got two Rotweillers and a Doberman, eh?" came the unsolicited census from a guy in a gray tracksuit with a wispy five-day beard. The feeble stubble was an attempt to conceal a rosy colony of chin zits, the more prominent of which were begging to be squeezed. His blue cap with the white old English D was on cockeyed and he had to remove his Walkman headphones to hear me repeat myself.

"I said are you really a Tiger fan or is that just so much headgear?"

"No way, the Tigers suck, that's just my hat, but you got a nice dog there man. You could put a saddle on that dog!"

"Thanks," I said as I inverted the top of the cage and tupperwared it into the bottom, and balanced the whole business on a luggage cart, our other bags following on top.

"C'mon honey, let's go," I said and Judy led Brutus behind me, leaving his throng of admirers. We made inquiries, found a precious grassy patch outside the concrete sprawl of Terminal 1 and Brutus squatted for his inaugural Ontario pee.

"He was such a good boy!" was Judy's review of the proceedings.

"He was good," I concurred.

Brutus' three weeks in Yorkville must have seemed, to him, like doing hard time. He curled on the Persian rug in the dark oak hallway and slept through the holidays dreaming of ducks and pheasants and twice daily sniffings of Dornoch's butt and his solemn responsibilities back at Foxglove.

Brutus kept the famished denizens of the coyote pack at a respectful distance from the worn front door of Foxglove Farm and the tasty feline delights therein. Dornoch knew. He was used to insisting on the earliest of exits from the farmhouse most mornings. I held him off as long as I could, making coffee first and needing to see a sliver of dawn before I let him out on these winter mornings. As soon as that door opened he'd bounce outside in swaggering confidence, embracing the day and the hunt.

But Brutus' three-week vacation changed everything. Upon our return Dornoch still wanted out, but my coffee cup steamed in the open doorway as he hesitated, sniffing the air, sometimes for a full minute. He was back in his Shaugnessy Golf Course survival mode, where he could never relax and needed all his formidable wits to outsmart the coyotes.

Chubby, dozy Zsu Zsu was another story. "If it wasn't for Brutus the coyotes would have had her ages ago," Judy maintained. "She's such a ditz." The elderly Yum Yum was taking no chances, preferring the safety and comfort of the litter box to the seventeen acres of options outside the house.

Though he was a gentle big guy, we still muzzled Brutus on his brief washroom breaks down Hazelton Avenue. We weren't so much worried about him biting a Prada swathed fashion plate with four-inch heels on her winter boots, strutting past our house, arms full of gift-wrapped presents. Nor were we overly concerned about him gnawing on one of the strident slick-sters emerging into the slush from their turbocharged Porsche Cayennes, working their cell phones, setting up lunches at Sassafraz. At least not for them.

It's just that we knew either occurrence would spell the end of Brutus; and to that end, we were taking no chances. So it came to pass that the daily highlight of the yellow dog's Yule was an icy, muzzled stroll down Hazelton Avenue where most of his canine counterparts sported knit coats and little black booties. For Brutus each outing amounted to a fleeting, barefoot sniff of downtown Canada for a tenta-tive, squatting pee.

"The booties keep the salt off their paws," advised Judy.

On Christmas Day he tolerated a pair of reindeer antlers on his head while Harmony rode him in the hallway like a horse.

My goodness, but wasn't he glad to get back to the farm!!

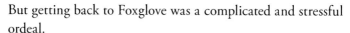

But getting back to Foxglove was a complicated and stressful ordeal.

It was New Years Day, a couple of hours past brunch, and the atmosphere at Pearson International was lazy and benign. There seemed to be as many airport employees as travelers and the leisurely pace suited both just fine. My hangover was not much worse than usual. Timing was the issue; timing and Judy's uncompromising commitment to the comfort and safety of Brutus.

"Don't get your braids in a knot, he'll be fine," I said, re-ferring to her New Year's Day pigtails. But her concern was compounding.

First, the flight back west is always longer by about sixty

minutes owing to prevailing headwinds. This meant an extra hour of cramped confinement for Brutus in the chilly cargo bay.

Judy was concerned and delayed coaxing him into the cage until the latest possible moment. First he had a cool drink in a plastic bowl from the water fountain and another trip to the grassy patch outside the terminal. Back inside, Judy held the leash but her back was turned as she rearranged the blanket in the cage and Brutus raised the eyebrows of a few of our fellow travelers when his snout and substantial pink tongue indicated his inclination to drink straight from the fountain next to the cash machine in Terminal 1.

"He's drooling in the fountain Jude," I observed. You're just visiting; I have to live here."

"What do you feed him?" came the first question from the Brutus groupies that were beginning to gather as Judy fluffed up his blanket to get it just so.

"I live on double eggnogs and hot turkey sandwiches with leftover stuffing," came my reply.

Then our flight was delayed as flights can be, further compromising Judy's plans for Brutus' comfort. At the special cargo counter she had him out of the cage again on his leash as she lobbied with the crew there for the latest possible loading. Behind her back a mid-sized hound in a mid-sized cage was likewise flying west and I watched in silence as Brutus came nose to nose with his startled fellow traveler. The ensuing junkyard exchange, the snarling, growling and woofing, provided a brief respite from the tedium of Terminal 1.

Finally, goodbyes were said and "Brutus is such a good boy!!" assessments were repeatedly uttered as he was dollied away.

Over half an hour later Judy and I were crammed into our

nasty economy seats, belts buckled and eager to be on our way. I had a National Post and had already solved the chess puzzle, studied the celebrity obituary roster for 2004 and was tackling the cryptic crossword.

"Please put away your tray table sir," directed the flight attendant.

But fifteen more minutes passed even though the doors of the 767 were shut, the plane full and everyone seated. Then that same hostess was crouching next to Judy's aisle seat and the news wasn't good.

"We're sorry, but we just can't get your dog on this flight. There's an unusual amount of regular luggage and no room for the cage. We're going to put him on a Vancouver flight at six."

"There's no way!" said Judy. "That's three hours from now. He can't be left in his cage that long. *This* flight was already delayed!"

"I'm sure he'll be in good hands," said the attendant.

"*I'm* not getting off this plane," was my contribution which Judy ignored as she started grinding the attendant.

"I arranged this weeks ago. Our dog is a living thing. That extra luggage shouldn't have priority over something that's alive. This plane has a heated cargo area. That's *specifically* why we're on this flight. Let me talk to the agent," Judy insisted.

I buried my nose in the crossword as Judy headed for the exit. Fifteen more minutes passed as I felt the weight of the stares of a couple of hundred weary souls. Finally her blond pigtails reappeared and bounced towards me past executive class and approached our seats, deep in the bowels of steerage. Girding my loins for a New Years Day showdown, I contemplated my options.

One, hang around Terminal 1 for another three hours;

fielding questions from Brutus admirers with what was now an insistent, gnawing headache. Or two, stay in my seat, fly alone, solve that puzzle with a double gin and tonic and spend the first quarter of 2005 in the doghouse. A full three-month sentence to Casa Bow-Wow. Thirteen weeks in Chez Robert, with earliest parole around Valentine's Day.

There was no utter triumph in the blue eyes framed by the fat yellow braids, as Judy stood by her seat and gave me the matter of fact update.

"I've got Brutus on a plane that leaves in one hour. The cargo bay is heated. We're on it too, in business class."

I could only smile, as I felt the girds flying from my loins.

Seventy-five minutes later I passed the puzzle over to Judy. "It's a tough one today, see what you can do."

I was in Seat 2A and she was in 2B. I took a swig of gin and tonic as the plane backed from the gate.

"You couldn't get Brutus into business class?" I asked, tugging on a pigtail.

CHAPTER 38

"The Rough God Comes Riding"—Van Morrison

ET TU BRUTE?

THE ONE-TWO PUNCH OF THE CARIBBEAN CRUISE FOLLOWED by Christmas had me puffed up like the Hindenberg.

On January 4th 2005, dismayed by the tightness of the waist of my suit pants, I put myself on the Atkins Diet. I dropped two inches of girth and probably six pounds in about a week. Bacon, eggs, steak and cheese ad nauseum.

"You've really done well," Judy encouraged.

Then snail mail arrived from my doctor indicating that a September blood profile showed high levels of "bad" cholesterol. Overnight I was supposed to start wolfing down the carbs I had been avoiding while avoiding the fats I had been wolfing.

Whole Foods is a sprawling organic grocery across the street from our Yorkville house on Hazelton. There's aisle after aisle of choices of foodstuffs for hungry Toronto folk who are determined to live to a hundred and fifty and then turn over a green planet to their progeny. Just about everything Whole Foods offers seems to be crying out for a tasty dose of salt and fat and nitrates. Several acres of vitamins and healthy holistic crap interface with organic hygiene products where a wide array of earth-friendly deodorants don't even begin to curtail a smelly sweat. Half a pound of bacon can be had for $13.99, masquerading as "Smoked, Sliced, Side of Pork." There's a full measure of passive-aggressive guilt meted out at checkout where the most sensitive choice is no bag, paper is an acceptable preference, and my insistence on plastic has me painted with the same brush as the alcoholic skipper of a floundered Exxon freighter. One time our emaciated cashier had to strike her counter with a roll of dimes six or seven times before she could make change for a twenty. "Get some red meat into you girl!!" was Judy's motherly advice.

Back in Toronto and alone in mid January, I was at Whole Foods when my cellular rang. It was Judy. I told her about the letter from my doctor and the sludgy condition of my arteries.

"There are fifty aisles of food here and the only thing I can have now is a Java Log," I whined, referring to the artificial fire logs that are made with recycled coffee grounds.

"And *it'll* probably keep me up all night!"

Feeling even sorrier for myself than usual, I bought a couple of Java Logs, a box of Meuslix and a carton of skim milk.

Back at the house I poured a double Glenlivet that had been aged in a French oak cask, fired up a Java log, and booked an early Tango flight online for the next morning. I'd get back by noon and surprise her.

When I saw Judy she told me that Brutus had chased a coyote that morning and nearly ran him down after a couple of hundred yards. He had bust right into Jessell's field in pursuit, straight through the barbed wire as if it wasn't there. He was still establishing that the big yellow sheriff was back in town after three weeks of eastern furlough.

The following evening the three of us were relaxing in

front of the fire in the library and enjoying a Napoleon biog-
raphy on the plasma screen.

"I really can't figure out what he saw in that Josephine," I
said, upon seeing an unflattering portrait of the Empress.

"Oh that doesn't look right," Judy fretted.

"Look at his belly; he's swollen."

I cast a glance at Bonaparte's silk breeches, then saw that
Judy was attending to Brutus whose abdomen looked about
to burst.

"Welcome to the club Brutus," I quipped; but he hadn't
indulged in the eggnogs and turkey and stuffing and plum
pudding with hard sauce that I had. To the contrary, Brutus
seemed to possess a rather modest Christmas appetite on his
Yorkville sojourn.

We own nothing in this life. We kind of rent, without even
the modicum of proprietorship afforded by leasing. Wherever
our distorted sense of permanence might be focused, there are
no ironclad deeds. Even month-to-month is a myth. It's more
like day-to-day, hour-to-hour, and minute-to-minute. There's
more of the Indonesian village awaiting the tsunami than
Gibraltar, from what I've encountered. We're merely passing
through, whether, at the time, we feel we own the right to
a clean toilet at the Bosco's, or the God given right to build
whatever the fuck we want onto our cash paid log cabin in
Tiddley Cove. Upscale vagrants, we sift and winnow through
the foulness of the dumpster. We shuffle our streets with shopping carts woven from deeds, portfolios, and online accounts,
brimming with summer homes and *pied a terres* and positions
in mid-cap securities, each with a solid, long-term upside.

We didn't own the houses with the pools, nor those for

which we overpaid. We didn't own the bargains. We didn't own the Shaughnessy estate nor the Dutch Colonial at Angus and Nanton.

We have a more honest relationship with the cars. We lease them whether Lexus or Rover. We're under less illusion; the meter's ticking; we take the best off the newness of them; we turn them in whether they smell of ripe pooch or whether they don't.

"Don't let me lose you," I had said.

Its ashes to ashes, isn't that what they say?

Ignorance is truly bliss. Dogs have it good.

No series of tests; no early detection; no chemo, no radiation, no support groups, no false hope.

That big yellow dog nearly ran down that coyote just three days before they shaved a patch on his leg to find a vein.

Desperate, incredulous, Judy had sought second and third opinions, and a prescription for codeine painkillers. The pills were for him; they haven't made the drug that could ease her pain.

She had 70 cc of fluid drained from his gut. She did her best to find sleep at his side by the fire in the library. Suddenly he hadn't been able to manage the stairs to our bedroom.

I heard as much of the prognosis as she could manage on my cellular in The Maple Leaf Lounge at Vancouver International. I was off again. Two days later I cancelled my Toronto meetings and headed back home. When I saw him I stifled a gasp; in only a couple of days much of the young brawn of his head and neck and back had seemed to have just melted into his abdomen.

Just before midnight I helped her hoist him into the back of the Rover. It was a three-way effort; Brutus summoned what resolve he could to haul himself on to the tailgate for one last ride.

Brutus' ashes have been on Judy's night table for a week now; a heavy box indeed. He had just turned three. He was just passing through.

We don't really own Point Grey Road amid the snapping sails at the Kisilano Yacht Club and the sunsets from the log on the beach. We could no more possess that place than we could chain high tide to the dock. These days there's a green and white "For Sale" sign at Point Grey Road.

And we don't own the elegant red brick house on Hazelton near Avenue Road and Bloor. The realtor came by last night. We signed things. I shoveled a bit of the walk for the realtor's visit, finally a concession to winter. By morning it was covered again as we headed for the airport.

We never owned Brutus, although I guess we had his papers in a drawer somewhere. And we never did possess his bounding through the golden fields of Foxglove Farm and the jingle of the tags on his collar as he stirred his lanky bones for another trip to the barn with his best pal. That heavy leather collar hangs silent on the handle of the mudroom door.

And we never owned Foxglove Farm; not really. No one ever has. Not the Russian immigrants who planted the Acacias down the driveway in 1901, not Alma Ziegler, no one since. But for now we're still visiting. It's only February fifth and the blossoms are stirring; maybe we'll fix that gate.

We went to a concert once. It was May of 1998 at GM Place, the hockey arena that Vancouverites call "The Garage." Front row center for Van Morrison, Joni Mitchell and Bob Dylan. A year later I found the ticket stubs in the pocket of a tweed jacket that I had loved once, but seldom wear these days. I don't even know where those tickets are now.

Van kicked things off and wore his trademark black fedora and directed his tight, talented band with a shrug here and a finger pop there. As great as he was, the man was even more memorable when we saw him for two more shows within the next twenty-four hours at The Queen Elizabeth Theatre. Then we walked home over The Burrard Street Bridge above the ocean and under the stars to the Kits Beach townhouse. Frank Sinatra had died that day and Van had paid tribute with "*That's Life,*" James Brown style.

Joni was cool and detached and didn't play wooden once. No open-tuned Martin, no capoed Gibson; she never even had an acoustic on stage. Just a high-tech Fender, both flanged and phased, and a synthesized bass-sliding manager ex-husband named Larry Klein and a couple of other rawboned boys. Everything was electric and jazzy and once removed; not one of the old gems except an electrified *Big Yellow Taxi* to end her set. No *Circle Game* no *Carey* no *Both Sides Now* no *Case of You* no *River.* In fact, for me, no Joni.

She actually made eye contact with me and held my gaze for seven seconds. I think she knew she was breaking my heart.

"We've lost you," I might have said.

Bob Dylan, though just ten feet from us, mugged larger than life for the crowd of twenty thousand. From the front row he was a caricature. Small and old.

He sang *Forever Young.*

And once I launched a perfect spiral sixty yards against a crisp blue October sky. There were scarlets and there were ambers. I know there were.

Robert E. L. Trowbridge

Was born in Calgary, Alberta in 1950. Residing in Vancouver, British Columbia since 1982, he and his wife Judy bought Foxglove Farm in 2002. President of a national insurance firm, Robert Trowbridge divides his time between Foxglove in B.C.'s Fraser Valley and Toronto, Ontario, where Judy and he live in a Yorkville brownstone. Robert and Judy, pictured above, have four children and a new grandson. "Foxglove" is Robert Trowbridge's first book.

ISBN 141208019-3

9 781412 080194